THE MATING SEASON

P.G. Wodehouse was born in Guildford, Surrey, in 1881 and educated at Dulwich College. After working for the Hong Kong and Shanghai Bank for two years, he left to earn his living as a journalist and storywriter.

During his lifetime he wrote over ninety books, and his work has won worldwide acclaim. He was hailed by the *Times* as 'A comic genius recognized in his lifetime as a classic and an old master of farce.' P.G. Wodehouse said: 'I believe there are two ways of writing novels. One is mine, making a sort of musical comedy without music and ignoring real life altogether; the other is going right deep down into life and not caring a damn.'

In 1975 he was created a Knight of the British Empire and he died on St Valentine's Day in the same year at the age of ninety-three.

D1494969

P.G. Wodehouse

THE MATING SEASON

ARENA

An Arena Book
Published by Arrow Books Limited
62–65 Chandos Place, London WC2N 4NW

An imprint of Century Hutchinson Limited

London Melbourne Sydney Auckland
Johannesburg and agencies throughout
the world

First published in Great Britain
by Herbert Jenkins Ltd 1949

Arena edition 1989

© P.G. Wodehouse 1949

Phototypeset by Input Typesetting Ltd, London

Printed and bound in Great Britain by
The Guernsey Press Co. Ltd, Guernsey, C.I.

ISBN 0 09965710 4

THE MATING SEASON

=1=

WHILE I would not go so far, perhaps, as to describe the heart as actually leaden, I must confess that on the eve of starting to do my bit of time at Deverill Hall I was definitely short on chirpiness. I shrank from the prospect of being decanted into a household on chummy terms with a thug like my Aunt Agatha, weakened as I already was by having had her son Thomas, one of our most prominent fiends in human shape, on my hands for three days.

I mentioned this to Jeeves, and he agreed that the set-up could have been juicier.

'Still,' I said, taking a pop, as always, at trying to focus the silver lining, 'it's flattering, of course.'

'Sir?'

'Being the People's Choice, Jeeves. Having these birds going around chanting "We Want Wooster".'

'Ah, yes, sir. Precisely. Most gratifying.'

But half a jiffy. I'm forgetting that you haven't the foggiest what all this is about. It so often pans out that way when you begin a story. You whizz off the mark all pep and ginger, like a mettlesome charger going into its routine, and the next thing you know, the customers are up on their hind legs, yelling for footnotes.

Let me get into reverse and put you abreast.

My Aunt Agatha, the one who chews broken bottles and kills rats with her teeth, arriving suddenly in London from her rural lair with her son Thomas, had instructed me in her authoritative way to put the latter up in my flat for three days while he visited dentists and Old Vics and things preparatory to leaving for his school at Bramley-on-Sea and, that done, to proceed to Deverill Hall, King's Deverill, Hants., the residence of some pals of hers, and lend my services to the village concert. Apparently they wanted to stiffen up the programme with a bit of metropolitan talent, and I had been recommended by the vicar's niece.

And that, of course, was that. It was no good telling her that

I would prefer not to touch young Thos with a ten-foot pole and that I disliked taking on blind dates. When Aunt Agatha issues her orders, you fill them. But I was conscious, as I have indicated, of an uneasiness as to the shape of things to come, and it didn't make the outlook any brighter to know that Gussie Fink-Nottle would be among those present at Deverill Hall. When you get trapped in the den of the Secret Nine, you want something a lot better than Gussie to help you keep the upper lip stiff.

I mused a bit.

'I wish I had more data about these people, Jeeves,' I said. 'I like on these occasions to know what I'm up against. So far, all I've gathered is that I am to be the guest of a landed proprietor called Harris or Hacker or possibly Hassock.'

'Haddock, sir.'

'Haddock, eh?'

'Yes, sir. The gentleman who is to be your host is a Mr Esmond Haddock.'

'It's odd, but that name seems to strike a chord, as if I'd heard it before somewhere.'

'Mr Haddock is the son of the owner of a widely advertised patent remedy known as Haddock's Headache Hokies, sir. Possibly the specific is familiar to you.'

'Of course. I know it well. Not so sensationally good as those pick-me-ups of yours, but none the less a sound stand-by on the morning after. So he's one of those Haddocks, is he?'

'Yes, sir. Mr Esmond Haddock's late father married the late Miss Flora Deverill.'

'Before they were both late, of course?'

'The union was considered something of a *mésalliance* by the lady's sisters. The Deverills are a very old county family – like so many others in these days, impoverished.'

'I begin to get the scenario. Haddock, though not as posh as he might be on the father's side, foots the weekly bills?'

'Yes, sir.'

'Well, no doubt he can afford to. There's gold in them thar Hokies, Jeeves.'

'So I should be disposed to imagine, sir.'

A point struck me which often does strike me when chewing the fat with this honest fellow – viz. that he seemed to know a hell of a lot about it. I mentioned this, and he explained that it was one of those odd chances that had enabled him to get the inside story.

'My Uncle Charlie holds the post of butler at the Hall, sir. It is from him that I derive my information.'

'I didn't know you had an Uncle Charlie. Charlie Jeeves?'

'No, sir. Charlie Silversmith.'

I lit a rather pleased cigarette. Things were beginning to clarify.

'Well, this is a bit of a goose. You'll be able to give me all the salient facts, if salient is the word I want. What sort of a joint is this Deverill Hall? Nice place? Gravel soil? Spreading views?'

'Yes, sir.'

'Good catering?'

'Yes, sir.'

'And touching on the personnel. Would there be a Mrs Haddock?'

'No, sir. The young gentleman is unmarried. He resides at the Hall with his five aunts.'

'*Five?*'

'Yes, sir. The Misses Charlotte, Emmeline, Harriet and Myrtle Deverill and Dame Daphne Winkworth, relict of the late P. B. Winkworth, the historian. Dame Daphne's daughter, Miss Gertrude Winkworth, is, I understand, also in residence.'

On the cue 'five aunts' I had given at the knees a trifle, for the thought of being confronted with such a solid gaggle of aunts, even if those of another, was an unnerving one. Reminding myself that in this life it is not aunts that matter but the courage which one brings to them, I pulled myself together.

'I see,' I said. 'No stint of female society.'

'No, sir.'

'I may find Gussie's company a relief.'

'Very possibly, sir.'

'Such as it is.'

'Yes, sir.'

I wonder, by the way, if you recall this Augustus, on whose activities I have had occasion to touch once or twice before now? Throw the mind back. Goofy to the gills, face like a fish, horn-rimmed spectacles, drank orange juice, collected newts, engaged to England's premier pill, a girl called Madeline Bassett . . . Ah, you've got him? Fine.

'Tell me, Jeeves,' I said, 'how does Gussie come to be mixed up with these bacteria? Surely a bit of an inscrutable mystery that he, too, should be headed for Deverill Hall?'

'No, sir. It was Mr Fink-Nottle himself who informed me.'

'You've seen him, then?'

'Yes, sir. He called while you were out.'

'How did he seem?'

'Low-spirited, sir.'

'Like me, he shrinks from the prospect of visiting this ghastly shack?'

'Yes, sir. He had supposed that Miss Bassett would be accompanying him, but she has altered her arrangements at the last moment and gone to reside at The Larches, Wimbledon Common, with an old school friend who has recently suffered a disappointment in love. It was Miss Bassett's view that she needed cheering up.'

I was at a loss to comprehend how the society of Madeline Bassett could cheer anyone up, she being from topknot to shoe sole the woman whom God forgot, but I didn't say so. I merely threw out the opinion that this must have made Gussie froth a bit.

'Yes, sir. He expressed annoyance at the change of plan. Indeed, I gathered from his remarks, for he was kind enough to confide in me, that there has resulted a certain coolness between himself and Miss Bassett.'

'Gosh!' I said.

And I'll tell you why I goshed. If you remember Gussie Fink-Nottle, you will probably also remember the chain of circumstances which led up, if chains do lead up, to this frightful Bassett getting the impression firmly fixed in her woollen head that Bertram Wooster was pining away for love of her. I won't go into details now, but it was her conviction that if ever she felt like severing relations with Gussie, she had only to send out a hurry call for me and I would come racing round, all ready to buy the licence and start ordering the wedding cake.

So, knowing my view regarding this Bassett, M., you will readily understand why this stuff about coolnesses drew a startled 'Gosh!' from me. The thought of my peril had never left me, and I wasn't going to be really easy in my mind till these two were actually centre-aisling. Only when the clergyman had definitely pronounced sentence would Bertram start to breathe freely again.

'Ah, well,' I said, hoping for the best. 'Just a lovers' tiff, no doubt. Always happening, these lovers' tiffs. Probably by this time a complete reconciliation has been effected and the laughing Love God is sweating away at the old stand once more with knobs on. Ha!' I proceeded as the front-door bell tootled, 'someone waits without. If it's young Thos, tell him that I shall expect him to be in readiness, all clean and rosy, at seven forty-five tonight to accompany me to the performance of *King Lear* at the Old Vic, and it's no good him trying to do a sneak. His mother said he had got to go to the Old Vic, and he's jolly well going.'

'I think it is more probable that it is Mr Pirbright, sir.'

'Old Catsmeat? What makes you think that?'

'He also called during your absence and indicated that he would return later. He was accompanied by his sister, Miss Pirbright.'

'Good Lord, really? Corky? I thought she was in Hollywood.'

'I understand that she has returned to England for a vacation, sir.'

'Did you give her tea?'

'Yes, sir. Master Thomas played host. Miss Pirbright took the young gentleman off subsequently to see a picture.'

'I wish I hadn't missed her. I haven't seen Corky for ages. Was she all right?'

'Yes, sir.'

'And Catsmeat? How was he?'

'Low-spirited, sir.'

'You're mixing him up with Gussie. It was Gussie, if you recall, who was low-spirited.'

'Mr Pirbright also.'

'There seems to be a lot of low-spiritedness kicking about these days.'

'We live in difficult times, sir.'

'True. Well, bung him in.'

He oozed out, and a few moments later oozed in again.

'Mr Pirbright,' he announced.

He had called his shots correctly. A glance at the young visitor was enough to tell me that he was low-spirited.

=2=

A ND, mind you, it isn't often that you find the object under advisement in this condition. A singularly fizzy bird, as a rule. In fact, taking him by and large, I should say that of all the rollicking lads at the Drones Club, Claude Cattermole Pirbright is perhaps the most rollicking, both on the stage and off.

I say 'on the stage', for it is behind the footlights that he earns his weekly envelope. He comes of a prominent theatrical family. His father was the man who wrote the music of *The Blue Lady* and other substantial hits which I unfortunately missed owing to being in the cradle at the time. His mother was Elsie Cattermole, who was a star in New York for years. And his sister Corky has been wowing the customers with her oomph and *espièglerie*, if that's the word I want, since she was about sixteen.

It was almost inevitable, therefore, that, looking about him on coming down from Oxford for some walk in life which would ensure the three squares a day and give him time to play a bit of county cricket, he should have selected the sock and buskin. To-day he is the fellow managers pick first when they have a Society comedy to present and want someone for 'Freddie', the lighthearted friend of the hero, carrying the second love interest. If at such a show you see a willowy figure come bounding on with a tennis racket, shouting 'Hallo, girls' shortly after the kick-off, don't bother to look at the programme. That'll be Catsmeat.

On such occasions he starts off sprightly and continues sprightly till closing time, and it is the same in private life. There, too, his sprightliness is a byword. Pongo Twistleton and Barmy Phipps, who do each year at the Drones smoker the knockabout Pat and Mike cross-talk act of which he is the author and producer, have told me that when rehearsing them in their lines and business, he is more like Groucho Marx than anything human.

Yet now, as I say, he was low-spirited. It stuck out a mile.

13

His brow was sicklied o'er with the pale cast of thought and his air that of a man who, if he had said 'Hallo, girls', would have said it like someone in a Russian drama announcing that Grandpapa had hanged himself in the barn.

I greeted him cordially and said I was sorry I had been out when he had come seeking an audience before, especially as he had had Corky with him.

'I should have loved a chat with Corky,' I said. 'I had no idea she was back in England. Now I'm afraid I've missed her.'

'No, you haven't.'

'Yes, I have. I leave to-morrow for a place called Deverill Hall in Hampshire to help at the village concert. It seems that the vicar's niece insisted on having me in the troupe, and what's puzzling me is how this girl of God heard of me. One hadn't supposed one's reputation was so far flung.'

'You silly ass, she's Corky.'

'Corky?'

I was stunned. There are few better eggs in existence than Cora ('Corky') Pirbright, with whom I have been on the matiest of terms since the days when in our formative years we attended the same dancing class, but nothing in her deportment had ever given me the idea that she was related to the clergy.

'My Uncle Sidney is the vicar down there, and my aunt's away at Bournemouth. In her absence, Corky is keeping house for him.'

'My God! Poor old Sid! She tidies his study, no doubt?'

'Probably.'

'Straightens his tie?'

'I wouldn't be surprised.'

'And tells him he smokes too much, and every time he gets comfortably settled in an armchair boosts him out of it so that she can smooth the cushions. He must be feeling as if he were living in the book of Revelations. But doesn't she find a vicarage rather slow after Hollywood?'

'Not a bit. She loves it. Corky's different from me. I wouldn't be happy out of show business, but she was never really keen on it, though she's been such a success. I don't think she would have gone on the stage at all, if it hadn't been for Mother wanting her to so much. Her dream is to marry someone who lives in the country and spend the rest of her life knee-deep in

14

cows and dogs and things. I suppose it's the old Farmer Giles strain in the Pirbrights coming out. My grandfather was a farmer. I can just remember him. Yards of whiskers, and always bellyaching about the weather. Messing about in the parish and getting up village concerts is her dish.'

'Any idea what she wants me to give the local yokels? Not the "Yeoman's Wedding Song", I trust?'

'No. You're billed to do the Pat part in that cross-talk act of mine.'

This came under the head of tidings of great joy. Too often at these binges the Brass Hats in charge tell you off to render the 'Yeoman's Wedding Song', which for some reason always arouses the worst passions of the tough eggs who stand behind the back row. But no rustic standees have ever been known not to eat a knockabout cross-talk act. There is something about the spectacle of Performer A sloshing Performer B over the head with an umbrella and Performer B prodding Performer A in the midriff with a similar blunt instrument that seems to speak to their depths. Wearing a green beard and given adequate assistance by my supporting cast, I could confidently anticipate that I should have the clientele rolling in the aisles.

'Right. Fine. Splendid. I can now face the future with an uplifted heart. But if she wanted someone for Pat, why didn't she get you? You being a seasoned professional. Ah, I see what must have happened. She offered you the role and you drew yourself up haughtily, feeling that you were above this amateur stuff.'

Catsmeat shook the lemon sombrely.

'It wasn't that at all. Nothing would have pleased me more than to have performed at the King's Deverill concert, but the shot wasn't on the board. Those women at the Hall hate my insides.'

'So you've met them? What are they like? A pretty stiffish nymphery, I suspect.'

'No, I haven't met them. But I'm engaged to their niece, Gertrude Winkworth, and the idea of her marrying me gives them the pip. If I showed myself within a mile of Deverill Hall, dogs would be set on me. Talking of dogs, Corky bought one this morning at the Battersea Home.'

'God bless her,' I said, speaking absently, for my thoughts

15

were concentrated on this romance of his and I was trying to sort out his little ball of worsted from the mob of aunts and what-have-you of whom Jeeves had spoken. Then I got her placed. Gertrude, daughter of Dame Daphne Winkworth, relict of the late P. B. Winkworth, the historian.

'That's what I came to see you about.'

'Corky's dog?'

'No, this Gertrude business. I need your help. I'll tell you the whole story.'

On Catsmeat's entry I had provided him with a hospitable whisky and splash, and of this he had downed up to this point perhaps a couple of sips and a gulp. He now knocked back the residuum, and it seemed to touch the spot, for when it was down the hatch he spoke with animation and fluency.

'I should like to start by saying, Bertie, that since the first human crawled out of the primeval slime and life began on this planet nobody has ever loved anybody as I love Gertrude Winkworth. I mention this because I want you to realize that what you're sitting in on is not one of those light summer flirtations but the real West End stuff. I love her!'

'That's good. Where did you meet her?'

'At a house in Norfolk. They were doing some amateur the-atricals and roped me in to produce. My God! Those twilight evenings in the old garden, with the birds singing sleepily in the shrubberies and the stars beginning to peep out in the – '

'Right ho. Carry on.'

'She's wonderful, Bertie. Why she loves me, I can't imagine.'

'But she does?'

'Oh yes, she does. We got engaged, and she returned to Deverill Hall to break the news to her mother. And when she did, what do you think happened?'

Well, of course, he had rather given away the punch of his story at the outset.

'The parent kicked?'

'She let out a yell you could have heard at Basingstoke.'

'Basingstoke being – '

'About twenty miles away as the crow flies.'

'I know Basingstoke. Bless my soul yes, know it well.'

'She – '

'I've stayed there as a boy. An old nurse of mine used to live at Basingstoke in a semi-detached villa called Balmoral. Her name was Hogg, oddly enough. Nurse Hogg. She suffered from hiccups.'

Catsmeat's manner became a bit tense. He looked like a village standee hearing the 'Yeoman's Wedding Song'.

'Listen, Bertie,' he said, 'suppose we don't talk about Basingstoke or about your nurse either. To hell with Basingstoke and to hell with your ruddy nurse, too. Where was I?'

'We broke off at the point where Dame Daphne Winkworth was letting out a yell.'

'That's right. Her sisters, when informed that Gertrude was proposing to marry the brother of the Miss Pirbright down at the Vicarage and that this brother was an actor by profession, also let our yells.'

I toyed with the idea of asking if these, too, could have been heard at Basingstoke, but wiser counsels prevailed.

'They don't like Corky, and they don't like actors. In their young days, in the reign of Queen Elizabeth, actors were looked on as rogues and vagabonds, and they can't get it into their nuts that the modern actor is a substantial citizen who makes his sixty quid a week and salts most of it away in sound Government securities. Why, dash it, if I could think of some way of doing down the income-tax people, I should be a rich man. You don't know of a way of doing down the income-tax people do you, Bertie?'

'Sorry, no. I doubt if even Jeeves does. So you got the bird?'

'Yes. I had a sad letter from Gertrude saying no dice. You may ask why don't we elope?'

'I was just going to.'

'I couldn't swing it. She fears her mother's wrath.'

'A tough character, this mother?'

'Of the toughest. She used to be headmistress of a big girls' school. Gertrude was a member of the chain gang and has never got over it. No, elopements seem to be out. And here's the snag, Bertie. Corky has wangled a contract for me with her studio in Hollywood, and I may have to sail at any moment. It's a frightful situation.'

I was silent for a moment. I was trying to remember something I had read somewhere about something not quenching something, but I couldn't get at it. However, the general idea was that if a girl loves you and you are compelled to leave her in storage for a while, she will wait for you, so I put this point, and he said that was all very well but I didn't know all. The plot, he assured me, was about to thicken.

'We now come,' he said, 'to the hellhound Haddock. And this is where I want you to rally round, Bertie.'

I said I didn't get the gist, and he said of course I didn't get the damned gist, but couldn't I wait half a second, blast me, and give him a chance to explain, and I said Oh, rather, certainly.

'Haddock!' said Catsmeat, speaking between clenched teeth and exhibiting other signs of emotion. 'Haddock the Home Wrecker! Do you know anything about this Grade A louse, Bertie?'

'Only that his late father was the proprietor of those Headache Hokies.'

'And left him enough money to sink a ship. I'm not suggesting, of course, that Gertrude would marry him for his money. She would scorn such raw work. But in addition to having more cash than you could shake a stick at, he's a sort of Greek god in appearance and extremely magnetic. So Gertrude says. And, what is more, I gather from her letters that pressure is being brought to bear on her by the family. And you can imagine what the pressure of a mother and four aunts is like.'

I began to grasp the trend.

'You mean Haddock is trying to move in?'

'Gertrude writes that he is giving her the rush of a lifetime. And this will show you the sort of flitting and sipping butterfly the hound is. It's only a short while ago that he was giving Corky a similar rush. Ask her when you see her, but tactfully, because she's as sore as a gumboil about it. I tell you, the man is a public menace. He ought to be kept on a chain in the interests of pure womanhood. But we'll fix him, won't we?'

'Will we?'

'You bet we will. Here's what I want you to do. You'll agree that even a fellow like Esmond Haddock, who appears to be the nearest thing yet discovered to South American Joe, couldn't press his foul suit in front of you?'

'You mean he would need privacy?'

'Exactly. So the moment you are inside Deverill Hall, start busting up his sinister game. Be always at Gertrude's side. Stick to her like glue. See that he doesn't get her alone in the rose garden. If a visit to the rose garden is mooted, include yourself in. You follow me, Bertie?'

'I follow you, yes,' I said, a little dubiously. 'What you have in mind is something on the lines of Mary's lamb. I don't know if you happen to know the poem – I used to recite it as a child – but, broadly, the nub was that Mary had a little lamb with fleece as white as snow, and everywhere that Mary went the lamb was sure to go. You want me to model my technique on that of Mary's lamb?'

'That's it. Be on the alert every second, for the peril is frightful. Well, to give you some idea, his most recent suggestion is that Gertrude and he shall take sandwiches one of these mornings and ride out to a place about fifteen miles away, where there are cliffs and things. And do you know what he plans to do when they get there? Show her the Lovers' Leap.'

'Oh, yes?'

'Don't say "Oh, yes?" in that casual way. Think, man. Fifteen miles there, then the Lovers' Leap, then fifteen miles back. The imagination reels at the thought of what excesses a fellow like Esmond Haddock may commit on a thirty-mile ride with a Lovers' Leap thrown in half-way. I don't know what day the expedition is planned for, but whenever it is, you must be with it from start to finish. If possible riding between them. And for God's sake don't take your eye off him for an instant at the Lovers' Leap. That will be the danger spot. If you notice the slightest disposition on his part, when at the Lovers' Leap, to lean towards her and whisper in her ear, break up the act like lightning. I'm relying on you, Bertie. My life's happiness depends on you.'

Well, of course, if a man you've been at private school, public school and Oxford with says he's relying on you, you have no option but to let yourself be relied on. To say that the assignment was one I liked would be over-stating the facts, but I right-hoed, and he grasped my hand and said that if there were more fellows like me in it the world would be a better place – a view which differed sharply from that of my Aunt Agatha, and one which I had a hunch was going to differ sharply from that of Esmond Haddock. There might be those at Deverill Hall who would come to love Bertram, but my bet was that E. Haddock's name would not be on the roster.

'Well, you've certainly eased my mind,' said Catsmeat, having released the hand and then re-grabbed and re-squeezed it. 'Knowing that you are on the spot, working like a beaver in my interests, will mean everything. I have been off my feed for some little time now, but I'm going to enjoy my dinner tonight. I only wish there was something I could do for you in return.'

'There is,' I said.

A thought had struck me, prompted no doubt by his mention of the word 'dinner'. Ever since Jeeves had told me about the coolness which existed between Gussie Fink-Nottle and Madeline Bassett I had been more than a bit worried at the thought of Gussie dining by himself that night.

I mean, you know how it is when you've had one of these lovers' tiffs and then go off to a solitary dinner. You start brooding over the girl with the soup and wonder if it wasn't a mug's game hitching up with her. With the fish this feeling deepens, and by the time you're through with the *poulet rôti au cresson* and are ordering the coffee you've probably definitely to the conclusion that she's a rag and a bone and a hank of hair and that it would be madness to sign her on as a life partner.

What you need on these occasions is entertaining company, so that your dark thoughts may be diverted, and it seemed to me that here was the chance to provide Gussie with some.

'There is,' I said. 'You know Gussie Fink-Nottle? He's low-spirited, and there are reasons why I would prefer that he isn't alone tonight, brooding. Could you give him a spot of dinner?'

Catsmeat chewed his lip. I knew what was passing in his mind. He was thinking, as others have thought, that the first essential for an enjoyable dinner-party is for Gussie not to be at it.

'Give Gussie Fink-Nottle dinner?'

'That's right.'

'Why don't you?'

'My Aunt Agatha wants me to take her son Thomas to the Old Vic.'

'Give it a miss.'

'I can't. I should never hear the last of it.'

'Well, all right.'

'Heaven bless you, Catsmeat,' I said.

So Gussie was off my mind. It was with a light heart that I retired to rest that night. I little knew, as the expression is, what the morrow was to bring forth.

Though, as a matter of fact, in its early stages the morrow brought forth some pretty good stuff. As generally happens on these occasions when you are going to cop it in the quiet evenfall, the day started extremely well. Knowing that at 2.53 I was to shoot young Thos off to his seaside Borstal, I breakfasted with a song on my lips, and at lunch, I recall, I was in equally excellent fettle.

I took Thos to Victoria, bunged him into his train, slipped him a quid and stood waving a cousinly hand till he was out of sight. Then, after looking in at Queen's Club for a game or two of rackets, I went back to the flat, still chirpy.

Up till then everything had been fine. As I put hat on hat-peg and umbrella in umbrella-stand, I was thinking that if God wasn't in His heaven and all right with the world, these conditions prevailed as near as made no matter. Not the suspicion of an inkling, if you see what I mean, that round the corner lurked the bitter awakening, stuffed eelskin in hand, waiting to sock me on the occiput.

The first thing to which my attention was drawn on crossing the threshold was that there seemed to be a lot more noise going on than was suitable in a gentleman's home. Through the closed door of the sitting-room the ear detected the sound of a female voice raised in what appeared to be cries of encouragement and, mingled with this female voice, a loud barking, as of hounds on the trail. It was as though my boudoir had been selected by the management of the Quorn or the Pytchley as the site for their most recent meet, and my first instinct, as that of any householder would have been, was to look into this. Nobody can call Bertram Wooster a fussy man, but there are moments when he feels he has to take a firm stand.

I opened the door, accordingly, and was immediately knocked base over apex by some solid body with a tongue like an anteater's. This tongue it proceeded to pass enthusiastically over my upper slopes and, the mists clearing away, I perceived that what I was tangled up with was a shaggy dog of mixed parentage. And standing beside us, looking down like a mother watching the gambols of her first-born, was Catsmeat's sister Corky.

'Isn't he a lamb?' she said. 'Isn't he an absolute seraph?'

I was not able wholly to subscribe to this view. The animal appeared to have an agreeable disposition and to have taken an immediate fancy to me, but physically it was no beauty-prize winner. It looked like Boris Karloff made up for something.

Corky, on the other hand, as always, distinctly took the eye. Two years in Hollywood had left her even easier to look at than when last seen around these parts.

This young prune is one of those lissom girls of medium height, constructed on the lines of Gertrude Lawrence, and her map had always been worth more than a passing glance. In repose, it has a sort of meditative expression, as if she were a pure white soul thinking beautiful thoughts, and, when animated, so dashed animated that it boosts the morale just to look at her. Her eyes are a kind of browny-hazel and her hair rather along the same lines. The general effect is of an angel who eats lots of yeast. In fine, if you were called upon to pick something to be cast on a desert island with, Hedy Lamarr might be your first choice, but Corky Pirbright would inevitably come high up in the list of Hon. Mentions.

'His name's Sam Goldwyn,' she proceeded, hauling the animal off the prostrate form. 'I bought him at the Battersea Home.'

I rose and dried the face.

'Yes, so Catsmeat told me.'

'Oh, you've seen Catsmeat? Good.'

At this point she seemed to become aware that we had skipped the customary pip-pippings, for she took time out to say how nice it was to see me again after all this time. I said how nice it was to see her again after all this time, and she asked me how I was, and I said I was fine. I asked her how she was, and she said she was fine. She enquired if I was still as big a chump as ever, and I satisfied her curiosity at this point.

'I looked in yesterday, hoping to see you,' she said, 'but you were out.'

'Yes, Jeeves told me.'

'A small boy with red hair entertained me. He said he was your cousin.'

'My Aunt Agatha's son and, oddly enough, the apple of her eye.'

'Why oddly enough?'

'He's the King of the Underworld. They call him The Shadow.'

'I liked him. I gave him fifty of my autographs. He's going to sell them to the boys at his school and expects to get sixpence apiece. He has long admired me on the screen, and we hit it off together like a couple of Yes-men. Catsmeat didn't seem to take to him so much.'

'He once put a drawing-pin on Catsmeat's chair.'

'Ah, that would account for the imperfect sympathy. Talking of Catsmeat, did he give you the Pat and Mike script?'

'Yes, I've got it. I was studying it in bed last night.'

'Good. It was sporting of you to rally round.'

I didn't tell her that my rallying round had been primarily due to *force majeure* on the part of an aunt who brooks, if that's the word, no back-chat. Instead, I asked who was to be my partner in the merry *mélange* of fun and topicality, sustaining the minor but exacting role of Mike, and she said an artiste of the name of Dobbs.

'Police Constable Dobbs, the local rozzer. And in this connection, Bertie, there is one thing I want to impress upon you with all the emphasis at my disposal. When socking Constable Dobbs with your umbrella at the points where the script calls for it, don't pull your punches. Let the blighter have it with every ounce of wrist and muscle. I want to see him come off that stage a mass of contusions.'

It seemed to me, for I am pretty quick, that she had it in for this Dobbs. I said so, and she concurred, a quick frown marring the alabaster purity of her brow.

'I have. I'm devoted to my poor old Uncle Sidney, and this uncouth bluebottle is a thorn in his flesh. He's the village atheist.'

'Oh, really? An atheist, is he? I never went in for that sort of thing much myself. In fact, at my private school I once won a prize for Scripture Knowledge.'

'He annoys Uncle Sidney by popping out at him from side streets and making offensive cracks about Jonah and the Whale. This cross-talk act has been sent from heaven. In ordinary life, I mean, you get so few opportunities of socking cops with umbrellas, and if ever a cop needed the treatment, it is Ernest Dobbs. When he isn't smirching Jonah and the Whale with his low sneers, he's asking Uncle Sidney where Cain got his wife. You can't say that sort of thing is pleasant for a sensitive vicar, so hew to the line, my poppet, and let the chips fall where they may.'

She had stirred the Wooster blood and aroused the Wooster chivalry. I assured her that by the time they struck up 'God Save The King' in the old village hall Constable Dobbs would know he had been in a fight, and she thanked me prettily.

'I can see you're going to be good, Bertie. And I don't mind telling you your public is expecting big things. For days the whole village has been talking of nothing else but the coming visit of Bertram Wooster, the great London comic. You will be the high spot of the programme. And goodness knows it can do with a high spot or two.'

'Who are the performers?'

'Just the scourings of the neighbourhood . . . and Esmond Haddock. He's singing a song.'

The way she spoke that name, with a sort of frigid distaste as if it soiled her lips, told me that Catsmeat had not erred in saying that she was as sore as a gumboil about E. Haddock's in-and-out running. Remembering that he had warned me to approach the subject tactfully, I picked my words with care.

'Ah, yes. Esmond Haddock. Catsmeat was telling me about Esmond Haddock.'

'What did he tell you?'

'Oh, this and that.'

'Featuring me?'

'Yes, to a certain extent featuring you.'

'What did he say?'

'Well, he seemed to hint, unless I misunderstood him, that the above Haddock hadn't, as it were, done right by our Nell. According to Catsmeat, you and this modern Casanova were at one time holding hands, but after flitting and sipping for a while he cast you aside like a worn-out glove and attached himself to Gertrude Winkworth. Quite incorrect, probably. I expect he got the whole story muddled up.'

She came clean. I suppose a girl who has been going about for some weeks as sore as a gumboil, and with the heart cracked in two places gets to feel that maidenly pride is all very well but that what eases the soul is confession. And, of course, making me her confidant was not like spilling the inside stuff to a stranger. No doubt the thought crossed her mind that we had attended the same dancing class, and it may be that a vision of the child Wooster in a Little Lord Fauntleroy suit and pimples rose before her eyes.

'No, he didn't get the story muddled up. We were holding hands. But Esmond didn't cast me aside like a worn-out glove, I cast him aside like a worn-out glove. I told him I wouldn't have any more to do with him unless he asserted himself and stopped crawling to those aunts of his.'

'He crawls to his aunts, does he?'

'Yes, the worm.'

I could not pass this. Better men than Esmond Haddock have crawled to their aunts, and I said so, but she didn't seem to be listening. Girls seldom do listen to me, I've noticed. Her face was drawn and her eyes had a misty look. The lips, I observed, were a-quiver.

'I oughtn't to call him a worm. It's not his fault, really. They brought him up from the time he was six, oppressing him daily, and it's difficult for him to cast off the shackles, I suppose. I'm very sorry for him. But there's a limit. When it came to being scared to tell them we were engaged, I put my foot down. I said he'd got to tell them, and he turned green and said Oh, he couldn't, and I said All right, then, let's call the whole thing off. And I haven't spoken to him since, except to ask him to sing this song at the concert. And the unfortunate part of it all is, Bertie, that I'm crazier about him than ever. Just to think of him makes me want to howl and chew the carpet.'

At this point she buried her face in Sam Goldwyn's coat, ostensibly by way of showing a proprietress's affection, but really, I could see, being shrewd, in order to dry the starting tears. Personally, for the animal niffed to heaven, I would have preferred to use my cambric handkerchief, but girls will be girls.

'Oh, well,' she said, coming to the surface again.

It was a bit difficult to know how to carry on. A "There, there, little woman" might have gone well, or it might not. After thinking it over for a moment, I too-badded.

'Oh, it's all right,' she said, stiffening the upper lip. 'Just one of those things. When do you go down to Deverill?'

'This evening.'

'How do you feel about it?'

'Not too good. A certain coolness in the feet. I'm never at my best in the society of aunts and, according to Jeeves, they assemble in gangs at Deverill Hall. There are five of them, he says.'

'That's right.'

'It's a lot.'

'Five too many. I don't think you'll like them, Bertie. One's deaf, one's dotty, and they're all bitches.'

'You use strong words, child.'

'Only because I can't think of any stronger. They're awful. They've lived all their lives at that mouldering old Hall, and they're like something out of a three-volume novel. They judge everybody by the county standard. If you aren't county, you don't exist. I believe they swooned for weeks when their sister married Esmond's father.'

'Yes, Jeeves rather suggested that in their opinion he soiled the escutcheon.'

'Nothing to the way I would have soiled it. Being in pix, I'm the scarlet woman.'

'I've often wondered about that scarlet woman. Was she scarlet all over, or was it just that her face was red? However, that is not germane to the issue. So that's how it is, is it?'

'That's how it is.'

I was rather glad that at this juncture the hound Sam Goldwyn made another of his sudden dives at my abdomen with the slogan 'Back to Bertram' on his lips, for it enabled me to bridge over an emotional moment. I was considerably concerned. What was to be done about it, I didn't know, but there was no gainsaying that when it came to making matrimonial plans, the Pirbrights were not a lucky family.

Corky seemed to be feeling this, too.

'It would happen, wouldn't it,' she said, 'that the only one of all the millions of men I've met that I've ever wanted to marry can't marry me because his aunts won't let him.'

'It's tough on you,' I agreed.

'And just as tough on poor old Catsmeat. You wouldn't think, just seeing him around, that Catsmeat was the sort of man to break his heart over a girl, but he is. He's full of hidden depths, if you really know him. Gertrude means simply everything to him. And I doubt if she will be able to hold out against a combination of Esmond and her mother and the aunts.'

'Yes, he told me pressure was being applied.'

'How did you think he seemed?'

'Low-spirited.'

'Yes, he's taking it hard,' said Corky.

Her face clouded. Catsmeat has always been her ewe lamb, if you understand what I mean by ewe lamb. It was plain that she mourned for him in spirit, and no doubt at this point we should have settled down to a long talk about his spot of bother, examining it from every angle and trying to decide what was to be done for the best, had not the door opened and he blown in in person.

'Hallo, Catsmeat,' I said.

'Hallo, Catsmeat, darling,' said Corky.

'Hallo,' said Catsmeat.

I looked at Corky. She looked at me. I rather think we pursed our lips and, speaking for myself, I know I raised my eyebrows. For the demeanour of this Pirbright was that of a man who has abandoned hope, and the voice in which he had said 'Hallo' had been to all intents and purposes a voice from the tomb. The whole set-up, in short, such as to occasion pity and terror in the bosoms of those who wished him well.

He sank into a chair and closed his eyes, and for some moments remained motionless. Then, as if a bomb had suddenly exploded inside the bean, he shot up with a stifled cry, clasping his temples, and I began to see daylight. His deportment, so plainly that of a man aware that only prompt action in the nick of time has prevented his head splitting in half, told me that we had been mistaken in supposing that this living corpse had got that way purely through disappointed love. I touched the bell, and Jeeves appeared.

'One of your special morning-afters, if you please, Jeeves.'

'Very good, sir.'

He shimmered out, and I subjected Catsmeat to a keen glance. I am told by those who know that there are six varieties of hangover – the Broken Compass, the Sewing Machine, the

Comet, the Atomic, the Cement Mixer and the Gremlin Boogie, and his manner suggested that he had got them all.

'So you were lathered last night?' I said.

'I was perhaps a mite polluted,' he admitted.

'Jeeves has gone for one of his revivers.'

'Thank you, Bertie, thank you,' said Catsmeat in a low, soft voice, and closed his eyes again.

His intention obviously was to restore his tissues with a short nap, and personally I would have left him alone and let him go to it. But Corky was of sterner stuff. She took his head in both hands and shook it, causing him to shoot ceilingwards, this time with a cry so little stifled that it rang through the room like the death rattle of a hundred expiring hyenas. The natural consequence was that Sam Goldwyn began splitting the welkin, and with the view of taking him off the air I steered him to the door and bunged him out. I returned to find Corky ticking Catsmeat off in no uncertain manner.

'You promised me faithfully you wouldn't get pie-eyed, you poor fish,' she was saying with sisterly vehemence. 'What price the word of the Pirbrights?'

'That's all right "What price the word of the Pirbrights?" ' retorted Catsmeat with some spirit. 'When I gave the word of the Pirbrights that I wouldn't get pie-eyed, I didn't know I should be dining with Gussie Fink-Nottle. Bertie will bear me out that it is not humanly possible to get through an evening alone with Gussie without large quantities of stimulants.'

I nodded.

'He's quite right,' I said. 'Even at the peak of his form Gussie isn't everybody's dream-comrade, and last night I should imagine he was low-spirited.'

'Very low-spirited,' said Catsmeat. 'In my early touring days I have sometimes arrived at Southport on a rainy Sunday morning. Gussie gave me that same sense of hopeless desolation. He sat there with his lower jaw drooping, goggling at me like a codfish – '

'Gussie,' I explained to Corky, 'has had a lovers' tiff with his betrothed.'

' – until after a bit I saw that there was only one thing to be done, if I was to survive the ordeal. I told the waiter to bring a magnum and leave it at my elbow. After that, things seemed to get better.'

'Gussie, of course, drank orange juice?'

'Throughout,' said Catsmeat with a slight shudder.

I could see that even though he had made this manly, straight-forward statement, Corky was still threatening to do the heavy sister and heap reproaches on a man who was in no condition to receive them, for even the best of women cannot refrain from saying their say the morning after, so I hastened to continue the conversation on a neutral note.

'Where did you dine?'

'At the Dorchester.'

'Go anywhere after dinner?'

'Oh, yes.'

'Where?'

'Oh, hither and thither. East Dulwich, Ponder's End, Limehouse – '

'Why Limehouse?'

'Well, I had always wanted to see it, and I may have had some idea of comparing its blues with mine. As to East Dulwich and Ponder's End, I am not sure. Perhaps I heard someone recommend them, or possibly I just felt that the thing to do was to get about and see fresh faces. I had chartered a taxi for the evening and we roamed around, taking in the sights. Eventually we fetched up in Trafalgar Square.'

'What time was this?'

'About five in the morning. Have you ever been in Trafalgar Square at five in the morning? Very picturesque, that fountain in the first early light of the dawn. It was as we stood on its brink with the sun just beginning to gild the house-tops that I got an idea which I can now see, though it seemed a good one at the time, was a mistake.'

'What was that?'

'It struck me as a possibility that there might be newts in the fountain, and knowing how keen Gussie is on newts I advised him to wade in and hunt around.'

'With all his clothes on?'

'Yes, he had his clothes on. I remember noticing.'

'But you can't go wading in the Trafalgar Square fountain with all your clothes on.'

'Yes, you can. Gussie did. My recollection of the thing is a trifle blurred, but I seem to recall that he took a bit of persuading. Yes, I've got it now,' said Catsmeat, brightening. 'I told him to wade, and he wouldn't wade, and I said if he didn't wade I would bean him with my magnum. So he waded.'

'You still had the magnum?'

'This was another one, which we had picked up in Limehouse.'

'And Gussie waded?'

'Yes, Gussie waded.'

'I wonder he wasn't pinched.'

'He was,' said Catsmeat. 'A cop came along and gaffed him, and this morning he was given fourteen days without the option at Bosher Street police court.'

The door opened. Sam Goldwyn came bounding in and flung himself on my chest as if we had been a couple of lovers meeting at journey's end.

He was followed by Jeeves, bearing a salver with a glass on it containing one of his dynamite specials.

=4=

W<small>HEN</small> I was a piefaced lad of some twelve summers, doing my stretch at Malvern House, Bramley-on-Sea, the private school conducted by the Rev. Aubrey Upjohn, I remember hearing the Rev. Aubrey give the late Sir Philip Sidney a big buildup because, when wounded at the battle of somewhere and offered a quick one by a companion in arms, he told the chap who was setting them up to leave him out of that round and slip his spot to a nearby stretcher-case, whose need was greater than his. This spirit of selfless sacrifice, said the Rev. Aubrey, was what he would like to see in you boys – particularly you, Wooster, and how many times have I told you not to gape at me in that half-witted way? Close your mouth, boy, and sit up.

Well, if he had been one of our little circle, he would have seen it now. My primary impulse was to charge across and grab that glass from that salver and lower it at a gulp, for if ever I needed a bracer, it was then. But I stayed my hand. Even in that dreadful moment I was able to tell myself that Catsmeat's need was greater than mine. I stood back, shimmying in every limb, and he got the juice and drained it, and after going through the motions of a man struck by lightning, always the immediate reaction to these pick-me-ups of Jeeves's, said 'Ha!' and looked a lot better.

I passed a fevered hand across the brow.

'Jeeves!'

'Sir?'

'Do you know what?'

'No, sir.'

'Gussie Fink-Nottle is in stir.'

'Indeed, sir?'

I passed another hand across the brow, and the blood pressure rose several notches. I ought, I suppose, to have got it into my nut by this time that no news item, however front page, is going to make Jeeves roll his eyes and leap about, but that 'Indeed, sir?' stuff of his never fails to get the Wooster goat.

'Don't say "Indeed, sir?" I repeat. Wading in the Trafalgar Square fountain at five ack emma this morning, Augustus Fink-Nottle was apprehended by the police and is in the coop for fourteen days. And he's due at Deverill Hall this evening.'

Catsmeat, who had closed his eyes, opened them for a moment.

'Shall I tell you something?' he said. 'He won't be there.'

He reclosed the eyes, and I passed a third hand across the brow.

'You see the ghastly position, Jeeves? What is Miss Bassett going to say? What will her attitude be when she learns the facts? She opens to-morrow's paper. She sees that loved name in headlines in the police court section . . .'

'No, she doesn't,' said Catsmeat. 'Because Gussie, showing unexpected intelligence, gave his name as Alfred Duff Cooper.'

'Well, what's going to happen when he doesn't turn up at the Hall?'

'Yes, there's that,' said Catsmeat, and fell into a refreshing sleep.

'I'll tell you what Miss Bassett is going to say. She is going to say . . . Jeeves!'

'Sir?'

'You are letting your attention wander.'

'I beg your pardon, sir. I was observing the dog. If you notice, sir, he has commenced to eat the sofa cushion.'

'Never mind about the dog.'

'I think it would be advisable to remove the little fellow to the kitchen, sir,' he said with respectful firmness. Jeeves is a great stickler for having things just right. 'I will return as soon as he is safely immured.'

He withdrew, complete with dog, and Corky caught the speaker's eye. For some moments she had been hovering on the outskirts with the air of one not completely abreast of the continuity.

'But, Bertie,' she said, 'why all the excitement and agony? I could understand this Mr Fink-Nottle being a little upset, but why are you skipping like the high hills?'

I was glad that Jeeves had temporarily absented himself from the conference-table, as it would have been impossible for me to unbosom myself freely about Madeline Bassett in his presence.

Naturally he knows all the circumstances *in re* the Bassett, and I know he knows them, but we do not discuss her. To do so would be bandying a woman's name. The Woosters do not bandy a woman's name. Nor, for the matter of that, do the Jeeveses.

'Hasn't Catsmeat told you about me and Madeline Bassett?'
'Not a word.'
'Well, I'll tell you why I'm skipping like the high hills,' I said, and proceeded to do so.

The Bassett-Wooster imbroglio or mix-up will, of course, be old stuff to those of my public who were hanging on my lips when I told of it before, but there are always new members coming along, and for the benefit of these new members I will give a brief what's-it-called of the facts.

The thing started at Brinkley Court, my Aunt Dahlia's place in Worcestershire, when Gussie and I and this blighted Bassett were putting in a spell there during the previous summer. It was one of those cases you so often read about where Bloke A loves a girl but fears to speak and a friend of his, Bloke B, out of the kindness of his heart, offers to pave the way for him with a few well-chosen words – completely overlooking, poor fathead, the fact that by doing so he will be sticking his neck out and simply asking for it. What I'm driving at is that Gussie, though very much under the influence, could not bring himself to start the necessary *pourparlers*, and like an ass I told him to leave this to me.

And so, steering the girl out into the twilight one evening, I pulled some most injudicious stuff about there being hearts at Brinkley Court that ached for love of her. And the first thing I knew, she was saying that of course she had guessed how I felt, for a girl always knows, doesn't she, but she was so, so sorry it could not be, for she was sold on Gussie. But, she went on, and it was this that had made peril lurk ever since, if there should come a time when she found that Gussie was not the rare, stainless soul she thought him, she would hand him his hat and make me happy.

And, as I have related elsewhere, there had been moments when it had been touch and go, notably on the occasion when Gussie got lit up like a candelabra and in that condition presented the prizes to the young scholars of Market Snodsbury

Grammar School. She had scratched his nomination then, though subsequently relenting, and it could not but be that she would scratch it again, should she discover that the man on whom she looked as a purer, loftier spirit than other men had received an exemplary sentence for wading in the Trafalgar Square fountain. Nothing puts an idealistic girl off a fellow more than the news that he is doing fourteen days in the jug.

All this I explained to Corky, and she said Yes, she saw what I meant.

'I should think you do see what I mean. I shan't have a hope. Let Madeline Bassett become hep to what has occurred, and there can be but one result. Gussie will get the bum's rush, and the bowed figure you will see shambling down the aisle at her side, while the customers reach for their hats and the organ plays "The Voice That Breathed O'er Eden", will be that of Bertram Wilberforce Wooster.'

'I didn't know your name was Wilberforce.'

I explained that except in moments of great emotion one hushed it up.

'But Bertie, I can't understand why you don't want to shamble down aisles at her side. I've seen a photograph of her at the Hall, and she's a pippin.'

This is a very common error into which people fall who have never met Madeline Bassett but have only seen her photograph. As far as the outer crust is concerned, there is little, I fully realize, to cavil at in this pre-eminent bit of bad news. The eyes are large and lustrous, the features delicately moulded, the hair, nose, teeth and ears well up to, if not above, the average standard. Judge her by the photograph alone, and you have something that would be widely accepted as a pin-up girl.

But there is a catch, and a very serious catch.

'You ask me why I do not wish to shamble down aisles at her side,' I said. 'I will tell you. It is because, though externally, as you say, a pippin, she is the sloppiest, mushiest, sentimentalest young Gawd-help-us who ever thought the stars were God's daisy chain and that every time a fairy hiccoughs a wee baby is born. She is squashy and soupy. Her favourite reading is Christopher Robin and Winnie the Pooh. I can perhaps best sum it up by saying that she is the ideal mate for Gussie Fink-Nottle.'

'I've never met Mr Fink-Nottle.'

'Well, ask the man who has.'

She stood pondering. It was plain that she appreciated the gravity of the situation.

'Then you think that, if she finds out, you will be in for it?'

'Definitely and indubitably. I shall have no option but to take the rap. If a girl thinks you love her, and comes and says she is returning her betrothed to store and is now prepared to sign up with you, what can you do except marry her? One must be civil.'

'Yes, I see. Difficult. But how are you going to keep her from finding out? When she hears that Mr Fink-Nottle hasn't arrived at the Hall, she's bound to make inquiries.'

'And those inquiries, once made, must infallibly lead her to the awful truth? Exactly. But there is always Jeeves.'

'You think he will be able to fix things?'

'He never fails. He wears a number fourteen hat, eats tons of fish, and moves in a mysterious way his wonders to perform. See, here he comes, looking as intelligent as dammit. Well, Jeeves? Have you speared a solution?'

'Yes, sir. But – '

'You see,' I said to Corky. I paused, knitting the brow a bit. 'Did I hear you use the word "but", Jeeves? Why "but"?'

'It is merely that I entertained a certain misgiving as to whether the solution which I am about to put forward would meet with your approval, sir.'

'If it's a solution, that's all I want.'

'Well, sir, to obviate the inquiries which would inevitably be set on foot, should Mr Fink-Nottle not present himself at Deverill Hall this evening, it would appear to be essential that a substitute, purporting to be Mr Fink-Nottle, should take his place.'

I reeled.

'You aren't suggesting that I should check in at this leper colony as Gussie?'

'Unless you can persuade one of your friends to do so, sir.'

I laughed. One of those hollow, mirthless ones.

'You can't go about London asking people to pretend to be Gussie Fink-Nottle. At least, you can, I suppose, but what a hell of a life. Besides, there isn't time to . . .' I paused. 'Catsmeat!' I cried.

Catsmeat opened his eyes.

'Hallo, there,' he said, seeming much refreshed. 'How's it coming?'

'It's come. Jeeves has found the way.'

'I thought he would. What does he suggest?'

'He thinks . . . What was it, Jeeves?'

'To obviate the inquiries which would inevitably be set on foot should Mr Fink-Nottle not present himself at Deverill Hall this evening – '

'Follow this closely, Catsmeat.'

' – it would appear to be essential that a substitute, purporting to be Mr Fink-Nottle, should take his place.'

Catsmeat nodded, and said he considered that very sound.

'You mean Bertie, of course?'

I massaged his coat sleeve tenderly.

'We thought of you,' I said.

'Me?'

'Yes.'

'You want me to say I'm Gussie Fink-Nottle?'

'That's right.'

'No,' said Catsmeat. 'A thousand times no. What a revolting idea!'

The shuddering horror with which he spoke made me realize how deeply his experiences of the previous night must have affected him. And, mind you, I could understand his attitude. Gussie is a fellow you can take or leave alone, and anyone having him as a constant companion from eight at night till five on the following morning might well become a bit allergic to him. I began to see that a good deal of silver-tongued eloquence would be needed in order to obtain service and co-operation from C. C. Pirbright.

'It would enable you to be beneath the same roof as Gertrude Winkworth,' I urged.

'Yes,' said Corky, 'you would be at your Gertrude's side.'

'Even to be at my Gertrude's side,' said Catsmeat firmly, 'I won't have people going about thinking I'm Gussie Fink-Nottle. Besides, I couldn't get away with it. I shouldn't be even adequate in the role. I'm much too obviously a man of intelligence and brains and gifts and all that sort of thing, and Gussie must have been widely publicized as the fat-headedest ass in creation. After five minutes' conversation with me the old folks would penetrate the deception like a dose of salts. No, what you want if you are putting on an understudy for Gussie Fink-Nottle is someone *like* Gussie Fink-Nottle, so that the eye is deceived. You get the part, Bertie.'

A cry escaped me.

'You don't think I'm like Gussie?'

'You might be twins.'

'I still think you're a chump, Catsmeat,' said Corky. 'If you were at Deverill Hall you could protect Gertrude from Esmond Haddock's advances.'

'Bertie's attending to that. I agree that I would much enjoy a brief visit to Deverill Hall, and if only there were some other way . . . But I won't say I'm Gussie Fink-Nottle.'

I bowed to the inev.

'Right ho,' I said, with one of those sighs. 'In all human affairs there has got to be a goat or Patsy doing the dirty work, and in the present crisis I see it has got to be me. It generally happens that way. Whenever there is a job to be taken on of a kind calculated to make Humanity shudder, the cry goes up "Let Wooster do it". I'm not complaining, I'm just mentioning it. Very well. No need to argue. I'll be Gussie.'

'Smiling, the boy fell dead. That's the way I like to hear you talk,' said Catsmeat. 'On the way down be thinking out your business.'

'What do you mean – my business?'

'Well, for instance, would it or would it not be a good move to kiss Gussie's girl's godmother when you meet? Those are the little points you will have to give thought to. And now, Bertie, if you don't mind, I'll be pushing along to your bedroom and taking a short nap. Too many interruptions in here, and sleep is what I must have, if I am to face the world again. What was it I heard you call sleep the other day, Jeeves?'

'Tired Nature's sweet restorer, sir.'

'That was it. And you said a mouthful.'

He crawled off, and Corky said she would have to be going too. A hundred things to attend to.

'Well, it all looks pretty smooth now, thanks to your quick

thinking, Jeeves,' she said. 'The only nuisance is that there will be disappointment in the village when they hear they're going to get a Road Company Number Four Fink-Nottle as Pat, and not the celebrated Bertram Wooster. I rather played you up, Bertie, in the advance billing and publicity. Still, it can't be helped. Good-bye. We shall meet at Philippi. Good-bye, Jeeves.'

'Good-bye, miss.'

'Here, half a second,' I said. 'You're forgetting your dog.'

She paused at the door.

'Oh, I had been meaning to tell you about that, Bertie. I want you to take him to the Hall with you for a day or two, so as to give me time to prepare Uncle Sidney's mind. He's not too keen on dogs, and Sam will have to be broken to him gently.'

I put in an instant *nolle prosequi*.

'I'm not going to appear at the Hall with a dog like that. It would ruin my prestige.'

'Mr Fink-Nottle's prestige, you mean. And I don't suppose he has any. As Catsmeat said, they have been told all about him, and will probably be relieved that you aren't rolling in with half a dozen bowls of newts. Well, good-bye again.'

'Hey!' I yipped, but she had gone.

I turned to Jeeves.

'So, Jeeves!'

'Yes, sir.'

'What do you mean, "Yes, sir"?'

'I was endeavouring to convey my appreciation of the fact that your position *is* in many respects somewhat difficult, sir. But I wonder if I might call your attention to an observation of the Emperor Marcus Aurelius. He said: "Does aught befall you? It is good. It is part of the destiny of the Universe ordained for you from the beginning. All that befalls you is part of the great web." '

I breathed a bit stertorously.

'He said that, did he?'

'Yes, sir.'

'Well, you can tell him from me he's an ass. Are my things packed?'

'Yes, sir.'

'The two-seater is at the door?'

'Yes, sir.'

'Then lead me to it, Jeeves. If I'm to get to this lazar-house before midnight, I'd better be starting.'

WELL, I did get there before midnight, of course, but I was dashed late, all the same. As might have been expected on a day like this, the two-seater, usually as reliable as an Arab steed, developed some sort of pox or sickness half-way through the journey, with the result that the time schedule was shot to pieces and it was getting on for eight when I turned in at the main gates. A quick burst up the drive enabled me to punch the front-door bell at about twenty to.

I remember once when he and I arrived at a country house where the going threatened to be sticky, Jeeves, as we alighted, murmured in my ear the words 'Childe Roland to the Dark Tower came, sir', and at the time I could make nothing of the crack. Subsequent inquiry, however, revealed that this Roland was one of those knights of the Middle Ages who spent their time wandering to and fro, and that on fetching up one evening at a dump known as the Dark Tower he had scratched the chin a bit dubiously, not liking the look of things.

It was the same with me now. I admired Deverill Hall, I could appreciate that it was a fine old pile, with battlements and all the fixings, and if the Deverill who built it had been with me at the moment, I would have slapped him on the back and said 'Nice work, Deverill'. But I quailed at the thought of what lay within. Behind that massive front door lurked five aunts of early Victorian vintage and an Esmond Haddock who, when he got on to the fact that I was proposing to pull a Mary's lamb on him, was quite likely to forget the obligations of a host and break my neck. Considerations like these prevent one feasting the eye on Tudor architecture with genuine enjoyment and take from fifty to sixty per cent off the entertainment value of spreading lawns and gay flower-beds.

The door opened, revealing some sixteen stone of butler.

'Good evening, sir,' said this substantial specimen. 'Mr Wooster?'

'Fink-Nottle,' I said hastily, to correct this impression.

As a matter of fact, it was all I could do to speak at all, for the sudden impact of Charlie Silversmith had removed the breath almost totally. He took me right back to the days when I was starting out as a *flâneur* and man about town and used to tremble beneath butlers' eyes and generally feel very young and bulbous.

Older now and tougher, I am able to take most of these fauna in my stride. When they open front doors to me, I shoot my cuffs nonchalantly. 'Aha, there, butler,' I say. 'How's tricks?' But Jeeves's Uncle Charlie was something special. He looked like one of those steel engravings of nineteenth-century statesmen. He had a large, bald head and pale, protruding gooseberry eyes, and those eyes, resting on mine, heightened the Dark Tower feeling considerably. The thought crossed my mind that if something like this had popped out at Childe Roland, he would have clapped spurs to his charger and been off like a jack-rabbit.

Sam Goldwyn, attached by a stout cord to the windscreen, seemed to be thinking along much the same lines, for, after one startled glance at Uncle Charlie, he had thrown his head back and was now uttering a series of agitated howls. I sympathized with his distress. A South London dog belonging to the lower middle classes or, rather, definitely of the people, I don't suppose he had ever seen a butler before, and it was a dashed shame that he should have drawn something like Uncle Charlie first crack out of the box. With an apologetic jerk of the thumb I directed the latter's attention to him.

'A dog,' I said, this seeming about as good a way as any other of effecting the introductions, and Uncle Charlie gave him an austere look, as if he had found him using a fish fork for the entrée.

'I will have the animal removed to the stables, sir,' he said coldly, and I said Oh, thanks, that would be fine.

'And now,' I said, 'I'd better be nipping along and dressing, what? I don't want to be late for dinner.'

'Dinner has already commenced, sir. We dine at seven-thirty punctually. If you would care to wash your hands, sir,' he said, and indicated a door to the left.

In the circles in which I move it is pretty generally recognized that I am a resilient sort of bimbo, and in circumstances where others might crack beneath the strain, may frequently be seen rising on stepping-stones of my dead self to higher things. Look in at the Drones and ask the first fellow you meet 'Can the fine spirit of the Woosters be crushed?' and he will offer you attractive odds against such a contingency. However tough the going, he will say, and however numerous what are called the slings and arrows of outrageous fortune, you will still find Bertram in there swinging.

But I had never before been thrust into the position of having to say I was Gussie Fink-Nottle and slap on top of that of having to dine in a strange house without dressing, and I don't mind admitting that for an instant everything went black. It was a limp and tottering Bertram Wooster who soaped, rinsed and dried the outlying portions and followed Uncle Charlie to the dining-room. And what with the agony of feeling like a tramp cyclist and the embarrassment of having to bolt my rations with everybody, or so it seemed to my inflamed imag., clicking their tongues and drumming on the table and saying to one another in undertones what a hell of a nuisance this hold-up was, because they wanted the next course to appear so that they could start digging in and getting theirs, it was not for some time that I was sufficiently restored to be able to glance around the board and take a dekko at the personnel. There had been introductions of a sort, of course – I seemed to recall Uncle Charlie saying 'Mr Fink-Nottle' in a reserved sort of voice, as if wishing to make it clear that it was no good blaming *him* – but they hadn't really registered.

As far as the eye could reach, I found myself gazing on a surging sea of aunts. There were tall aunts, short aunts, stout aunts, thin aunts, and an aunt who was carrying on a conversation in a low voice to which nobody seemed to be paying the slightest attention. I was to learn later that this was Miss Emmeline Deverill's habitual practice, she being the aunt of whom Corky had spoken as the dotty one. From start to finish of every meal she soliloquized. Shakespeare would have liked her.

At the top of the table was a youngish bloke in a well-cut dinner jacket which made me more than ever conscious of the travel-stained upholstery in which I had been forced to appear. E. Haddock, presumably. He was sitting next to a girl in white, so obviously the junior member of the bunch that I deduced that here we had Catsmeat's Gertrude.

Drinking her in, I could see how Catsmeat had got that way. The daughter of Dame Daphne, relict of the late P. B. Winkworth, was slim and blonde and fragile, in sharp contradistinction to her mother, whom I had now identified as the one on my left, a rugged light-heavyweight with a touch of Wallace Beery in her make-up. Her eyes were blue, her teeth pearly, and in other respects she had what it takes. I was quite able to follow Catsmeat's thought processes. According to his own statement, he had walked with this girl in an old garden on twilight evenings, with the birds singing sleepily in the shrubberies and the stars beginning to peep out, and no man of spirit could do that with a girl like this without going under the ether.

I was musing on these two young hearts in springtime and speculating with a not unmanly touch of sentiment on their chances of spearing the happy ending, when the subject of the concert came up.

The conversation at the table up to this point had been pretty technical stuff, not easy for the stranger within the gates to get a toe-hold on. You know the sort of thing I mean. One aunt saying that she had had a letter from Emily by the afternoon post, and another aunt saying Had she said anything about Fred and Alice, and the first aunt saying Yes, everything was all right about Fred and Alice, because Agnes had now told Edith what Jane had said to Eleanor. All rather mystic.

But now an aunt in spectacles said she had met the vicar that evening and the poor old gook was spitting blood because his niece, Miss Pirbright, insisted on introducing into the programme of the concert what she described as a knockabout cross-talk act by Police Constable Dobbs and Agatha Worplesdon's nephew, Mr Wooster. What a knockabout cross-talk act was, she had no idea. Perhaps you can tell us, Augustus?

I was only too glad to have the opportunity of saying a few words, for, except for a sort of simpering giggle at the outset, I hadn't uttered since joining the party, and I felt it was about time, for Gussie's sake, that I came out of the silence. Carry along on these lines much longer, and the whole gang would be at their desks writing letters to the Bassett entreating her to think twice before entrusting her happiness to a dumb brick who would probably dish the success of the honeymoon by dashing off in the middle of it to become a Trappist monk.

'Oh, rather,' I said. 'It's one of those Pat and Mike things. Two birds come on in green beards, armed with umbrellas, and one bird says to the other bird "Who was that lady I saw you coming down the street with?" and the second bird says to the first bird "Faith and begob, that was no lady, that was my wife." And then the second bird busts the first bird over the bean with his umbrella, and the first bird, not to be behindhand, busts the second bird over the head with *his* umbrella. And so the long day wears on.'

It didn't go well. There was a sharp intake of breath from one and all.

'Very vulgar!' said one aunt.

'Terribly vulgar!' said another.

'Disgustingly vulgar,' said Dame Daphne Winkworth. 'But how typical of Miss Pirbright to suggest such a performance at a village concert.'

The rest of the aunts didn't say 'You betcher' or 'You've got something there, Daph', but their manner suggested these words. Lips were pursed and noses looked down. I began to get on to what Catsmeat had meant when he had said that these females did not approve of Corky. Her stock was plainly down in the cellar and the market sluggish.

'Well, I am glad,' said the aunt in spectacles, 'that it is this Mr Wooster and not you, Augustus, who is disgracing himself by taking part in this degrading horseplay. Imagine how Madeline would feel!'

'Madeline would never get over it,' said a thin aunt.

'Dear Madeline is so spiritual,' said Dame Daphne Winkworth.

A cold hand seemed to clutch at my heart. I felt like a Gadarene swine that has come within a toucher of doing a nose-dive over the precipice. You'll scarcely believe it, but it had never so much as crossed my mind that Madeline Bassett, on learning that her lover had been going about in a green beard socking policemen with umbrellas, would be revolted to the depths of her soul. Why, dash it, the engagement wouldn't go on functioning for a minute after the news had reached her. You can't be too careful how you stir up these romantic girls with high ideals.

A Gussie in a green beard would be almost worse than a Gussie in the cooler.

It gave me a pang to hand in my portfolio, for I had been looking forward to a sensational triumph, but I know when I'm licked. I resolved that bright and early tomorrow morning word must be sent to Corky that Bertram was out and that she would have to enlist the services of another artist for the role of Pat.

'From all I have heard of Mr Wooster,' said an aunt with a beaky nose, continuing the theme, 'this kind of vulgar foolery will be quite congenial to him. By the way, where *is* Mr Wooster?'

'Yes,' chimed in the aunt with spectacles. 'He was to have arrived this afternoon, and he has not even sent a telegram.'

'He must be a most erratic young man,' said a third aunt, who would have been the better for a good facial.

Dame Daphne took command of the conversation like a head-mistress at a conference of her subordinates.

' "Erratic",' she said, 'is a kindly term. He appears to be completely irresponsible. Agatha tells me that sometimes she despairs of him. She says she often wonders if the best thing would not be to put him in a home of some kind.'

You may picture the emotions of Bertram on learning that his flesh and blood was in the habit of roasting the pants off him in this manner. One doesn't demand much in the way of gratitude, of course, but when you have gone to the expense and inconvenience of taking an aunt's son to the Old Vic, you are justified, I think, in expecting her to behave like an aunt who has had her son taken to the Old Vic – in expecting her, in other words, to exhibit a little decent feeling and a modicum of the live-and-let-live spirit. How sharper than a serpent's tooth, I remember Jeeves saying once, it is to have a thankless child, and it isn't a dashed sight better having a thankless aunt.

I flushed darkly, and would have drained my glass if it had contained anything restorative. But it didn't. Champagne of a sound vintage was flowing like water elsewhere, Uncle Charlie getting a stiff wrist pouring the stuff, but I, in deference to Gussie's known tastes, had been served with that obscene beverage which is produced by putting half an orange on a squeezer and pushing.

'There seems,' proceeded Dame Daphne in the cold and disapproving voice which in the old days she would have employed when rebuking Maud or Beatrice for smoking gaspers in the shrubbery, 'to be no end to his escapades. It is not so long ago that he was arrested and fined for stealing a policeman's helmet in Piccadilly.'

I could put her straight there, and did so.

'That,' I explained, 'was due to an unfortunate oversight. In pinching a policeman's helmet, as of course I don't need to tell you, it is essential before lifting to give a forward shove in order to detach the strap from the officer's chin. This Wooster omitted to do, with the results you have described. But I think you ought to take into consideration the fact that the incident occurred pretty late on Boat Race night, when the best of men are not quite themselves. Still, be that as it may,' I said, quickly sensing that I had not got the sympathy of the audience and adroitly changing the subject, 'I wonder if you know the one about the strip-tease dancer and the performing flea. Or, rather, no, not that one,' I said, remembering that it was a *conte* scarcely designed for the gentler sex and the tots. 'The one about the two men in the train. It's old, of course, so stop me if you've heard it before.'

'Pray go on, Augustus.'

'It's about these two deaf men in the train.'

'My sister Charlotte has the misfortune to be deaf. It is a great affliction.'

The thin aunt bent forward.

'What is he saying?'

'Augustus is telling us a story, Charlotte. Please go on, Augustus.'

Well, of course, this had damped the fire a bit, for the last thing one desires is to be supposed to be giving a maiden lady the horse's laugh on account of her physical infirmities, but it was too late now to take a bow and get off, so I had a go at it.

'Well, there were these two deaf chaps in the train, don't you know, and it stopped at Wembley, and one of them looked out of the window and said "This is Wembley", and the other said "I thought it was Thursday", and the first chap said "Yes, so am I".'

I hadn't had much hope. Right from the start something had

seemed to whisper in my ear that I was about to lay an egg. I laughed heartily to myself, but I was the only one. At the point where the aunts should have rolled out of their seats like one aunt there occurred merely a rather ghastly silence as of mourners at a death-bed, which was broken by Aunt Charlotte asking what I had said.

I would have been just as pleased to let the whole thing drop, but the stout aunt spoke into her ear, spacing her syllables carefully.

'Augustus was telling us a story about two men in a train. One of them said "To-day is Wednesday", and the other said "I thought it was Thursday", and the first man said "Yes, so did I".'

'Oh?' said Aunt Charlotte, and I suppose that about summed it up.

Shortly after this, the browsing and sluicing being concluded, the females rose and filed from the room. Dame Daphne told Esmond Haddock not to be too long over his port, and popped off. Uncle Charlie brought the decanter, and also popped off. And Esmond Haddock and I were alone together, self wondering how chances were for getting a couple of glassfuls.

I moved up to his end of the table, licking the lips.

=6=

Esmond Haddock, seen close to, fully bore out Catsmeat's description of him as a Greek god, and I could well understand the concern of a young lover who saw his girl in danger of being steered into rose gardens by such a one. He was a fine, upstanding – sitting at the moment, of course, but you know what I mean – broad-shouldered bozo of about thirty, with one of those faces which I believe, though I should have to check up with Jeeves, are known as Byronic. He looked like a combination of a poet and an all-in wrestler.

It would not have surprised you to learn that Esmond Haddock was the author of sonnet sequences of a fruity and emotional nature which had made him the toast of Bloomsbury, for his air was that of a man who could rhyme 'love' and 'dove' as well as the next chap. Nor would you have been astonished if informed that he had recently felled an ox with a single blow. You would simply have felt what an ass the ox must have been to get into an argument with a fellow with a chest like that.

No, what was extraordinary was that this superman was in the habit, as testified to by the witness Corky, of crawling to his aunts. But for Corky's evidence I would have said, looking at him, that there sat a nephew capable of facing the toughest aunt and making her say Uncle. Not that you can ever tell, of course, by the outward appearance. Many a fellow who looks like the dominant male and has himself photographed smoking a pipe curls up like carbon paper when confronted with one of these relatives.

He helped himself to port, and there was a momentary silence, as so often occurs when two strong men who have not been formally introduced sit face to face. He worked painstakingly through his snootful, while I continued to fix my bulging eyes on the decanter. It was one of those outsize decanters, full to the brim.

He swigged away for some little while before opening the

conversation. His manner was absent, and I got the impression that he was thinking deeply. Presently he spoke.

'I say,' he said, in an odd, puzzled voice. 'That story of yours.'

'Oh, yes?'

'About the fellows in the train.'

'Quite.'

'I was a bit *distrait* when you were telling it, and I think I may possibly have missed the point. As I got it, there were two men in a train, and it stopped at a station.'

'That's right.'

'And one of them said "This is Woking", and the other chap said "I'm thirsty". Was that how it went?'

'Not quite. It was Wembley the train stopped at, and the fellow said he thought it was Thursday.'

'Was it Thursday?'

'No, no, these chaps were deaf, you see. So when the first chap said "This is Woking", the other chap, thinking he had said "Wednesday", said "So am I". I mean — '

'I see. Yes, most amusing,' said Esmond Haddock.

He refilled his glass, and I think that as he did so he must have noticed the tense, set expression on my face, rather like that of a starving wolf giving a Russian peasant the once-over, for he started, as if realizing that he had been remiss.

'I say, I suppose it's no good offering you any of this?'

I felt the table-talk could not have taken a more satisfactory turn.

'Well, do you know,' I said, 'I wouldn't mind trying it. It would be an experience. It's whisky, or claret or something, isn't it?'

'Port. You may not like it.'

'Oh, I think I shall.'

And a moment later I was in a position to state that I did. It was a very fine old port, full of buck and body, and though my better self told me that it should be sipped, I lowered a beakerful at a gulp.

'It's good,' I said.

'It's supposed to be rather special. More?'

'Thanks.'

'I'll have another myself,' he said. 'One needs a lot of bracing up these days, I find. Do you know the expression "These are the times that try men's souls"?'

'New to me. Your own?'

'No, I heard it somewhere.'

'It's very neat.'

'It is, rather. Another?'

'Thanks.'

'I'll join you. Shall I tell you something?'

'Do.'

I inclined the ear invitingly. Three goblets of the right stuff had left me with a very warm affection for this man. I couldn't remember when I had liked a fellow more at a first meeting, and if he wanted to tell me his troubles, I was prepared to listen as attentively as any barman to an old and valued customer.

'The reason I mentioned the times that try men's souls is that I am right up against those identical times at this very moment. My soul is on the rack. More port?'

'Thanks. I find this stuff rather grows on you. Why is your soul on the rack, Esmond? You don't mind me calling you Esmond?'

'I prefer it. I'll call you Gussie.'

This, of course, came as rather an unpleasant shock, Gussie being to my mind about the ultimate low in names. But I quickly saw that in the role I had undertaken I must be prepared to accept the rough with the smooth. We drained our glasses, and Esmond Haddock refilled them. A princely host, he struck me as.

'Esmond,' I said, 'you strike me as a princely host.'

'Thank you, Gussie,' he replied. 'And you're a princely guest. But you were asking me why my soul was on the rack. I will tell you, Gussie. I must begin by saying that I like your face.'

I said I liked his.

'It is an honest face.'

I said his was, too.

'A glance at it tells me that you are trustworthy. By that I mean that I can trust you.'

'Quite.'

'If I couldn't, I wouldn't, if you follow what I mean. Because what I am about to tell you must go no further, Gussie.'

'Not an inch, Esmond.'

'Well, then, the reason my soul is on the rack is that I love a girl with every fibre of my being, and she has given me the brush-off. Enough to put anyone's soul on the rack, what?'

'I should say so.'

'Her name . . . But naturally I can't mention names.'

'Of course not.'

'Not cricket.'

'Not at all.'

'So I will merely say that her name is Cora Pirbright. Corky to her pals. You don't know her, of course. I remember when I told her you were coming here she said she had heard from mutual friends that you were a freak of the first water and practically dotty, but she had never met you. But she is probably familiar to you on the screen. The name she goes by professionally is Cora Starr. You've seen her?'

'Oh, rather.'

'An angel in human shape, didn't you think?'

'Definitely.'

'That was my view, too, Gussie. I was in love with her long before I met her. I had frequently seen her pictures in Basingstoke. And when old Pirbright, the vicar here, mentioned that his niece was coming to keep house for him and that she was just back from Hollywood and I said "Oh really? Who is she?" and he said "Cora Starr", you could have knocked me down with a feather, Gussie.'

'I bet I could, Esmond. Proceed. You are interesting me strangely.'

'Well, she arrived. Old Pirbright introduced us. Our eyes met.'

'They would, of course.'

'And it wasn't more than about two days after that that we talked it over and agreed that we were twin souls.'

'And then she gave you the brusheroo?'

'And then she gave me the brusheroo. But mark this, Gussie. Even though she has given me the brusheroo, she is still the lodestar of my life. My aunts . . . More port?'

'Thanks.'

'My aunts, Gussie, will try to kid you that I love my cousin Gertrude. Don't believe a word of it. I'll tell you how that mistake arose. Shortly after Corky handed me my papers, I went to the pictures in Basingstoke, and in the thing they were showing there was a fellow who had been turned down by a girl, and in order to make her think a bit and change her mind he started surging around another girl.'

'To make her jealous?'

'Exactly. I thought it a clever idea.'

'Very clever.'

'And it occurred to me that if I started surging round Gertrude, it might make Corky change her mind. So I surged.'

'I see. A bit risky, wasn't it?'

'Risky?'

'Suppose you overdid it and got too fascinating. Broke her heart, I mean.'

'Corky's heart?'

'No, your cousin Gertrude's heart.'

'Oh, that's all right. She's in love with Corky's brother. No chance of breaking Gertrude's heart. We might drink to the success of my scheme, don't you think, Gussie?'

'An excellent idea, Esmond.'

I was, as you may imagine, profoundly bucked. What this meant was that the dark menace of Esmond Haddock had passed from Catsmeat's life. No more need for him to worry about that rose garden. You could unleash Esmond Haddock in the rose gardens with Gertrude Winkworth by the hour, and no business would result. I raised my glass and emptied it to Catsmeat's happiness. Whether or not a tear stole into my eye, I couldn't say, but I should think it very probable.

It was a pity, of course, that, being supposed never to have met Corky, I couldn't electrify Esmond Haddock and bring the sunshine breezing back into his life by telling him what she had told me – viz. that she loved him still. All I could do was to urge him not to lose hope, and he said he hadn't lost hope, not by a jugful.

'And I'll tell you why I haven't lost hope, Gussie. The other day a very significant thing happened. She came to me and asked me to sing a song at this ghastly concert she's getting up. Well, of course, it wasn't a thing I would have gone out of my way to do, had the circumstances been different. I've never sung at a village concert. Have you?'

'Oh, rather. Often.'

'A terrible ordeal, was it not?'

'Oh, no. I enjoyed it. I don't say it was all jam for the audience, but a good time was had by me. You feel nervous at the prospect, do you, Esmond?'

'There are moments, Gussie, when the thought of what is before me makes me break into a cold perspiration. But then I say to myself that I'm the young Squire and pretty popular around these parts, so I'll probably get by all right.'

'That's the attitude.'

'But you're wondering why I said it was significant that she should have come to me and asked me to sing a song at this foul concert. I'll tell you. I take it as definite evidence that the old affection still lingers. Well, I mean, if it didn't would she come asking me to sing at concerts? I am banking everything on that song, Gussie. Corky is an emotional girl, and when she hears that audience cheering me to the echo, it will do something to her. She will melt. She will relent. I wouldn't be surprised if she didn't say "Oh, Esmond!" and fling herself into my arms. Always provided, of course, that I don't get the bird.'

'You won't get the bird.'

'You think not?'

'Not a chance. You'll go like a breeze.'

'You're a great comfort, Gussie.'

'I try to be, Esmond. What are you going to sing? The "Yeoman's Wedding Song"?'

'No, it's a thing written by my Aunt Charlotte, with music by my Aunt Myrtle.'

I pursed the lips. This didn't sound too good. Nothing that I had seen of Aunt Charlotte had led me to suppose that the divine fire lurked within her. One didn't want to condemn her unheard, of course, but I was prepared to bet that anything proceeding from her pen would be well on the lousy side.

'I say,' said Esmond Haddock, struck by an idea, 'would you mind if I just ran through it for you now?'

'Nothing I'd like better.'

'Except perhaps another spot of port?'

'Except that, perhaps. Thanks.'

Esmond Haddock drained his glass.

'I won't sing the verse. It's just a lot of guff about the sun is high up in the sky and the morn is bright and fair, and so forth.'

'Quite.'

'The chorus is what brings home the bacon. It goes like this.'

He assumed the grave, intent expression of a stuffed frog, and let it rip.

' "Hallo, hallo, hallo, hallo . . ." '

I raised a hand.

'Just a second. What are you supposed to be doing? Telephoning?'

'No, it's a hunting song.'

'Oh, a hunting song? I see. I thought it might be one of those "I'm going to telephone ma baby" things. Right ho.'

He resumed.

' "Hallo, hallo, hallo, hallo!
   A-hunting we will go, pom pom,
   A-hunting we will go, Gussie." '

I raised the hand again.

'I don't like that.'

'What?'

'That "pom pom".'

'Oh, that's just in the accompaniment.'

'And I don't like that "Gussie". It lets the side down.'

'Did I say "Gussie"?'

'Yes. You said "A-hunting we will go, pom pom, a-hunting we will go, Gussie".'

'Just a slip of the tongue.'

'It isn't in the script?'

'No, it isn't in the script.'

'I'd leave it out on the night.'

'I will. Shall I continue?'

'Do.'

'Where was I?'

'Better start again at the beginning.'

'Right. Another drop of port?'

'Just a trickle, perhaps.'

'Well, then, starting again at the beginning and omitting, as before, all the-sun-is-high-up-in-the-sky stuff, "Hallo, hallo, hallo, hallo! A-hunting we will go, pom pom, a-hunting we will go. To-day's the day, so come what may, a-hunting we will go".'

I began to see that I had been right about Charlotte. This wouldn't do at all. Young Squire or no young Squire, a songster

55

singing this sort of thing at a village concert was merely asking for the raspberry.

'All wrong,' I said.

'All wrong?'

'Well, think it out for yourself. You start off "A-hunting we will go, a-hunting we will go", and then, just as the audience is all keyed up for a punch line, you repeat that a-hunting we will go. There will be a sense of disappointment.'

'You think so, Gussie?'

'I'm sure of it, Esmond.'

'Then what would you advise?'

I pondered a moment.

'Try this,' I said. ' "Hallo, hallo, hallo, hallo! A-hunting we will go, my lads, a-hunting we will go, pull up our socks and chase the fox and lay the blighter low." '

'I say, that's good!'

'Stronger, I think?'

'Much stronger.'

'How do you go on from there?'

He switched on the stuffed-frog expression once more:

' "Oh, hearken to the merry horn!
Over brake and over thorn
Upon this jolly hunting morn
A-hunting we will go." '

I weighed this.

'I pass the first two lines,' I said. ' "Merry horn." "Brake and thorn." Not bad at all. At-a-girl, Charlotte, we always knew you had it in you! But not the finish.'

'You don't like it?'

'Weak. Very weak. I don't know what sort of standees you get at King's Deverill, but if they're like the unshaven thugs behind the back row at every village concert I've ever known, you're simply inviting them to chi-yike and make a noise like tearing calico. No, we must do better than that. Born . . . corn . . . pawn . . . torn . . . Ha!' I said, reaching out for the decanter, 'I think I have it. "Oh, hearken to the merry horn! Over brake and over thorn we'll ride although our bags get torn! What ho! What ho! What ho!" '

I had more or less expected it to knock him cold and it did.

For an instant he was speechless with admiration, then he said it lifted the whole thing and he couldn't thank me enough.

'It's terrific!'

'I was hoping you would like it.'

'How do you think of these things?'

'Oh, they just come to one.'

'We might run through the authorized version, old man, shall we?'

'No time like the present, dear old chap.'

It's curious how, looking back, you can nearly always spot where you went wrong in any binge or enterprise. Take this little slab of community singing of ours, for instance. In order to give the thing zip, I stood on my chair and waved the decanter like a baton, and this, I see now, was a mistake. It helped the composition enormously, but it tended to create a false impression in the mind of the observer, conjuring up a picture of drunken revels.

And if you are going to say that on the present occasion there was no observer, I quietly reply that you are wrong. We had just worked through the 'brake and thorn' and were going all out for the rousing finish, when a voice spoke behind us.

It said:

'Well!'

There are, of course, many ways of saying 'Well!' The speaker who had the floor at the moment – Dame Daphne Winkworth – said it rather in the manner of the prudish Queen of a monarch of Babylon who has happened to wander into the banqueting hall just as the Babylonian orgy is beginning to go nicely.

'*Well!*' she said.

Of course, what Corky had told me about Esmond Haddock's aunt-fixation ought to have prepared me for it, but I must say I was shocked at his deportment at this juncture. It was the deportment of a craven and a worm. Possibly stimulated by my getting on a chair, he had climbed onto the table and was using a banana as a hunting-crop, and he now came down like an apologetic sack of coals, his whole demeanour so crushed and cringing that I could hardly bear to look at him.

'It's all right, Aunt Daphne!'

'All right!'

'We were rehearsing. For the concert, you know. With the concert so near, one doesn't want to lose a minute.'

'Oh? Well, we are expecting you in the drawing-room.'

'Yes, Aunt Daphne.'

'Gertrude is waiting to play backgammon with you.'

'Yes, Aunt Daphne.'

'If you feel capable of playing backgammon.'

'Oh, yes, Aunt Daphne.'

He slunk from the room with bowed head, and I was about to follow, when the old geezer checked me with an imperious gesture. One noted a marked increase in the resemblance to Wallace Beery, and the thought crossed my mind that life for the unfortunate moppets who had drawn this Winkworth as a headmistress must have been like Six Weeks on Sunny Devil's Island. Previous to making her acquaintance, I had always supposed the Rev. Aubrey Upjohn to be the nearest thing to the late Captain Bligh of the *Bounty* which the scholastic world had provided to date, but I could see now that compared with old Battling Daphne he was a mere prelim boy.

'Augustus, did you bring a great, rough dog with you this evening?' she demanded.

It shows how the rush and swirl of events at Deverill Hall had affected me when I say that for an instant nothing stirred.

'Dog?'

'Silversmith says it belongs to you.'

'Oh, ah,' I said, memory returning to its throne. 'Yes, yes, yes, of course. Yes, to be sure. You mean Sam Goldwyn. But he's not mine. He belongs to Corky.'

'To *whom?*'

'Corky Pirbright. She asked me to put him up for a day or two.'

The mention of Corky's name, as had happened at the dinner-table, caused her to draw in her breath and do a quick-take-um. There was no getting away from the fact that the girl's popularity at Deverill Hall was but slight.

'Is Miss Pirbright a great friend of yours?'

'Oh, rather,' I said, remembering too late that this scarcely squared with what Corky had told Esmond Haddock. I was glad that he was no longer with us. 'She was a trifle dubious about springing the animal on her uncle without a certain amount of preliminary spade-work, he being apparently not very dog-minded, so she turned it over to me. It's in the stables.'

'It is not in the stables.'

'Then Silversmith was pulling my leg. He said he would have it taken there!'

'He did have it taken there, but it broke loose and came rushing into the drawing-room just now like a mad thing.'

I saw that here was where the soothing word was required.

'Sam Goldwyn isn't dotty,' I assured her. 'I wouldn't say he was one of our great minds, but he's perfectly compos. In re his rushing into the drawing-room, that was because he thought I was there. He has conceived a burning passion for me and counts every minute lost when he is not in my society. No doubt his first act on being tied up in the stables was to start gnawing through the rope in order to be free to come and look for me. Rather touching.'

Her manner suggested that she did not think it in the least touching. Her eye was alight with anti-Sam sentiment.

'Well, it was most unpleasant. We had left the french windows open, as the night was so warm, and suddenly this disgusting brute came galloping in. My sister Charlotte received a nervous shock from which it will take her a long time to recover. The animal leaped upon her back and chased her all over the room.'

I did not give the thought utterance, for if there is one thing the Woosters are, it is tactful, but it did occur to me that this had come more or less as a judgment on Charlotte for writing all that Hallo-hallo-hallo-hallo, a-hunting-we-will-go stuff and would be a lesson to her next time she took pen in hand. She was now in a position to see the thing from the fox's point of view.

'And when we rang for Silversmith, the creature bit him.'

I must confess to feeling a thrill of admiration as I heard these words. 'You're a better man than I am, Gunga Din', I came within a toucher of saying. I wouldn't have bitten Silversmith myself to please a dying grandmother.

'I'm frightfully sorry,' I said. 'Is there anything I can do?'

'No, thank you.'

'I have considerable influence with this hound. I might be able to induce him to call it a day and go back to the stables and get his eight hours.'

'It will not be necessary. Silversmith succeeded in overpowering the animal and locking it in a cupboard. Now that you tell me its home is at the Vicarage, I will send it there at once.'

'I'll take him, shall I?'

'Pray do not trouble. I think it would be better if you were to go straight to bed.'

This seemed to me the most admirable suggestion. From the moment when the females had legged it from the dinner-table, I had been musing somewhat apprehensively on the quiet home evening which would set in as soon as Esmond and I were through with the port. You know what these quiet home evenings are like at country houses where the personnel of the ensemble is mainly feminine. You get backed into corners and shown photograph albums. Folk songs are sung at you. You find the head drooping like a lily on its stem and have to keep jerking it back into position one with an effort that taxes the frail strength to the utmost. Far, far better to retire to my sleeping quarters now, especially as I was most anxious to get in touch with Jeeves, who long 'ere this must have arrived by train with the heavy luggage.

I am not saying that this woman's words, with their underlying suggestion that I was fried to the tonsils, had not wounded me. It was all too plainly her opinion that, if let loose in drawing-rooms, I would immediately proceed to create an atmosphere reminiscent of a waterfront saloon when the Fleet is in. But the Woosters are essentially fair-minded, and I did not blame her for holding these views. I could quite see that when you come into a dining-room and find a guest leaping about on a chair with a decanter in his hand, singing Hallo, hallo, hallo, hallo, a-hunting we will go, my lads, a-hunting we will go, you are pretty well bound to fall into a certain train of thought.

'I do feel a little fatigued after my journey,' I said.

'Silversmith will show you to your room,' she replied, and I perceived that Uncle Charlie was in our midst. I had not seen or heard him arrive. Like Jeeves, he had manifested himself silently out of the void. No doubt these things run in families.

'Silversmith.'

'Madam?'

'Show Mr Fink-Nottle to his room,' said Dame Daphne,

though I could see that she was feeling that 'help' would have been more the *mot juste*.

'Very good, madam.'

I noticed that the man was limping slightly, seeming to suggest that Sam Goldwyn had connected with his calf, but I forbore to probe and question, realizing that the subject, like the calf, might be a sore one. I followed him up the stairs to a well-appointed chamber and wished him a cheery good night.

'Oh, Silversmith,' I said.

'Sir?'

'Has my man arrived?'

'Yes, sir.'

'You might send him along.'

'Very good, sir.'

He withdrew, and a few minutes later there entered a familiar form.

But it wasn't the familiar form of Jeeves. It was the familiar form of Claude Cattermole Pirbright.

7

WELL, I suppose if I had been a Seigneur of the Middle Ages – somebody like Childe Roland, for instance – in the days when you couldn't throw a brick without beaning a magician or a wizard or a sorcerer and people were always getting changed into something else, I wouldn't have given the thing a second thought. I would just have said 'Ah, so Jeeves has had a spell cast on him and been turned into Catsmeat, has he? Too bad. Still, that's life', and carried on regardless, calling for my pipe and my bowl and my fiddlers three.

But nowadays you tend to lose this easy outlook, and it would be wilfully deceiving my public to say that I did not take it big. I stared at the man, my eyes coming out of the parent sockets like a snail's and waving about on their stems.

'Catsmeat!' I yipped.

He waggled his head frowningly, like a conspirator when a fellow-conspirator has said the wrong thing.

'Meadowes,' he corrected.

'What do you mean, Meadowes?'

'That is my name while I remain in your employment. I'm your man.'

A solution occurred to me. I have already mentioned that the port which I had swigged perhaps a little too freely in Esmond Haddock's society was of a fine old vintage and full of body. It now struck me that it must have had even more authority than I had supposed and that Dame Daphne Winkworth had been perfectly correct in assuming that I was scrooched. And I was about to turn my face to the wall and try to sleep it off, when he proceeded.

'Your valet. Your attendant. Your gentleman's personal gentleman. It's quite simple. Jeeves couldn't come.'

'What!'

'No.'

'You mean Jeeves isn't going to be at my side?'

'That's right. So I am taking his place. What are you doing?'

'Turning my face to the wall.'

'Why?'

'Well, wouldn't you turn your face to the wall if you were trapped in a place like this with everybody thinking you were Gussie Fink-Nottle and without Jeeves to comfort and advise? Oh, hell! Oh, blast! Oh, damn! Why couldn't Jeeves come? Is he ill?'

'I don't think so. I speak only as a layman, of course, not as a medical man, but the last I saw of him he seemed pretty full of vitamins. Sparkling eyes. Rosy cheeks. No, Jeeves isn't ill. What stopped him coming was the fact that his Uncle Charlie is the butler here.'

'Why the devil should that stop him?'

'My good Bertie, use your intelligence, if any. Uncle Charlie knows that Jeeves is your keeper. No doubt Jeeves writes him weekly letters, saying how happy he is with you and how nothing would ever induce him to switch elsewhere. Well, what would happen if he suddenly showed up in attendance on Gussie Fink-Nottle? I'll tell you what would happen. Uncle Charlie's suspicions would be aroused. "Something fishy here," he would say to himself. And before you knew where you were he would be tearing off your whiskers and denouncing you. Obviously Jeeves couldn't come.'

I was forced to admit that there was something in this. But I still chafed.

'Why didn't he tell me?'

'It only occurred to him after you had left.'

'And why couldn't he have squared Silversmith?'

'That point came up when we were discussing the thing, and Jeeves said his Uncle Charlie was one of those fellows who can't be squared. A man of very rigid principles.'

'Every man has his price.'

'Not Jeeves's Uncle Charlie. My gosh, Bertie, what a lad! He received me when I arrived, and my bones turned to water. Do you remember the effect King Solomon had on the Queen of Sheba at their first meeting? My reactions were somewhat similar. "The half was not told unto me," I said to myself. If it hadn't been for Queenie leading me from the presence and buoying me up with a quick cooking sherry, I might have swooned in my tracks.'

'Who's Queenie?'

'Haven't you met her? The parlourmaid. Delightful girl. Engaged to the village policeman, a fellow named Dobbs. Have you ever tasted cooking sherry, Bertie? Odd stuff.'

I felt that we were wandering from the nub. This was no time for desultory chit-chat about cooking sherry.

'But, look here, dash it, I can understand Jeeves's reasons for backing out, but I can't see why you had to come.'

He raised a couple of eyebrows.

'You can't see why I had to come? Didn't you yourself say with your own lips, when we were discussing the idea of me understudying Gussie, that this was the one place where I ought to be? It's vital that I should be on the spot, seeing Gertrude constantly, pleading with her, reasoning with her, trying to break down her sales resistance.' He paused, and gave me a penetrating look. 'You've nothing against my being here, have you?'

'Well . . .'

'So!' he said, and his voice was cold and hard, like a picnic egg. 'You have some far-fetched objection to the scheme, have you? You don't want me to win the girl I love?'

'Of course I want you to win the bally girl you love.'

'Well, I can't do it by mail.'

'But I don't see why you've got to be at the Hall. Why couldn't you have stayed at the Vicarage?'

'You couldn't expect Uncle Sidney to have Corky *and* me on the premises. The mixture would be too rich.'

'At the inn, then.'

'There isn't an inn. Only what they call beer-houses.'

'You could have got a bed at a cottage.'

'And shared it with the cottager? No, thanks. How many beds do you think these birds have?'

I relapsed into a baffled silence. But it is never any good repining on these occasions. When I next spoke, I doubt if Catsmeat spotted the suspicion of a tremor in the voice. We Woosters are like that. In moments of mental anguish we resemble those Red Indians who, while getting cooked to a crisp at the stake, never failed to be the life and soul of the party.

'Have you seen her?' I asked.

'Gertrude? Yes, just before I came up here. I was in the hall, and she suddenly appeared from the drawing-room.'

'I suppose she was surprised.'

'Surprised is right. She swayed and tottered. Queenie said "Oh, miss, are you ill?" and rushed off to get sal volatile.'

'Oh, Queenie was there?'

'Yes, Queenie was there with her hair in a braid. She had just been telling me how worried she was about her betrothed's spiritual outlook. He's an atheist.'

'So Corky told me.'

'And every time she tries to make him see the light, he just twirls his moustache and talks Ingersoll at her. This upsets the poor girl.'

'She's very pretty.'

'Extraordinarily pretty. I don't remember ever having seen a prettier parlourmaid.'

'Gertrude. Not Queenie.'

'Oh, Gertrude. Well, dash it, you don't need to tell me that. She's the top. She begins where Helen of Troy left off.'

'Did you get a chance to talk to her?'

'Unfortunately no. A couple of aunts came out of the drawing-room, and I had to leg it. That's the trouble about being a valet. You can't mix. By the way, Bertie, I've found out something of the utmost importance. That Lovers' Leap binge is fixed for next Thursday. Queenie told me. She's cutting the sandwiches. I hope you haven't weakened? You are still in your splendid, resolute frame of mind of yesterday? I can rely on you to foil and battle that foul blot, Esmond Haddock?'

'I like Esmond Haddock.'

'Then you ought to be ashamed of yourself.'

I smiled an indulgent smile.

'It's all right, Catsmeat. You can simmer down. Gertrude Winkworth means nothing to Esmond Haddock. He's not really pursuing her with his addresses.'

'Don't be an ass. How about the Lovers' Leap? What price the sandwiches?'

'All that stuff is just to make Corky jealous.'

'What!'

'He thinks it will bring her round. You see, he didn't give Corky the brush-off. You had your facts twisted. She gave him the brush-off, because they had differed on a point of policy, and she is still the lodestar of his life. I had this from his own lips. We got matey over the port. So you can cease to regard him as a menace.'

He gaped at me. You could see hope beginning to dawn.

'Is this official?'

'Absolutely.'

'You say Corky is the lodestar of his life?'

'That's what he told me.'

'And all this rushing Gertrude is just a ruse?'

'That's right.'

Catsmeat expelled a deep breath. It sounded like the final effort of a Dying Rooster.

'My gosh, you've taken a weight off my mind.'

'I thought you'd be pleased.'

'You bet I'm pleased. Well, good night.'

'You're off?'

'Yes, I shall leave you now, Bertie, much as I enjoy your society, because I have man's work to do elsewhere. When I was chatting with Queenie, she happened to mention that she knows where Uncle Charlie keeps the key of the cellar. So long. I shall hope to see more of you later.'

'Just a second. Will you be seeing Corky shortly?'

'First thing to-morrow morning. I must let her know I'm here and put her in touch with the general situation, so that she will be warned against making any floaters. Why?'

'Tell her from me that she has got to find somebody else for Pat.'

'You're walking out on the act?'

'Yes, I am,' I said, and put him abreast.

He listened intelligently, and said he quite understood.

'I see. Yes, I think you're right. I'll tell her.'

He withdrew, walking on the tips of his toes and conveying in his manner the suggestion that if he had had a hat and that hat had contained roses, he would have started strewing them from it, and for a while the thought that I had been instrumental in re-sunshining a pal's life bucked me up no little.

But it takes more than that to buck a fellow up permanently who is serving an indeterminate sentence in a place like Deverill

Hall, and it was not long before I was in sombre mood again, trying to find the bluebird but missing it by a wide margin.

I have generally found on these occasions when the heart is heavy that the best thing to do is to curl up with a good goose-flesher and try to forget, and fortunately I had packed among my effects one called *Murder At Greystone Grange*. I started to turn its pages now, and found that I couldn't have made a sounder move. It was one of those works in which Baronets are constantly being discovered dead in libraries and the heroine can't turn in for a night without a Thing popping through a panel in the wall of her bedroom and starting to chuck its weight about, and it was not long before I was so soothed that I was able to switch off the light and fall into a refreshing sleep, which lasted, as my refreshing sleeps always do, till the coming of the morning cup of tea.

My last thought, just before the tired eyelids closed, was that I had had an idea that I had heard the front-door bell ring and a murmur of distant voices, seeming to indicate the blowing-in of another guest.

It was Silversmith who brought me my tea ration, and though his manner, on the chilly side, suggested that the overnight activities of Sam Goldwyn still rankled, I had a dash at setting the conversational ball rolling. I always like, if I can, to establish matey relations between tea bringer and tea recipient.

'Oh, good morning, Silversmith, good morning,' I said. 'What sort of a day is it, Silversmith? Fine?'

'Yes, sir.'

'The lark on the wing and the snail on the thorn and all that?'

'Yes, sir.'

'Splendid. Oh, Silversmith,' I said, 'I don't know if it was but a dream, but latish last night I fancied I heard the front-door bell doing its stuff and a good lot of off-stage talking going on. Was I right? Did someone arrive after closing time?'

'Yes, sir. Mr Wooster.'

He gave me a cold look, as if to remind me that he would prefer not to be drawn into conversation with the man responsible for introducing Sam Goldwyn into his life, and vanished, leaving not a wrack behind.

And it was, as you may well imagine, a pensive Bertram with a puzzled frown on his face who propped himself against the pillows and sipped from the teacup. I could make nothing of this.

'Mr Wooster', the man had said, and only two explanations seemed to offer themselves – (a) that, like the fellows in the train at Wembley, I had not heard correctly and (b) that I had recently been in the presence of a butler who had been having a couple.

Neither theory satisfied me. From boyhood up my hearing has always been of the keenest, and as for the possibility of Silversmith having had one over the eight, I dismissed that instanter. It is a very frivolous butler who gets a load before nine in the morning, and I have gone sadly astray in my delineation of character if I have given my public the impression that Jeeves's Uncle Charlie was frivolous. You could imagine Little Lord Fauntleroy getting a skinful, but not Silversmith.

And yet he had unquestionably said 'Mr Wooster'.

I was still pondering like billy-o and nowhere near spiking a plausible solution of the mystery, when the door opened and the ghost of Jeeves entered, carrying a breakfast tray.

8

I SAY 'the ghost of Jeeves' because in that first awful moment that was what I had the apparition docketed as. The words 'What ho! A spectre!' trembled on my lips, and I reacted rather like the heroine of *Murder At Greystone Grange* on discovering that the Thing had come to doss in her room. I don't know if you have ever seen a ghost, but the general effect is to give you quite a start.

Then the scent of bacon floated to the nostrils, and feeling that it was improbable that a wraith would be horsing about the place with dishes of eggs and b., I calmed down a bit. That is to say, I stopped upsetting the tea and was able to stutter. It is true that all I said was 'Jeeves!' but that wasn't such bad going for one whose tongue had so recently been tangled up with the uvula, besides cleaving to the roof of the mouth.

He dumped the tray on my lap.

'Good morning, sir,' he said. 'I fancied that you would possibly wish to enjoy your breakfast in the privacy of your apartment, rather than make one of the party in the dining-room.'

Cognizant as I was of the fact that in that dining-room there would be five aunts, one of them deaf, one of them dotty, one of them Dame Daphne Winkworth, and all of them totally unfit for human consumption on an empty stomach, I applauded the kindly gesture; all the more heartily because it had just occurred to me that in a house like this, where things were sure to be run on old-fashioned lines rather than in a manner of keeping with the trend of modern thought, the butler probably waited at the breakfast-table.

'Does he?' I asked. 'Does Silversmith minister to the revellers at the morning meal?'

'Yes, sir.'

'My God!' I said, paling beneath the tan. 'What a man, Jeeves!'

'Sir?'

'Your Uncle Charlie.'

'Ah, yes, sir. A forceful personality.'

'Forceful is correct. What's that thing of Shakespeare's about someone having an eye like Mother's?'

'An eye like Mars, to threaten and command, is possibly the quotation for which you are groping, sir.'

'That's right. Uncle Charlie has an eye like that. You really call him Uncle Charlie?'

'Yes, sir.'

'Amazing. To me, to think of him as Uncle Charlie is like thinking of him as Jimmy or Reggie, or, for the matter of that, Bertie. Used he in your younger days to dandle you on his knee?'

'Quite frequently, sir.'

'And you didn't quail? You must have been a child of blood and iron.' I addressed myself to the platter once more. 'Extraordinarily good bacon, this, Jeeves.'

'Home cured, I understand, sir.'

'And made, no doubt, from contented pigs. Kippers, too, not to mention toast, marmalade and, unless my senses deceive me, an apple. Say what you will of Deverill Hall, its hospitality is lavish. I don't know if you have ever noticed it, Jeeves, but a good, spirited kipper first thing in the morning seems to put heart into you.'

'Very true, sir, though I myself am more partial to a slice of ham.'

For some moments we discussed the relative merits of ham and kippers as buckers-up of the morale, there being much, of course, to be said on both sides, and then I touched on something which I had been meaning to touch on earlier. I can't think how it came to slip my mind.

'Oh, Jeeves,' I said, 'I knew there was something I wanted to ask you. What in the name of everything bloodsome are you doing here?'

'I fancied that you might possibly be curious on that point, sir, and I was about to volunteer an explanation. I have come here in attendance on Mr Fink-Nottle. Permit me, sir.'

He retrieved the slab of kipper which a quick jerk of the wrist had caused me to send flying from the fork, and replaced it on the dish. I stared at him wide-eyed as the expression is.

'Mr Fink-Nottle?'

'Yes, sir.'

'But Gussie's not here?'

'Yes, sir. We arrived at a somewhat late hour last night.'

A sudden blinding light flashed upon me.

'You mean it was Gussie to whom Uncle Charlie was referring when he said that Mr Wooster had punched the time-clock? I'm here saying I'm Gussie, and now Gussie has blown in, saying he's me?'

'Precisely, sir. It is a curious and perhaps somewhat complex situation that has been precipitated – '

'You're telling me, Jeeves!'

Only the fact that by doing so I should have upset the tray prevented me turning my face to the wall. When Esmond Haddock in our exchanges over the port had spoken of the times that try men's souls, he hadn't had a notion of what the times that try men's souls can really be, if they spit on their hands and get right down to it. I levered up a forkful of kipper and passed it absently over the larynx, endeavouring to adjust the faculties to a set-up which even the most intrepid would have had to admit was a honey.

'But how did Gussie get out of stir?'

'The magistrate decided on second thoughts to substitute a fine for the prison sentence, sir.'

'What made him do that?'

'Possibly the reflection that the quality of mercy is not strained, sir.'

'You mean it droppeth as the gentle rain from heaven?'

'Precisely, sir. Upon the place beneath. His Worship would no doubt have taken into consideration the fact that it blesseth him that gives and him that takes and becomes the throned monarch better than his crown.'

I mused. Yes, there was something in that.

'What did he soak him? Five quid?'

'Yes, sir.'

'And Gussie brassed up and was free?'

'Yes, sir.'

I put my finger on the nub.

'Why?' I said.

I thought I had him there, but I hadn't. Where a lesser man would have shuffled his feet and twiddled his fingers and mumbled 'Yes, I see what you mean, that is the problem, is it not?'

he had his explanation all ready to serve and dished it up without batting an eyelid.

'It was the only course to pursue, sir. On the one hand, her ladyship, your aunt, was most emphatic in her desire that you should visit the Hall, and on the other Miss Bassett was equally insistent on Mr Fink-Nottle doing so. In the event of either of you failing to arrive, inquiries would have been instituted, with disastrous results. To take but one aspect of the matter, Miss Bassett is expecting to receive daily letters from Mr Fink-Nottle, giving her all the gossip of the Hall and describing in detail his life there. These will, of course, have to be written on the Hall notepaper and postmarked "King's Deverill".'

'True. You speak sooth, Jeeves. I never thought of that.'

I swallowed a sombre chunk of toast and marmalade. I was thinking how easily all this complex stuff could have been avoided, if only the beak had had the sense to fine Gussie in the first place, instead of as an afterthought. I have said it before, and I will say it again, all magistrates are asses. Show me a magistrate and I will show you a fathead.

I started on the apple.

'So here we are.'

'Yes, sir.'

'I'm Gussie and Gussie's me.'

'Yes, sir.'

'And ceaseless vigilance will be required if we are not to gum the game. We shall be walking on eggshells.'

'A very trenchant figure, sir.'

I finished the apple, and lit a thoughtful cigarette.

'Well, I suppose it had to be,' I said. 'But lay off the Marcus Aurelius stuff, because I don't think I could stand it if you talk about it all being part of the great web. How's Gussie taking the thing?'

'Not blithely, sir. I should describe him as disgruntled. I learn from Mr Pirbright – '

'Oh, you've seen Catsmeat?'

'Yes, sir, in the servants' hall. He was helping Queenie, the parlourmaid, with her crossword puzzle. He informed me that he had contrived to obtain an interview with Miss Pirbright and had apprised her of your reluctance to play the part of Pat in the Hibernian entertainment at the concert, and that Miss Pirbright fully appreciated your position and said that now that Mr Fink-Nottle had arrived he would, of course, sustain the role. Mr Pirbright has seen Mr Fink-Nottle and informed him of the arrangement, and it is this that has caused Mr Fink-Nottle to become disgruntled.'

'He shrinks from the task?'

'Yes, sir. He is also somewhat exercised in his mind by what he has heard the ladies of the Hall saying with regard to – '

'My doings?'

'Yes, sir.'

'The dog?'

'Yes, sir.'

'The port?'

'Yes, sir.'

'And the hallo, hallo, a-hunting we will go?'

'Yes, sir.'

I whooshed out a remorseful puff of smoke.

'Yes,' I said, 'I'm afraid I haven't given Gussie a very good send-off. Quite inadvertently I fear that I have established him in the eyes of mine hostesses as one of those whited sepulchres which try to kid the public that they drink nothing but orange juice and the moment that public's back is turned, start doing the *Lost Week-End* stuff with the port. Of course, I could put up a pretty good case for myself. Esmond Haddock thrust the decanter on me, and I was dying of thirst. You wouldn't blame a snowbound traveller in the Alps for accepting a drop of brandy at the hands of a St Bernard dog. Still, one hopes that they will keep it under their hats and not pass it along to Miss Bassett. One doesn't want spanners bunged into Gussie's romance.'

We were silent for a moment, musing on what the harvest would be, were anything to cause Madeline Bassett to become de-Gussied. Then I changed a distasteful subject.

'Talking of romances, I suppose Catsmeat confided in you about his?'

'Yes, sir.'

'I thought he would. Amazing, the way all these birds come to you and sob out their troubles on your chest.'

'I find it most gratifying, sir, and am always eager to lend such assistance as may lie within my power. One desires to give satisfaction. Shortly after your departure yesterday, Mr Pirbright devoted some little time to an exposition of the problems confronting him. It was after learning the facts that I ventured to suggest that he should take my place here as your attendant.'

'I wish one of you had thought to tip me off with a telegram. I should have been spared a nasty shock. The last thing one wants on top of what might be termed a drinking bout is to have a changeling ring himself in on you without warning. You'd look pretty silly yourself if you came into my room one morning with the cup of tea after a thick night and found Ernie Bevin or someone propped up in the bed. When you saw Catsmeat just now, did he tell you the Stop Press news?'

'Sir?'

'About Esmond Haddock and Corky.'

'Ah, yes, sir. He informed me of what you had said to him with reference to Mr Haddock's unswerving devotion to Miss Pirbright. He appeared greatly relieved. He feels that the principal obstacle to his happiness has now been removed.'

'Yes, Catsmeat's sitting pretty. One wishes one could say the same of poor old Esmond.'

'You think that Miss Pirbright does not reciprocate Mr Haddock's sentiments, sir?'

'Oh, she reciprocates them, all right. She freely admits that he is the lodestar of her life, and you're probably saying to yourself that in these circs everything should be hunkadory. I mean, if she's the lodestar of his life and he's the lodestar of hers, the thing ought to be in the bag. But you're wrong, and so is Esmond Haddock. His view, poor deluded clam, is that he will make such a whale of a hit with this song he's singing at the concert that when she hears the audience cheering him to the echo she will say "Oh, Esmond!" and fling herself into his arms. Not a hope.'

'No, sir?'

'Not a hope, Jeeves. There's a snag. The trouble is that she refuses to consider the idea of hitching up with him unless he defies his aunts, and he very naturally gets the vapours at the mere idea. It is what I have sometimes heard described as an impasse.'

'Why does the young lady wish Mr Haddock to defy his aunts, sir?'

'She says he has allowed them to oppress him from childhood, and it's time he threw off the yoke. She wants him to show her that he is a man of intrepid courage. It's the old dragon gag. In the days when knights were bold, as you probably know, girls used to hound fellows into going out and fighting dragons. I expect your old pal Childe Roland had it happen to him a dozen times. But dragons are one thing, and aunts are another. I have no doubt that Esmond Haddock would spring to the task of taking on a fire-breathing dragon, but there isn't the remotest chance of him ever standing up to Dame Daphne Winkworth, and the Misses Charlotte, Emmeline, Harriet and Myrtle Deverill and making them play ball.'

'I wonder, sir?'

'What do you mean, you wonder, Jeeves?'

'It crossed my mind as a possibility, sir, that were Mr Haddock's performance at the concert to be the success he anticipates, his attitude might become more resolute. I have not myself had the opportunity of studying the young gentleman's psychology, but from what my Uncle Charlie tells me I am convinced that he is one of those gentlemen on whom popular acclamation might have sensational effects. Mr Haddock's has been, as you say, a repressed life, and he has, no doubt, a very marked inferiority complex. The cheers of the multitude frequently act like a powerful drug upon young gentlemen with inferiority complexes.'

I began to grasp the gist.

'You mean that if he makes a hit he will get it up his nose to such an extent that he will be able to look his aunts in the eye and make them wilt?'

'Precisely, sir. You will recall the case of Mr Little.'

'Golly, yes, that's right. Bingo became a changed man, didn't he? Jeeves, I believe you've got something.'

'At least the theory which I have advanced is a tenable one, sir.'

'It's more than tenable. It's a pip. Then what we've got to do is to strain every nerve to see that he makes a hit. What are those things people have?'

'Sir?'

'Opera singers and people like that.'

'You mean a claque, sir?'

'That's right. The word was on the tip of my tongue. He must be provided with a claque. It will be your task, Jeeves, to move about the village, dropping a word here, standing a beer there, till the whole community is impressed with the necessity of cheering Esmond Haddock's song till their eyes bubble. I can leave this to you?'

'Certainly, sir. I will attend to the matter.'

'Fine. And now I suppose I ought to be getting up and seeing Gussie. There are probably one or two points he will want to discuss. Is there a ruined mill around here?'

'Not to my knowledge, sir.'

'Well, any landmark where you could tell him to meet me? I don't want to roam the house and grounds, looking for him. My aim is rather to sneak down the back stairs and skirt around the garden via the shrubberies. You follow me, Jeeves?'

'Perfectly, sir. I would suggest that I arrange with Mr Fink-Nottle to meet you in, say, an hour's time outside the local post office.'

'Right,' I said. 'Outside the post office in an hour or sixty minutes. And now, Jeeves, if you will be so good as to turn it on, the refreshing bath.'

9

WHAT with one thing and another, singing a bit too much in the bath and so on, I was about five minutes behind scheduled time in reaching the post office, and when I got there I found Gussie already at the tryst.

Jeeves, in speaking of this Fink-Nottle, had, if you remember, described him as disgruntled, and it was plain at a glance that the passage of time had done nothing to gruntle him. The eyes behind their horn-rimmed spectacles were burning with fury and resentment and all that sort of thing. He looked like a peevish halibut. In moment of emotion Gussie's resemblance to some marine monster always becomes accentuated.

'Well,' he said, starting in without so much as a What-ho. 'This is a pretty state of things!'

It seemed to me that a cheery, pep-giving word would be in order. I proceeded, accordingly, to shoot it across. Assenting to his opinion that the state of things was pretty, I urged him to keep the tail up, pointing out that though the storm clouds might lower, he was better off at Deverill Hall than he would have been in a dark dungeon with dripping walls and a platoon of resident rats, if that's where they put fellows who have been given fourteen days without the option at Bosher Street police court.

He replied curtly that he entirely disagreed with me.

'I would greatly have preferred prison,' he said. 'When you're in prison, you don't have people calling you Mr Wooster. How do you suppose I feel, knowing that everybody thinks I'm you?'

This startled me, I confess. Of all the things I had to worry about, the one that was gashing me like a knife most was the thought that the populace, beholding Gussie, were under the impression that there stood Bertram Wooster. When I reflected that the little world of King's Deverill would go to its grave believing that Bertram Wooster was an undersized gargoyle who looked like Lester de Pester in that comic strip in one of the

New York papers, the iron entered my soul. It was a bit of a
jar to learn that Gussie was suffering the same spiritual agonies.

'I don't know if you are aware,' he proceeded, 'what your
reputation is in these parts? In case you are under any illusions,
let me inform you that your name is mud. Those women at
breakfast were drawing their skirts away as I passed. They
shivered when I spoke to them. From time to time I would catch
them looking at me in a way that would have wounded a smash-
and-grab man. And, as if that wasn't bad enough, you seem in
a single evening to have made my name mud, too. What's all
this I hear about you getting tight last night and singing hunting
songs?'

'I didn't get tight, Gussie. Just pleasantly mellowed, as you
might say. And I sang hunting songs because my host seemed
to wish it. One has to humour one's host. So they mentioned
that, did they?'

'They mentioned it, all right. It was the chief topic of conversation at the breakfast-table. And what's going to happen if
they mention it to Madeline?'

'I advise stout denial.'

'It wouldn't work.'

'It might,' I said, for I had been giving a good deal of thought
to the matter and was feeling more optimistic than I had been.
'After all, what can they prove?'

'Madeline's godmother said she came into the dining-room
and found you on a chair, waving a decanter and singing A-
hunting we will go.'

'True. We concede that. But who is to say that that decanter
was not emptied exclusively by Esmond Haddock, who, you
must remember, was on the table, also singing A-hunting we
will go and urging his horse on with a banana? I feel convinced
that, should the affair come to Madeline's ears, you can get
away with it with stout denial.'

He pondered.

'Perhaps you're right. But all the same I wish you'd be more
careful. The whole thing has been most annoying and upsetting.'

'Still,' I said, feeling that it was worth trying, 'it's part of the
great web, what?'

'Great web?'

'One of Marcus Aurelius's cracks. He said: "Does aught befall

78

you? It is good. It is part of the destiny of the Universe ordained for you from the beginning. All that befalls you is part of the great web." '

From the brusque manner in which he damned and blasted Marcus Aurelius, I gathered that, just as had happened when Jeeves sprang it on me, the gag had failed to bring balm. I hadn't had much hope that it would. I doubt, as a matter of fact, if Marcus Aurelius's material is ever the stuff to give the troops at a moment when they have just stubbed their toe on the brick of Fate. You want to wait till the agony has abated.

To ease the strain, I changed the subject, asking him if he had been surprised to find Catsmeat in residence at the Hall, and immediately became aware that I had but poured kerosene on the flames. Heated though his observations on Marcus Aurelius had been, they were mildness itself compared with what he had to say about Catsmeat.

It was understandable, of course. If a fellow has forced you against your better judgment to go wading in the Trafalgar Square fountain at five in the morning, ruining your trousers and causing you to be pinched and jugged and generally put through it by the machinery of the Law, no doubt you do find yourself coming round to the view that what he needs is disembowelling with a blunt bread-knife. This, among other things, was what Gussie hoped some day to be able to do to Catsmeat, if all went well, and, as I say, one could follow the train of thought.

Presently, having said all he could think of on the topic of Catsmeat, he turned, as I had rather been expecting he would, to that of the cross-talk act of which the other was the originator and producer.

'What's all this Pirbright was saying about something he called a cross-talk act?' he asked, and I saw that we had reached a point in the exchanges where suavity and the honeyed word would be needed.

'Ah, yes, he mentioned that to you, did he not? It's an item on the programme of the concert which his sister is impresarioing at the village hall shortly. I was to have played Pat in it, but owing to the changed circumstances you will now sustain the role.'

'Will I! We'll see about that. What the devil is the damned thing?'

'Haven't you seen it? Pongo Twistleton and Barmy Phipps do it every year at the Drones smoker.'

'I never go to the Drones smoker.'

'Oh? Well, it's a . . . How shall I put it? . . . It's what is known as a cross-talk act. The principals are a couple of Irishmen named Pat and Mike, and they come on and . . . But I have the script here,' I said, producing it. 'If you glance through it, you'll get the idea.'

He took the script and studied it with a sullen frown. Watching him, I realized what a ghastly job it must be writing plays. I mean, having to hand over your little effort to a hardfaced manager and stand shuffling your feet while he glares at it as if it hurt him in a tender spot, preparatory to pushing it back at you with a curt 'It stinks'.

'Who wrote this?' asked Gussie, as he turned the final page, and when I told him that Catsmeat was the author he said he might have guessed it. Throughout his perusal, he had been snorting at intervals, and he snorted again, a good bit louder, as if he were amalgamating about six snorts into one snort.

'The thing is absolute drivel. It has no dramatic coherence. It lacks motivation and significant form. Who are these two men supposed to be?'

'I told you. A couple of Irishmen named Pat and Mike.'

'Well, perhaps you can explain what their social position is, for it is frankly beyond me. Pat, for instance, appears to move in the very highest circles, for he describes himself as dining at Buckingham Palace, and yet his wife takes in lodgers.'

'I see what you mean. Odd.'

'Inexplicable. Is it credible that a man of his class would be invited to dinner at Buckingham Palace, especially as he is apparently completely without social *savoir-faire*? At this dinner-party to which he alludes he relates how the Queen asked him if he would like some mulligatawny and he, thinking that there was nothing else coming, had six helpings, with the result that, to quote his words, he spent the rest of the evening sitting in a corner full of soup. And in describing the incident he prefaces his remarks at several points with the expressions "Begorrah" and "faith and begob". Irishmen don't talk like that. Have you ever read Synge's *Riders to the Sea*? Well, get hold of it and study it, and if you can show me a single character in it who says "Faith and begob", I'll give you a shilling. Irish-men are poets. They talk about their souls and mist and so on. They say things like "An evening like this, it makes me wish I was back in County Clare, watchin' the cows in the tall grass".'

He turned the pages frowningly, his nose wrinkled as if it had detected some unpleasant smell. It brought back to me the old days at Malvern House, Bramley-on-Sea, when I used to take my English essay to be blue-pencilled by the Rev. Aubrey Upjohn.

'Here's another bit of incoherent raving. "My sister's in the ballet." "You say your sister's in the ballet?" "Yes, begorrah, my sister's in the ballet." "What does your sister do in the ballet?" "She comes rushing in, and then she goes rushing out." "What does she have to rush like that for?" "Faith and begob, because it's a Rushin' ballet." It simply doesn't make sense. And now we come to something else that is quite beyond me, the word "*bus*". After the line "Because it's a Rushin' ballet" and in other places throughout the script the word "*bus*" in brackets occurs. It conveys nothing to me. Can you explain it?'

'It's short for "*business*". That's where you hit Mike with your umbrella. To show the audience that there has been a joke.'

Gussie started.

'Are these things jokes?'

'Yes.'

'I see. I *see*. Well, of course, that throws a different light on . . .' He paused, and eyed me narrowly. 'Did you say that I am supposed to strike my colleague with an umbrella?'

'That's right.'

'And if I understood Pirbright correctly, the other performer in this extraordinary production is the local policeman?'

'That's right.'

'The whole thing is impossible and utterly out of the question,' said Gussie vehemently. 'Have you any idea what happens when you hit a policeman with an umbrella? I did so on emerging from the fountain in Trafalgar Square, and I certainly do not intend to do it again.' A sort of grey horror came into his face, as if he had been taking a quick look into a past which he had hoped to forget. 'Well, let me put you quite straight, Wooster, as to what my stand is in this matter. I shall not say "Begorrah". I shall not say "Faith and begob". I shall not assault policemen with an umbrella. In short, I absolutely and positively refuse to have the slightest association with this degraded buffoonery. Wait till I meet Miss Pirbright. I'll tell her a thing or two. I'll show her she can't play fast and loose with human dignity like this.'

He was about to speak further, but at this point his voice died away in a sort of gurgle and I saw his eyes bulge. Glancing around, I perceived Corky approaching. She was accompanied by Sam Goldwyn and was looking, as is her wont, like a million dollars, gowned in some clinging material which accentuated rather than hid her graceful outlines, if you know what I mean.

I was delighted to see her. With Gussie in this non-cooperative mood, digging his feet in and refusing to play ball, like Balaam's ass, it seemed to me that precisely what was needed was the woman's touch. To decide to introduce them and leave her to take on the job of melting his iron front was with me the work of a moment.

I had high hopes that she would be able to swing the deal. Though differing from my Aunt Agatha in almost every possible respect, Corky has this in common with that outstanding scourge: she is authoritative. When she wants you to do a thing, you find yourself doing it. This has been so from her earliest years. I remember her on one occasion at our mutual dancing class handing me an antique orange, a blue and yellow mass of pips and mildew, and bidding me bung it at our instructress, who had incurred her displeasure for some reason which has escaped my recollection. And I did it without a murmur, though knowing full well how bitter the reckoning would be.

'Hoy!' I said, eluding the cheesehound's attempts to place his front paws on my shoulders and strop his tongue on my face. I jerked a thumb. 'Gussie,' I said.

Corky's face lit up in a tickled-to-death manner. She proceeded immediately to turn on the charm.

'Oh, is *this* Mr Fink-Nottle? How do you do, Mr Fink-Nottle? I *am* so glad to see you, Mr Fink-Nottle. How lucky meeting you. I wanted to talk to you about the act.'

'We've just been having a word or two on that subject,' I said, 'and Gussie's kicking a bit at playing Pat.'

'Oh, *no?*'

'I thought you might like to reason with him. I'll leave you to it,' I said and biffed off. Looking around as I turned the corner, I saw that she had attached herself with one slim hand to the lapel of Gussie's coat and with the other was making wide, appealing gestures, indicating to the most vapid and irreflective observer that she was giving him Treatment A.

Well pleased, I made my way back to the Hall, keeping an eye skinned for prowling aunts, and won through without disaster to my room. I was enjoying a thoughtful smoke there about half an hour later when Gussie came in, and I could see right away that this was not the morose, sullen Fink-Nottle who had so uncompromisingly panned the daylights out of Pat and Mike in the course of our recent get-together. His bearing was buoyant. His face glowed. He was wearing in his buttonhole a flower which had not been there before.

'Hallo, there, Bertie,' he said. 'I say, Bertie, why didn't you tell me that Miss Pirbright was Cora Starr, the film actress? I have long been one of her warmest admirers. What a delightful girl she is, is she not, and how unlike her brother, whom I consider and always shall consider England's leading louse. She has made me see this cross-talk act in an entirely new light.'

'I thought she might.'

'It's extraordinary that a girl as pretty as that should also have a razor-keen intelligence and that amazing way of putting her arguments with a crystal clarity which convinces you in an instant that she is right in every respect.'

'Yes, Corky's a persuasive young gumboil.'

'I would prefer that you did not speak of her as a gumboil. Corky, eh? That's what you call her, is it? A charming name.'

'What was the outcome of your conference? Are you going to do the act?'

'Oh, yes, it's all settled. She overcame my objections entirely. We ran through the script after you had left us, and she quite brought me round to her view that there is nothing in the least degrading in this simple, wholesome form of humour. Hokum, yes, but, as she pointed out good theatre. She is convinced that I shall go over big.'

'You'll knock 'em cold. I'm sorry I can't play Pat myself – '

'A good thing, probably. I doubt if you are the type.'

'Of course I'm the type,' I retorted hotly. 'I should have given a sensational performance.'

'Corky thinks not. She was telling me how thankful she was that you had stepped out and I had taken over. She said the part wants broad, robust treatment and you would have played it too far down. It's a part that calls for personality and the most precise timing, and she said that the moment she saw me she felt that here was the ideal Pat. Girls with her experience can tell in a second.'

I gave it up. You can't reason with hams, and twenty minutes of Corky's society seemed to have turned Augustus Fink-Nottle from a blameless newt-fancier into as pronounced a ham as ever drank small ports in Bodegas and called people 'laddie'. In another half jiffy, I felt, he would be addressing me as 'laddie'.

'Well, it's no use talking about it,' I said, 'because I could never have taken the thing on. Madeline wouldn't have approved of her affianced appearing in public in a green beard.'

'No, she's an odd girl.'

It seemed to me that I might wipe that silly smile off his face by reminding him of something he appeared to have forgotten.

'And how about Dobbs?'

'Eh?'

'When last heard from, you were a bit agitated at the prospect of having to slosh Police Constable Dobbs with your umbrella.'

'Oh, Dobbs? He's out. He's been given his notice. He came along when we were rehearsing and started to read Mike's lines, but he was hopeless. No technique. No personality. And he wouldn't take direction. Kept arguing every point with the management, until finally Corky got heated and began raising her voice, and he got heated and began raising his voice, and the upshot was that that dog of hers, excited no doubt by the uproar, bit him in the leg.'

'Good Lord!'

'Yes, it created an unpleasant atmosphere. Corky put the animal's case extremely well, pointing out that it had probably been pushed around by policemen since it was a slip of a puppy and so was merely fulfilling a legitimate aspiration if it took an occasional nip at one, but Dobbs refused to accept her view that the offence was one calling for a mere reprimand. He took the creature into custody and is keeping it at the police station until he has been able to ascertain whether this was its first bite.

Apparently a dog that has had only one bite is in a strong position legally.'

'Sam Goldwyn bit Silversmith last night.'

'Did he? Well, if that comes out, I'm afraid counsel for the prosecution will have a talking-point. But, to go on with my story, Corky, incensed, and quite rightly, by Dobbs's intransigent attitude, threw him out of the act and is getting her brother to play the part. There is the risk, of course, that the vicar will recognize him, which would lead to an unfortunate situation, but she thinks the green beard will form a sufficient disguise. I am looking forward to having Pirbright as a partner. I can think of few men whom it would give me more genuine pleasure to hit with an umbrella,' said Gussie broodingly, adding that the first time his weapon connected with Catsmeat's head, the latter would think he had been struck by a thunderbolt. It was plain that Time, the great healer, would have to put in a lot of solid work before he forgot and forgave.

'But I can't stay here talking,' he went on. 'Corky has asked me to lunch at the Vicarage, and I must be getting along. I just looked in to give you those poems.'

'Those what?'

'Those Christopher Robin poems. Here they are.'

He handed me a slim volume of verse, and I gave it the perplexed eye.

'What's this for?'

'You recite them at the concert. The ones marked with a cross. I was to have recited them, Madeline making a great point of it – you know how fond she is of the Christopher Robin poems – but now, of course, we have switched acts. And I don't mind telling you that I feel extremely relieved. There's one about the little blighter going hoppity-hoppity-hop which . . . Well, as I say, I feel extremely relieved.'

The slim volume fell from my nerveless fingers, and I goggled at him.

'But, dash it!'

'It's no good saying "But, dash it!" Do you think I didn't say "But, dash it!" when she forced these nauseous productions on me? You've got to do them. She insists. The first thing she will want to know is how they went.'

'But the tough eggs at the back of the row will rush the stage and lynch me.'

'I shouldn't wonder. Still, you've got one consolation.'

'What's that?'

'The thought that all that befalls you is part of the great web, ha, ha, ha,' said Gussie, and exited smiling.

And so the first day of my sojourn at Deverill Hall wore to a close, full to the brim of V-shaped depressions and unsettled outlooks.

10

A ND as the days went by, these unsettled outlooks became more unsettled, those V-shaped depressions even V-er. It was on a Friday that I had clocked in at Deverill Hall. By the morning of Tuesday I could no longer conceal it from myself that I was losing the old pep and that, unless the clouds changed their act and started dishing out at an early date a considerably more substantial slab of silver lining than they were coming across with at the moment, I should soon be definitely down among the wines and spirits.

It is bad to be trapped in a den of slavering aunts, lashing their tails and glaring at you out of their red eyes. It is unnerving to know that in a couple of days you will be up on a platform in a village hall telling an audience, probably well provided with vegetables, that Christopher Robin goes hoppity-hoppity-hop. It degrades the spirit to have to answer to the name of Augustus, and there are juicier experiences than being in a position where you are constantly asking yourself if an Aunt Agatha or a Madeline Bassett won't suddenly arrive and subject you to shame and exposure. No argument about that. We can take that, I think, as read.

But it was not these chunks of the great web that were removing the stiffening from the Wooster upper lip. No, the root of the trouble, the thing that was giving me dizzy spells and night sweats and making me look like the poor bit of human wreckage in the 'before taking' pictures in the advertisements of Haddocks' Headache Hokies, was the sinister behaviour of Gussie Fink-Nottle. Contemplating Gussie, I found my soul darkened by a nameless fear.

I don't know if you have ever had your soul darkened by a nameless fear. It's a most unpleasant feeling. I used to get it when I was one of the resident toads beneath the harrow at Malvern House, Bramley-on-Sea, on hearing the Rev. Aubrey Upjohn conclude a series of announcements with the curt crack that he would like to see Wooster in his study after evening prayers. On the present occasion I had felt it coming on during the conversation with Gussie which I have just related, and in the days that followed it had grown and grown until now I found myself what is known as a prey to the liveliest apprehension.

I wonder if you spotted anything in the conversation to which I refer? Did it, I mean, strike you as significant and start you saying 'What ho!' to yourself? It didn't? Then you missed the gist.

The first day I had had merely a vague suspicion. The second day this suspicion deepened. By nightfall on the third day suspicion had become a certainty. The evidence was all in, and there was no getting round it. Reckless of the fact that there existed at The Larches, Wimbledon Common, a girl to whom he had plighted his troth and who would be madder than a bull-pup entangled in a fly-paper were she to discover that he was moving in on another, Augustus Fink-Nottle had fallen for Corky Pirbright like a ton of bricks.

You may say 'Come, come, Bertram, you are imagining things' or 'Tush, Wooster, this is but an idle fancy', but let me tell you that I wasn't the only one who had noticed it. Five solid aunts had noticed it.

'Well, really,' Dame Daphne Winkworth had observed bitterly just before lunch, when Silversmith had blown in with the news that Gussie had once again telephoned to say he would be taking pot-luck at the Vicarage, 'Mr Wooster seems to live in Miss Pirbright's pocket. He appears to regard Deverill Hall as a hotel which he can drop into or stay away from as he feels inclined.'

And Aunt Charlotte, when the facts had been relayed to her through her ear-trumpet, for she was wired for sound, had said with a short, quick sniff that she supposed they ought to consider themselves highly honoured that the piefaced young bastard condescended to sleep in the bally place, or words to that effect.

Nor could one fairly blame them for blinding and stiffing. Nothing sticks the gaff into your chatelaine more than a guest being constantly AWOL, and it was only on the rarest occasions nowadays that Gussie saw fit to put on the nosebag at Deverill Hall. He lunched, tea-ed and dined with Corky. Since that first meeting outside the post office he had seldom left her side. The human poultice, nothing less.

You can readily understand, then, why there were dark circles beneath my eyes and why I had almost permanently now a fluttering sensation at the pit of the stomach, as if I had recently swallowed far more mice than I could have wished. It only needed a word from Dame Daphne Winkworth to Aunt Agatha to the effect that her nephew Bertram had fallen into the toils of a most undesirable girl – a Hollywood film actress, my dear – I could see her writing it as clearly as if I had been peeping over her shoulder – to bring the old relative racing down to Deverill Hall with her foot in her hand. And then what? Ruin, desolation and despair.

The obvious procedure, of course, when the morale is being given the sleeve across the windpipe like this, is to get in touch with Jeeves and see what he has to suggest. So, encountering the parlourmaid, Queenie, in the passage outside my room after lunch, I enquired as to his whereabouts.

'I say,' I said, 'I wonder if you happen to know where Jeeves is? Wooster's man, you know.'

She stood staring at me goofily. Her eyes, normally like twin stars, were dull and a bit reddish about the edges, and I should have described her face as drawn. The whole set-up, in short, seeming to indicate that here one had a parlourmaid who had either gone off her onion or was wrestling with a secret sorrow.

'Sir?' she said, in a tortured sort of voice.

I repeated my remarks, and this time they penetrated.

'Mr Jeeves isn't here, sir. Mr Wooster let him go to London. There was a lecture he wanted to be at.'

'Oh thanks,' I said, speaking dully, for this was a blow. 'You don't know when he'll be back?'

'No, sir.'

'I see. Thanks.'

I went on into my room and took a good, square look at the situation.

If you ask any of the nibs who move in diplomatic circles and are accustomed to handling tricky affairs of state, he will tell you that when matters have reached a deadlock, it is not a bit of good just sitting on the seat of the pants and rolling the eyes up to heaven – you have got to turn stones and explore avenues and take prompt steps through the proper channels. Only thus can you hope to find a formula. And it seemed to me, musing tensely, that in the present crisis something constructive might be accomplished by rounding up Corky and giving her a straight-from-the-shoulder talk, pointing out the frightful jeopardy in which she was placing an old friend and dancing-class buddy by allowing Gussie to spend his time frisking and bleating round her.

I left the room, accordingly, and a few minutes later might have been observed stealing through the sunlit grounds en route for the village. In fact, I was observed, and by Dame Daphne Winkworth. I was nearing the bottom of the drive and in another moment should have won through to safety, when somebody called my name – or, rather, Gussie's name – and I saw the formidable old egg standing in the rose garden. From the fact that she had a syringe in her hand I deduced that she was in the process of doing the local green-fly a bit of no good.

'Come here, Augustus,' she said.

It was the last thing I would have done, if given the choice, for even at the best of times this dangerous specimen put the wind up me pretty vertically, and she was now looking about ten degrees more forbidding than usual. Her voice was cold and her eye was cold, and I didn't like the way she was toying with that syringe. It was plain that for some reason I had fallen in her estimation to approximately the level of a green-fly, and her air was that of a woman who for two pins would press the trigger and let me have a fluid ounce of whatever the hell-brew was squarely in the mazzard.

'Oh, hallo,' I said, trying to be *debonair* but missing by a mile. 'Squirting the rose trees?'

'Don't talk to me about rose trees!'

'Oh, no, rather not,' I said. Well, I hadn't wanted to particularly. Just filling in with *ad lib* stuff.

'Augustus, what is this I hear?'

'I beg your pardon?'

'You would do better to beg Madeline's.'

Mystic stuff. I didn't get it. The impression I received was of a Dame of the British Empire talking through the back of her neck.

'When I was in the house just now,' she proceeded, 'a telegram

90

arrived for you from Madeline. It was telephoned from the post office. Sometimes they telephone, and sometimes they deliver personally.'

'I see. According to the whim of the moment.'

'Please do not interrupt. This time it happened that the message was telephoned, and as I was passing through the hall when the bell rang, I took it down.'

'Frightfully white of you,' I said, feeling that I couldn't go wrong in giving her the old oil.

I had gone wrong, however. She didn't like it. She frowned, raised the syringe, then, as if remembering in time that she was a Deverill, lowered it again.

'I have already asked you not to interrupt. I took down the message, as I say, and I have it here. No,' she said, having searched through her costume, 'I must have left it on the hall table. But I can tell you its contents. Madeline says she has not received a single letter from you since you arrived at the Hall, and she wishes to know why. She is greatly distressed at your abominable neglect, and I am not surprised. You know how sensitive she is. You ought to have been writing to her every day. I have no words to express what I think of your heartless behaviour. That is all, Augustus,' she said, and dismissed me with a gesture of loathing, as if I had been a green-fly that had fallen short of even the very moderate level of decency of the average run-of-the-mill green-fly. And I tottered off and groped my way to a rustic bench and sank onto it.

The information which she had sprung on me had, I need scarcely say, affected me like the impact behind the ear of a stocking full of wet sand. Only once in my career had I experienced an emotion equally intense, on the occasion when Freddie Widgeon at the Drones, having possessed himself of a motor horn, stole up behind me as I crossed Dover Street in what is known as a reverie and suddenly tooted the apparatus in my immediate ear.

It had never so much as occurred to me to suppose that Gussie was not writing daily letters to the Bassett. It was what he had come to this Edgar Allen Poe residence to do, and I had taken it for granted that he was doing it. I didn't need a diagram to show me what the run of events would be, if he persisted in this policy of ca'canny. A spot more silence on his part, and along

91

would come La Bassett in person to investigate, and the thought of what would happen then froze the blood and made the toes curl.

I suppose it may have been for a matter of about ten minutes that I sat there inert, the jaw drooping, the eyes staring sightlessly at the surrounding scenery. Then I pulled myself together and resumed my journey. It has been well said of Bertram Wooster that though he may sink onto rustic benches and for a while give the impression of being licked to a custard, the old spirit will always come surging back sooner or later.

As I walked, I was thinking hard and bitter thoughts of Corky, the *fons et origo*, if you know what I mean by *fons et origo*, of all the trouble. It was she who, by shamelessly flirting with him, by persistently giving him the flashing smile and the quick sidelong look out of the corner of the eye, had taken Gussie's mind off his job and slowed him up as our correspondent on the spot. Oh, Woman, Woman, I said to myself, not for the first time, feeling that the sooner the sex was suppressed, the better it would be for all of us.

At the age of eight, in the old dancing-class days, incensed by some incisive remarks on her part about my pimples, of which I had a notable collection at that time, I once forgot myself to the extent of socking Corky Pirbright on the top-knot with a wooden dumb-bell, and until this moment I had always regretted the unpleasant affair, considering my action a blot on an otherwise stainless record and, no matter what the provocation, scarcely the behaviour of a *preux chevalier*. But now, as I brooded on the Delilah stuff she was pulling, I found myself wishing I could do it again.

I strode on, rehearsing in my mind some opening sentence to be employed when we should meet, and not far from the Vicarage came upon her seated at the wheel of her car by the side of the road.

But when I confronted her and said I wanted a word with her, she regretted that it couldn't be managed at the moment. It was, she explained, her busy afternoon. In pursuance of her policy of being the Little Mother to her uncle, the sainted Sidney, she was about to take a bowl of strengthening soup to one of his needy parishioners.

'A Mrs Clara Wellbeloved, if you want to keep the record

straight,' she proceeded. 'She lives in one of those picturesque cottages of the High Street. And it's no good you waiting, because after delivering the bouillon I sit and talk to her about Hollywood. She's a great fan, and it takes hours. Some other time, my lamb.'

'Listen, Corky – '

'You are probably saying to yourself "Where's the soup?" I unfortunately forgot to bring it along, and Gussie has trotted back for it. What a delightful man he is, Bertie. So kind. So helpful. Always on hand to run errands, when required, and with a fund of good stories about newts. I've given him my autograph. Speaking of autographs, I heard from your cousin Thomas this morning.'

'Never mind about young Thos. What I want – '

She broke into speech again, as girls always do. I have had a good deal of experience of this tendency on the part of the female sex to refrain from listening when you talk to them, and it has always made me sympathize with those fellows who tried to charm the deaf adder and had it react like a Wednesday matinée audience.

'You remember I gave him fifty of my autographs, and he expected to sell them to his playmates at sixpence apiece? Well, he tells me that he got a bob, not sixpence, which will give you a rough idea of how I stand with the boys at Bramley-on-Sea. He says a genuine Ida Lupino only fetches ninepence.'

'Listen, Corky – '

'He wants to come and spend his midterm holiday at the Vicarage, and, of course, I've written to say that I shall be delighted. I don't think Uncle Sidney is too happy at the prospect, but it's good for a clergyman to have these trials. Makes him more spiritual, and consequently hotter at his job.'

'Listen, Corky. What I want to talk to you about – '

'Ah, here's Gussie,' she said, once more doing the deaf adder.

Gussie came bounding up with a look of reverent adoration on his face and a steaming can in his hands. Corky gave him a dazzling smile which seemed to go through him like a red-hot bullet through a pat of butter, and stowed the can away in the rumble seat.

'Thank you, Gussie darling,' she said. 'Well, good-bye all. I must rush.'

She drove off, Gussie standing gaping after her transfixed, like a goldfish staring at an ant's egg. He did not, however, remain transfixed long, because I got him between the third and fourth ribs with a forceful finger, causing him to come to life with a sharp 'Ouch!'

'Gussie,' I said, getting down to brass tacks and beating about no bushes. 'What's all this about you not writing to Madeline?'

'Madeline?'

'Madeline.'

'Oh, Madeline?'

'Yes, Madeline. You ought to have been writing to her every day.'

This seemed to annoy him.

'How on earth could I write to her every day? What chance do I get to write letters when my time is all taken up with memorizing my lines in this cross-talk act and thinking up effective business? I haven't a moment.'

'Well, you'll jolly well have to find a moment. Do you realize she's started sending telegrams about it? You must write to-day without fail.'

'What, to Madeline?'

'Yes, blast you, to Madeline.'

I was surprised to see that he was glowering sullenly through his windshields.

'I'll be blowed if I write to Madeline,' he said, and would have looked like a mule if he had not looked so like a fish. 'I'm teaching her a lesson.'

'You're what?'

'Teaching her a lesson. I'm not at all pleased with Madeline. She wanted me to come to this ghastly house, and I consented on the understanding that she would come, too, and give me moral support. It was a clear-cut gentlemen's agreement. And at the last moment she coolly backed out on the flimsy plea that some school friend of hers at Wimbledon needed her. I was extremely annoyed, and I let her see it. She must be made to realize that she can't do that sort of thing. So I'm not writing to her. It's a sort of system.'

I clutched at the brow. The mice in my interior had now got up an informal dance and were buck-and-winging all over the place like a bunch of Nijinskys.

'Gussie,' I said, 'once and for all, will you or will you not go back to the house and compose an eight-page letter breathing love in every syllable?'

'No, I won't,' he said and left me flat.

Baffled and despondent, I returned to the Hall. And the first person I saw there was Catsmeat. He was in my room, lying on the bed with one of my cigarettes in his mouth.

There was a sort of dreamy look on his dial, as if he were thinking of Gertrude Winkworth.

=11=

Observing me, he switched off the dreamy look.

'Oh, hallo, Bertie,' he said. 'I wanted to see you.'

'Oh, yes?' I riposted, quick as a flash, and I meant it to sting, for I was feeling a bit fed with Catsmeat.

I mean of his own free will he had taken on the job of valeting me, and in his capacity of my gentleman's personal gentleman should have been in and out all the time, brushing here a coat, pressing there a trouser and generally making himself useful, and I hadn't set eyes on him since the night we had arrived. One frowns on this absenteeism.

'I wanted to tell you the good news.'

I laughed hollowly.

'Good news? Is there such a thing?'

'You bet there's such a thing. Things are looking up. The sun is smiling through. I believe I'm going to swing this Gertrude deal. Owing to the footling social conventions which prevent visiting valets hobnobbing with the daughter of the house, I haven't seen her, of course, to speak to, but I've been sending her notes by Jeeves and she has been sending me notes by Jeeves, and in her latest she shows distinct signs of yielding to my prayers. I think about two more communications, if carefully worded, should do the trick. Don't actually buy the fish-slice yet, but be prepared.'

My pique vanished. As I have said before, the Woosters are fairminded. I knew what a dickens of a sweat these love letters are, a whole-time job calling for incessant concentration. If Catsmeat had been tied up with a lot of correspondence of this type, he wouldn't have had much time for attending to my wardrobe, of course. You can't press your suit and another fellow's trousers simultaneously.

'Well, that's fine,' I said, pleased to learn that, though the general outlook was so scaly, someone was getting a break. 'I shall watch your future progress with considerable interest. But pigeon-holing your love life for the moment, Catsmeat, a most frightful thing has happened, and I should be glad if you could come across with anything in the aid-and-comfort line. That criminal lunatic Gussie – '

'What's he been doing?'

'It's what he's not been doing that's the trouble. You could have flattened me with a toothpick just now when I found out that he hasn't written a single line to Madeline Bassett since he got here. And, what's more, he says he isn't going to write to her. He says he's teaching her a lesson,' I said, and in a few brief words placed the facts before him.

He looked properly concerned. Catsmeat's is a kindly and feeling heart, readily moved by the spectacle of an old friend splashing about in the gumbo, and he knows how I stand with regard to Madeline Bassett, because she told him the whole story one day when they met at a bazaar and the subject of me happened to come up.

'This is rather serious,' he said.

'You bet it's serious. I'm shaking like a leaf.'

'Girls of the Madeline Bassett type attach such importance to the daily letter.'

'Exactly. And if it fails to arrive, they come and make inquiries on the spot.'

'And you say Gussie was not to be moved?'

'Not an inch. I pleaded with him, I may say passionately, but he put his ears back and refused to co-operate.'

Catsmeat pondered.

'I think I know what's behind all this. The trouble is that Gussie at the moment is slightly off his rocker.'

'What do you mean, at the moment? And why slightly?'

'He's infatuated with Corky. Sorry to use such long words. I mean he's got a crush on her.'

'I know he has. So does everybody else for miles around. His crush is the favourite topic of conversation when aunt meets aunt.'

'There has been comment in the servants' hall, too.'

'I'm not surprised. I'll bet they're discussing the thing in Basingstoke.'

'You can't blame him, of course.'

'Yes, I can.'

'I mean, it isn't his fault, really. This is springtime, Bertie, the mating season, when, as you probably know, a livelier iris gleams upon the burnished dove and a young man's fancy lightly turns to thoughts of love. The sudden impact plumb spang in the middle of spring, of a girl like Corky on a fathead like Gussie, weakened by constantly swilling orange juice, must have been terrific. Corky, when she's going nicely, bowls over the strongest. No one knows that better than you. You were making a colossal ass of yourself over her at one time.'

'No need to rake up the dead past.'

'I only raked it up to drive home my point, which is that he is more to be pitied than censured.'

'She's the one that wants censuring. Why does she encourage him?'

'I don't think she encourages him. He just adheres.'

'She does encourage him. I've seen her doing it. She deliberately turns on the charm and gives him the old personality. Don't tell me that a girl like Corky, accustomed to giving Hollywood glamour men the brusheroo, couldn't put Gussie on ice, if she wanted to.'

'But she doesn't.'

'That's what I'm beefing about.'

'And I'll tell you why she doesn't. I haven't actually asked her, but I'm pretty sure she's working this Gussie continuity with the idea of sticking the harpoon into Esmond Haddock. To show him that if he doesn't want her, there are others who do.'

'But he does want her.'

'She doesn't know that. Unless you've told her.'

'I haven't.'

'Why not?'

'I wasn't sure if it would be the correct procedure. You see, he dished out all that stuff about his inner feelings under the seal of the confessional, as you might say, and he said he didn't want it to go any further. "This must go no further," he said. On the other hand, a word in season might quite easily reunite a couple of sundered hearts. The whole thing is extraordinarily moot.'

'I'd go ahead and tell her. Bung in the word in season. I'm all for reuniting sundered hearts.'

'Me, too. But I think we've left it too late. Already the Bassett is burning up the wires with telegrams asking what it's all about. A hot one just arrived. I found it on the hall table when I came in. It was the telegram of a girl on the verge of becoming fed to the eye teeth. I tell you, Catsmeat, I see no ray of light. I'm sunk.'

'No, you're not.'

'I am. When I told Gussie about this telegram, urging upon him that now was the time for all good men to come to the aid of the party, he merely as I say, stuck his ears back and said he was teaching the girl a lesson and not a smell of a letter should she get from him till that lesson had been learned. The man's *non compos*, and I repeat that I see no ray of light.'

'It seems to me it's all quite simple.'

'You mean you have something to suggest?'

'Of course I've something to suggest. I always have something to suggest. The thing's obvious. If Gussie won't write to this girl, you must write to her yourself.'

'But she doesn't want to hear from me. She wants to hear from Gussie.'

'And so she will, bless her heart. Gussie has sprained his wrist, so had to dictate the letter to you.'

'Gussie hasn't sprained his wrist.'

'Pardon me. He gave it a nasty wrench while stopping a runaway horse and at great personal risk saving a little child from a hideous death. A golden-haired child, if you will allow yourself to be guided by me, with blue eyes, pink cheeks and a lisp. I think a lisp is good box-office?'

I gasped. I had got his drift.

'Catsmeat, this is terrific! You'll write the thing?'

'Of course. It'll be pie. I've been writing Gertrude that sort of letter since I was so high.'

He seated himself at the table, took pen and paper and immediately became immersed in composition, as the expression is. I could see that it had been no idle boast on his part that the thing would be pie. He didn't even seem to have to stop and think. In almost no time he was handing me the finished script and bidding me get a jerk on and copy it out.

'It ought to go off at once, every moment being vital. Trot down to the post office with it yourself. Then she'll get it first thing in the morning. And now, Bertie, I must leave you. I promised to play gin rummy with Queenie, and I am already late. She wants cheering up, poor child. You've heard about her tragedy? The severing of her engagement to the flatty Dobbs?'

'No, really? Is her engagement off? Then that's why she was looking like that, I suppose. I ran into her after lunch,' I explained, 'and I got the impression that the heart was heavy. What went wrong?'

'She didn't like him being an atheist, and he wouldn't stop being an atheist, and finally he said something about Jonah and the Whale which it was impossible for her to overlook. This morning, she returned the ring, his letters and a china ornament with "A Present From Blackpool" on it, which he bought her last summer while visiting relatives in the north. It's hit her pretty hard, I'm afraid. She's passing through the furnace. She loves him madly and yearns to be his, but she can't take that stuff about Jonah and the Whale. One can only hope that gin rummy will do something to ease the pain. Right ho, Bertie, get on with that letter. It's not actually one of my best, perhaps, because I was working against time and couldn't prune and polish, but I think you'll like it.'

He was correct. I studied the communication carefully, and was enchanted with its virtuosity. If it wasn't one of his best, his best must have been pretty good, and I was not surprised that upon receipt of a series Gertrude Winkworth was weakening. There are letters which sow doubts as to whether this bit here couldn't have been rather more neatly phrased and that bit there gingered up a trifle, and other letters of which you say to yourself "This is the goods. Don't alter a word". This was one of the latter letters. He had got just the right modest touch into the passage about the runaway horse, and the lisping child was terrific. She stuck out like a sore thumb and hogged the show. As for the warmer portions about missing Madeline every minute and wishing she were here so that he could fold her in his arms and what not, they simply couldn't have been improved upon.

I copied the thing out, stuffed it in an envelope and took it down to the post office. And scarcely had it plopped into the box, when I was hailed from behind by a musical soprano and, turning, saw Corky heaving alongside.

12

I FELT profoundly bucked. The very girl I wanted to see. I grabbed her by the arm, so that she couldn't do another of her sudden sneaks.

'Corky,' I said, 'I want a long, heart to heart talk with you.'

'Not about Hollywood?'

'No, not about Hollywood.'

'Thank God. I don't think I could have stood any more Hollywood chatter this afternoon. I wouldn't have believed,' she said, proceeding, as always, to collar the conversation, 'that anybody except Louella Parsons and Hedda Hopper could be such an authority on the film world as is Mrs Clara Wellbeloved. She knows much more about it than I do, and I'll have been moving in celluloid circles two years come Lammas Eve. She knows exactly how many times everybody's been divorced and why, how much every picture for the last twenty years has grossed, and how many Warner brothers there are. She even knows how many times Artie Shaw has been married, which I'll bet he couldn't tell you himself. She asked if I had ever married Artie Shaw, and when I said No, seemed to think I was pulling her leg or must have done it without noticing. I tried to explain that when a girl goes to Hollywood she doesn't *have* to marry Artie Shaw, it's optional, but I don't think I convinced her. A very remarkable old lady, but a bit exhausting after the first hour or two. Did you say you wanted to speak to me about something.'

'Yes, I did.'

'Well, why don't you?'

'Because you won't let me get a word in edgeways.'

'Oh, have I been talking? I'm sorry. What's on your mind, my king?'

'Gussie.'

'Fink-Nottle?'

'Fink-Nottle is correct.'

'The whitest man I know.'

'The fatheadest man you know. Listen, Corky, I've just been talking to Catsmeat – '

'Did he tell you that he expects shortly to persuade Gertrude Winkworth to elope with him?'

'Yes.'

She smiled in a steely sort of way, like one of those women in the Old Testament who used to go about driving spikes into people's heads.

'I'm just waiting for that to happen,' she said, 'so that I can get a good laugh out of seeing Esmond's face when he finds out that his Gertrude has gone off with another. Most amusing it will be. Ha, ha,' she added.

That 'Ha, ha', so like the expiring quack of a duck dying of a broken heart, told me all I wanted to know. I saw that Catsmeat had not erred in his diagnosis of this young shrimp's motives in giving Gussie the old treatment, and I had no option but to slip her the lowdown without further delay. I tapped her on the shoulder, and bunged in the word in season.

'Corky,' I said, 'you're a chump. You've got a completely wrong angle on this Haddock. So far from being enamoured of Gertrude Winkworth, I don't suppose he would care, except in a distant, cousinly way, if she choked on a fish-bone. You are the lodestar of his life.'

'What!'

'I had it from his own lips. He was a bit pickled at the time, which makes it all the more impressive, because *in vino* what's-the-word.'

Her eyes had lighted up. She gave a quick gulp.

'He said I was the lodestar of his life?'

'With a "still" in front of the "lodestar". "Mark this," he said, helping himself to port, of which he was already nearly full. "Though she has given me the brusheroo, she is still the lodestar of my life." '

'Bertie, if you're kidding – '

'Of course I'm not.'

'I hope you're not, because if you are I shall put the curse of the Pirbrights on you, and it's not at all the sort of curse you will enjoy. Tell me more.'

I told her more. In fact I told her all. When I had finished, she laughed like a hyena and also, for girls never make sense, let fall a pearly tear or two.

'Isn't that just the sort of thing he would think up, bless him!' she said, alluding to the hot idea Esmond Haddock had brought back with him from the Basingstoke cinema. 'What a woolly lambkin that man is!'

I was not sure if 'woolly lambkin' was quite the phrase I would have used myself to describe Esmond Haddock, but I let it go, it being no affair of mine. If she elected to regard a fellow with a forty-six-inch chest and muscles like writhing snakes as a woolly lambkin, that was up to her. My task, having started a good thing, was to push it along.

'In these circs,' I said, 'you will probably be glad of a word of advice from a knowledgeable man of the world. Catsmeat appears to have obtained excellent results on the Gertrude front from pouring out his soul in the form of notes, and if you take my tip, you will do the same. Drop Esmond Haddock a civil line telling him you are aching for his presence, and he will lower the world's record racing round to the Vicarage to fold you in his arms. He's only waiting for the green light.'

She shook her head.

'No,' she said.

'Why no?'

'We should simply be where we were before.'

I saw what she was driving at, of course.

'I know what's in your mind,' I said. 'You are alluding to his civil disobedience *in re* defying his aunts. Well, let me assure you that that little difficulty will very shortly yield to treatment. Listen. Esmond Haddock is singing a hunting song at the concert, words by his Aunt Charlotte, music by his Aunt Myrtle. You don't dispute that.'

'All correct so far.'

'Well, suppose that hunting song is a smackerino.'

And in a few well-chosen words I informed her of Jeeves's tenable theory.

'You get the idea?' I concluded. 'The cheers of the multitude frequently act like a powerful drug on these birds with inferiority complexes. Rouse such birds, as, for instance, by whistling through your fingers and yelling "*Bis! Bis!*" when they sing hunting songs, and they become changed men. Their morale stiffens. Their tails shoot up like rockets. They find themselves regarding the tough eggs before whom they have always been accustomed to crawl as less than the dust beneath their chariot wheels. If Esmond Haddock goes with the bang I anticipate, it won't be long before those aunts of his will be climbing trees and pulling them up after them whenever he looks squiggle-eyed at them.'

My eloquence had not been wasted. She started considerably, and said something about 'Out of the mouths of babes and sucklings', going on to explain that the gag was not her own but one of her Uncle Sidney's. And in return I told her that the tenable theory I had been outlining was not mine, but Jeeves's. Each giving credit where credit was due.

'I believe he's right, Bertie.'

'Of course he's right. Jeeves is always right. It's happened before. Do you know Bingo Little?'

'Just to say Hallo to. He married some sort of female novelist, didn't he?'

'Rosie M. Banks, author of *Mervyn Keene, Clubman*, and *Only A Factory Girl*. And their union was blessed. In due season a bouncing baby was added to the strength. Keep your eye on that baby, for the plot centres round it. Well, since you last saw Bingo, Mrs Bingo, by using her substantial pull, secured for him the post of editor of *Wee Tots*, a journal for the nursery and the home, a very good job in most respects but with this flaw, that the salary attached to it was not all it might have been. His proprietor, P. P. Purkiss, being one of those parsimonious birds in whose pocket-books moths nest and raise large families. It was Bingo's constant endeavour, accordingly, to try to stick old Gaspard the Miser for a raise. All clear so far?'

'I've got it.'

'Week after week he would creep into P. P. Purkiss's presence and falter out apologetic sentences beginning "Oh, Mr Purkiss, I wonder if . . ." and "Oh, Mr Purkiss, do you think you could possibly . . ." only to have the blighter gaze at him with fishy eyes and talk about the tightness of money and the growing cost of pulp paper. And Bingo would say "Oh, quite, Mr Purkiss," and "I see, Mr Purkiss, yes I see," and creep out again. That's Act One.'

'But mark the sequel?'

'You're right, mark the sequel. Came a day when Bingo's bouncing baby, entered in a baby contest against some of the warmest competition in South Kensington, scooped in the first prize, a handsome all-day sucker, getting kissed in the process by the wife of a Cabinet Minister and generally fawned upon by all and sundry. And next morning Bingo, with a strange light on his face, strode into P. P. Purkiss's private office without knocking, banged the desk with his fist and said he wished to see an additional ten fish in his pay envelope from now on, and to suit everybody's convenience the new arrangement would come into effect on the following Saturday. And when P. P. Purkiss started to go into his act, he banged the desk again and said he hadn't come there to argue. "Yes or no, Purkiss!" he said, and P. P. Purkiss, sagging like a wet sock, said "Why, yes, yes, of course, most certainly, Mr Little", adding that he had been on the point of suggesting some such idea himself. Well, I mean, that shows you.'

It impressed her. No mistaking that. She uttered a meditative 'Golly!' and stood on one leg, looking like 'The Soul's Awakening'.

'And so,' I proceeded, 'we are going to strain every nerve to see that Esmond Haddock's hunting song is the high-spot of the evening. Jeeves is to go about the village, scattering beers, so as to assemble what is known as a claque and ensure the thunderous applause. You will be able to help in that direction, too.'

'Of course I will. My standing in the village is terrific. I have the place in my pocket. I must get after this right away. I can't wait. You don't mind me leaving you?'

'Not at all, not at all, or, rather, yes, I jolly well do. Before you go, we've got to get this Gussie thing straight.'

'What Gussie thing?'

I clicked my tongue.

'You know perfectly well what Gussie thing. For reasons into which we need not go, you have recently been making Augustus Fink-Nottle the plaything of an idle hour, and it has got to stop. I don't have to tell you again what will happen if you continue carrying on as of even date. In our conference at the flat I made the facts clear to the meanest intelligence. You are fully aware that should the evil spread, should sand be shoved into the gears of the Fink-Nottle–Bassett romance to such an extent that it

105

ceases to tick over, Bertram Wooster will be faced with the fate that is worse than death – viz. marriage. I feel sure that, now that you have been reminded of the hideous peril that looms, your good heart will not allow you to go on encouraging the above Fink-Nottle as, according to the evidence of five aunts, you are doing now. Appalled by the thought of poor old Wooster pressing the wedding trousers and packing the trunks for a honeymoon with that ghastly Bassett, you will obey the dictates of your better self and cool him off.'

She saw my point.

'You want me to restore Gussie to circulation?'

'Exactly.'

'Switch off the fascination? Release him from my clutches?'

'That's right.'

'Why, of course. I'll attend to it immediately.'

And on these very satisfactory terms we parted. A great weight had been lifted from my mind.

Well, I don't know what your experience has been, but mine is that there is very little percentage in having a weight lifted off your mind, because the first thing you know another, probably a dashed sight heavier, is immediately shoved on. It would appear to be a game you can't beat.

I had scarcely got back to my room, all soothed and relaxed, when in blew Catsmeat, and there was that in his mere appearance that chilled my merry mood like a slap in the eye with a wet towel. His face was grave, and his deportment not at all the sprightly deportment of a man who has recently been playing gin rummy with parlourmaids.

'Bertie,' he said, 'hold on tight to something. A very serious situation has arisen.'

The floor seemed to heave beneath me like a stage sea. The mice, which since that latter sequence and the subsequent chat with Corky had been taking a breather, sprang into renewed activity, as if starting training for some athletic sports.

'Oh, my sainted aunt!' I moaned, and Catsmeat said I might well say 'My sainted aunt', because she was the spearhead of the trouble.

'Here comes the bruise,' he said. 'When I was in the servants' hall a moment ago, Silversmith rolled in. And do you know what he had just been told by the girls higher up? He had been told that your Aunt Agatha is coming here. I don't know when, but in the next day or so. Dame Daphne Winkworth had a letter from her by the afternoon post, and in it she announced her intention of shortly being a pleasant visitor at this ruddy hencoop. So now what?'

13

Iᴛ was a Bertram Wooster with a pale, careworn face and a marked disposition to start at sudden noises who sat in his bedroom on the following afternoon, rising occasionally to pace the floor. Few, seeing him, would have recognized in this limp and shivering chunk of human flotsam the suave, dapper *boulevardier* of happier years. I was waiting for Catsmeat to return from the metropolis and make his report.

Threshing the thing out on the previous evening, we had not taken long in reaching the conclusion that it would be madness to attempt to cope with this major crisis ourselves, and that the whole conduct of the affair must at the earliest moment be handed over to Jeeves. And as Jeeves was in London and it might have looked odd for me to dash away from the Big House for the night, Catsmeat had gone up to confer with him. He had tooled off secretly in my two-seater, expecting to be back around lunch-time.

But lunch had come and gone, the duck and green peas turning to ashes in my mouth, and still no sign of him. It was past three when he finally showed up.

At the sight of him, my heart, throwing off its burden of care, did a quick soft-shoe dance. No fellow, I reasoned, unless he was bringing good news, could look so like the United States Marines. When last seen, driving off on his mission, his air had been sober and downcast, as if he feared that even Jeeves would have to confess himself snookered by this one. He was now gay, bobbish and boomps-a-daisy.

'Sorry I'm late,' he said. 'I had to wait for Jeeves's brain to gather momentum. He was a little slower off the mark than usual.'

I clutched his arm.

'Did he click?' I cried, quivering in every limb.

'Oh, yes, he clicked. Jeeves always clicks. But this time only after brooding for what seemed an eternity. I found him in the kitchen at your flat, sipping a cup of tea and reading Spinoza, and put our problem before him, bidding him set the little grey cells in operation without delay and think of some way of preventing your blasted aunt from fulfilling her evil purpose of coming to infest Deverill Hall. He said he would, and I went back to the sitting-room, where I took a seat, put my feet on the mantelpiece and thought of Gertrude. From time to time I would rise and look in at the kitchen and ask him how it was coming, but he motioned me away with a silent wave of the hand and let the brain out another notch. Finally he emerged and announced that he had got it. He had been musing, as always, on the psychology of the individual.'

'What individual? My Aunt Agatha?'

'Naturally, your Aunt Agatha. What other individual's psychology would you have expected him to muse on? Sir Stafford Cripps's? He then proceeded to outline a scheme which I think you will agree was a ball of fire. Tell me, Bertie, have you ever stolen a cub from a tigress?'

I said no, for one reason and another I never had, and he asked me what, if I ever did, I supposed the reactions of the tigress would be, always assuming that she was a good wife and mother. And I said that, while I didn't set myself up as an authority on tigresses, I imagined that she would be as sick as mud.

'Exactly. And you would expect the animal, the loss of its child having been drawn to its attention, to drop everything and start looking for it, would you not? It would completely revise it social plans, don't you think? If, for instance, it had arranged to visit other tigresses in a nearby cave, it would cancel the date and begin hunting around for clues. You agree?'

I said Yes, I thought this probable.

'Well, that is what Jeeves feels will happen in the case of your Aunt Agatha when she learns that her son Thomas has vanished from his school at Bramley-on-Sea.'

I can't tell you offhand what I had been expecting, but it certainly wasn't this. Having recovered sufficient breath to enable me to put the question, I asked what it was that he had said, and he repeated his words at dictation speed, and I said, 'But dash it!' and he said 'Well?'

'You aren't telling me that Jeeves is going to kidnap young Thos?'

He t'chk-t'chked impatiently.

'You don't have to kidnap dyed-in-the-wool fans like your cousin Thomas, if you inform them that their favourite film star is hoping that they will be able to get away and come and spend a few days at the Vicarage where she is staying. That is the message which Jeeves has gone to Bramley-on-Sea to deliver, and I confidently expect it to work like a charm.'

'You mean he'll run away from school?'

'Of course he'll run away from school. Like lightning. However, to clinch the thing, I empowered Jeeves in your name to offer a fee of five quid in the event of any hesitation. I gather from Jeeves, in whom he confided, that young Thomas is more than ordinarily out for the stuff just now. He's saving up to buy a camera.'

I applauded the shrewd thought, but I didn't think that this introduction of the sordid note would really be necessary. Thos is a boy of volcanic passions, the sort of boy who, if he had but threepence in the world, would spend it on a stamp, writing to Dorothy Lamour for her autograph, and the message which Catsmeat had outlined would, I felt, be in itself amply sufficient to get him on the move.

'Yes,' Catsmeat agreed, 'I think we should shortly have the young fellow with us. But not your Aunt Agatha, who will be occupied elsewhere. It's a pity she has to be temporarily deprived of her cub, of course, and one sympathizes with a mother's anxiety. It would have been nice if the thing could have been arranged some other way, but that's how it goes. One has simply got to say to oneself that into each life some rain must fall.'

My own view was that Aunt Agatha wouldn't be anxious so much as hopping mad.

'Thos,' I said, 'makes rather a speciality of running away from school. He's done it twice before this, once to attend a cup final and once to go hunting for buried treasure in the Caribbees, and I don't remember Aunt Agatha on either occasion as the stricken mother. Thos was the one who got stricken. Six of the best on the old spot, he tells me. This, I should imagine, will probably occur again, and I think that even if he takes the assignment on for love alone, I will slip him that fiver as added money.'

'It would be a graceful act.'

'After all, what's money? You can't take it with you.'

'The right spirit.'

'But isn't Corky going to be a bit at a loss when he suddenly shows up?'

'That's all fixed. I met her in the village and told her.'

'And she approved?'

'Wholeheartedly. Corky always approves of anything that seems likely to tend to start something.'

'She's a wonderful girl.'

'A very admirable character. By the way, she tells me you put in that word in season.'

'Yes. I thought she seemed braced.'

'That's how she struck me, too. Odd that she should be so crazy about Esmond Haddock. I've only seen him from a distance, of course, but I should have imagined he would have been a bit on the stiff side for Corky.'

'He's not really stiff. You should see him relaxing over the port.'

'Perhaps you're right. And, anyway, love's a thing you can't argue about. I suppose it would perplex thousands that Gertrude, bless her, loves me. Yet she does. And look at poor little Queenie. Heartbroken over the loss of a rozzer I wouldn't be seen in a ditch with. And talking of Queenie, I was thinking of taking her to the pictures in Basingstoke this afternoon, if you'll lend me your car.'

'Of course. You feel it would cheer her up?'

'It might. And I should like to slap balm on that wounded spirit, if it can be managed. It's curious how, when you're in love, you yearn to go about doing acts of kindness to everybody. I am bursting with a sort of yeasty benevolence these days, like one of those chaps in Dickens. I very nearly bought you a tie in London. Gosh! Who's that?'

Someone had knocked on the door.

'Come in,' I said, and Catsmeat dashed at the wardrobe and dashed out festooned in trousers and things. Striking the professional note.

Silversmith came navigating over the threshold. This majestic man always had in his deportment a suggestion of the ambassador about to deliver important State papers to a reigning monarch, and now the resemblance was heightened by the fact that in front of his ample stomach he was bearing a salver with a couple of telegrams on it. I gathered them in, and he went navigating out again.

Catsmeat replaced the trousers. He was quivering a little.

'What effect does that bloke have on you, Bertie?' he asked in a hushed voice, as if he were speaking in a cathedral. 'He paralyses me. I don't know if you are familiar with the works of Joseph Conrad, but there's a chap in his *Lord Jim* of whom he says "Had you been the Emperor of the East and West, you could not have ignored your inferiority in his presence". That's Silversmith. He fills me with an awful humility. He shrivels my immortal soul to the size of a parched pea. He's the living image of some of those old time pros who used to give me such a hell of a time when I first went on the stage. Well, go on. Open them.'

'You mean these telegrams?'

'What did you think I meant?'

'They're addressed to Gussie.'

'Of course they're addressed to Gussie. But they're for you.'

'We don't know that.'

'They must be. One's probably from Jeeves, telling you that the balloon has gone up.'

'But the other? It may be a tender bob's-worth from Madeline.'

'Ah, go on.'

I was firm.

'No, Catsmeat. The code of the Woosters restrains me. The code of the Woosters is more rigid than the code of the Catsmeats. A Wooster cannot open a telegram addressed to another, even if for the moment he is that other, if you see what I mean. I'll have to submit them to Gussie.'

'All right, if you see it that way. I'll be off, then, to try to bring a little sunshine into Queenie's life.'

He legged it, and I took a seat and went on being firm. The hour was then three-forty-five.

I continued firm till about five minutes to four.

The catch about the code of the Woosters is that if you start examining it with a couple of telegrams staring you in the face, one of them almost certainly containing news of vital import, you find yourself after a while beginning to wonder if it's really so hot, after all. I mean to say, the thought creeps in that maybe, if one did but know, the Woosters are priceless asses to let themselves be ruled by a code like that. By four o'clock I wasn't quite so firm as I had been. By ten past my fingers were definitely twitching.

It was at four-fifteen sharp that I opened the first telegram. As Catsmeat had predicted, it was a cautiously worded communication from Jeeves, handed in at Bramley-on-Sea and signed Bodger's Stores, guardedly intimating that everything had gone according to plan. The goods, it said, were in transit and would be delivered in a plain van in the course of the evening. Highly satisfactory.

I put a match to it and reduced it to ashes, for you can't be too careful, and having done so was concerned to find, as I looked at the other envelope, that my fingers were still twitching. I took the thing and twiddled it thoughtfully.

I can guess what you're going to say. You're going to say that, having perused the first one and mastered its contents, there was no need whatever for me to open the other, and you are perfectly right. But you know how it is. Ask the first lion cub you meet, and it will tell you that, once you've tasted blood, there is no pulling up, and it's the same with opening telegrams. Conscience whispered that this one, addressed to Gussie and intended for Gussie, was for Gussie's eyes alone, and I agreed absolutely. But I could no more stop myself opening it than you can stop yourself eating another salted almond.

I ripped the envelope, and the quick blush of shame mantled the cheek as my eye caught the signature 'Madeline'.

Then my eye caught the rest of the bally thing.

It read as follows:

Fink-Nottle
Deverill Hall
King's Deverill
Hants.

Letter received. Cannot understand why not had reassuring telegram. Sure you concealing accident terribly serious. Fever anxiety. Fear worst. Arriving Deverill Hall to-morrow afternoon. Love. Kisses. Madeline.

14

Yes, that was the torpedo that exploded under my bows, and I had the feeling you get sometimes that some practical joker has suddenly removed all the bones from your legs, substituting for them an unsatisfactory jelly. I re-read the thing, to make sure I had seen what I thought I had seen, and, finding I had, buried the face in the hands.

It was the being without advisers that made the situation so bleak. On these occasions when Fate, having biffed you in the eye, proceeds to kick you in the pants, you want to gather the boys about you and thresh things out, and there weren't any boys to gather. Jeeves was in London, Catsmeat in Basingstoke. It made me feel like a Prime Minister who starts to call an important Cabinet meeting and finds that the Home Secretary and the Lord President of the Council have nipped over to Paris and the Minister of Agriculture and Fisheries and the rest of the gang are at the dog races.

There seemed to be nothing to do but wait till Catsmeat, having sat through the news and the main feature and the two-reel Silly Symphony, wended homeward. And though Reason told me that he couldn't get back for another two hours or more and that even when he did get back it was about a hundred to eight against him having any constructive policy to put forward, I went down to the main gate and paced up and down, scanning the horizon like Sister what-was-her-name in that story one used to read.

The evening was well advanced, and the local birds had long since called it a day, when I spotted the two-seater coming down the road. I flagged it, and Catsmeat applied the brakes.

'Oh, hallo, Bertie,' he said in a subdued sort of voice, and when he had alighted and I had drawn him apart he explained the reason for his sober deportment.

'Most unfortunate,' he said, throwing a commiserating glance at the occupant of the other seat, who was staring before her with anguished eyes and from time to time taking a dab at them with her handkerchief. 'With these tough films so popular, I suppose I might have foreseen that something like this would happen. The picture was full of cops, scores of cops racing to and fro saying "Oh, so you won't talk?" and it was too much for poor little Queenie. Just twisted the knife in the wound, as you might say. She's better now, though still sniffing.'

I suppose if you went through the W1 postal district of London with a fine-tooth comb and a brace of bloodhounds, you wouldn't find more than about three men readier than Bertram Wooster to sympathize with a woman's distress, and in ordinary circumstances I would unquestionably have given a low, pitying whistle and said 'Too bad, too bad.' But I hadn't time now to mourn over stricken parlourmaids. All the mourning at my disposal was earmarked for Wooster, B.

'Read this,' I said.

He cocked an eye at me.

'Hallo!' he said, in what is known as a sardonic manner. 'So the code of the Woosters sprang a leak? I had an idea it would.'

I think he was about to develop the theme and be pretty dashed humorous at my expense, but at this moment he started to scan the document and the gist hit him in the eyeball.

'H'm!' he said. 'This will want a little management.'

'Yes,' I concurred.

'It calls for sophisticated handling. We shall have to think this over.'

'I've been thinking it over for hours.'

'Yes, but you've got one of those cheap substitute brains which are never any good. It will be different when a man like me starts giving it the cream of his intellect.'

'If only Jeeves were here!'

'Yes, we could use Jeeves. It's a pity he is not with us.'

'And it's a pity,' I couldn't help pointing out, though the man of sensibility dislikes rubbing these things in, 'that you started the whole trouble by making Gussie wade in the Trafalgar Square fountain.'

'True. One regrets that. Yet at the time it seemed so right, so inevitable. There he was, I mean, and there was the fountain. I felt very strongly that here was an opportunity which might not occur again. And while I would be the last to deny that the aftermath hasn't been too good, it was certainly value for money. A man who has seen Gussie Fink-Nottle chasing newts in the Trafalgar Square fountain in correct evening costume at five o'clock in the morning is a man who has lived. He has got something he can tell his grandchildren. But if we are apportioning the blame, we can go further back than that. Where the trouble started was when you insisted on me giving him dinner. Madness. You might have known something would crack.'

'Well, it's no good talking about it.'

'No. Action is what we want. Sharp, decisive action as dished out by Napoleon. I suppose you will shortly be going in and dressing for dinner?'

'I suppose so.'

'How soon after dinner will you be in your room?'

'As soon as I can jolly well manage it.'

'Expect me there, then, probably with a whole plan of campaign cut and dried. And now I really must be getting back to Queenie. She will be on duty before long and will want to powder her nose and remove the tear stains. Poor little soul! If you knew how my heart bleeds for that girl, Bertie, you would shudder.'

And, of course, it being so vital that we should get together with the minimum of delay, that night turned out to be the one night when it was impossible to take an early powder. Instead of the ordinary dinner, a regular binge had been arranged, with guests from all over the countryside. No fewer than ten of Hampshire's more prominent stiffs had been summoned to the trough, and they stuck on like limpets long after any competent chucker-out would have bounced them. No doubt, if you have gone to the sweat of driving twenty miles to a house to dine, you don't feel like just snatching a chop and dashing off. You hang on for the musical evening and the drinks at ten-thirty.

Be that as it may, it wasn't till close on midnight that the final car rolled away. And when I bounded to my room, off duty at last, there was no sign of Catsmeat.

There was, however, a note from him lying on the pillow, and I tore it open with a feverish flick of the finger.

It was dated eleven p.m., and its tone was reproachful. He rebuked me for what he described as sitting gorging and swilling with my fine friends when I ought to have been at the conference table doing a bit of honest work. He asked me if I thought he was going to remain seated on his fanny in my damned room all night, and hoped that I would have a hangover next day, as well as indigestion from too much rich food. He couldn't wait any longer, he said, it being his intention to take my car and drive to London so as to be at Wimbledon Common bright and early to-morrow morning for an interview with Madeline Bassett. And at that interview, he went on, concluding on a cheerier note, he would fix everything up just the same as Mother makes it, for he had got the idea of a lifetime, an idea so superb that I could set my mind, if I called it a mind, completely at rest. He doubted, he said, whether Jeeves himself, even if full to the brim of fish, could have dug up a better *modus operandi*.

Well, this was comforting, of course, always provided that one could accept the theory that he was as good as he thought he was. You never know with Catsmeat. In one of his school reports, which I happened to see while prowling about the Rev. Aubrey Upjohn's study one night in search of biscuits, the Rev. Aubrey had described him as 'brilliant but unsound', and if ever a headmaster with a face like a cassowary rang the bell and entitled himself to receive a cigar or a coco-nut, this headmaster was that headmaster.

However, I will own that his communication distinctly eased the spirit. It is a pretty well established fact that the heart bowed down with weight of woe to weakest hope will cling, and that's what mine did. It was in quite an uplifted frame of mind that I shed the soup and fish and climbed into the slumberwear. I rather think, though I wouldn't swear to it, that I sang a bar or two of a recent song hit.

I had just donned the dressing-gown and was preparing for a final cigarette, when the door opened and Gussie came in.

Gussie was in peevish mood. He hadn't liked the stiffs, and he complained with a good deal of bitterness at having had to waste in their society an evening which might have been spent *chez* Corky.

'You couldn't oil out of a big dinner-party,' I urged.

'No, that's what Corky said. She said it wouldn't do. *Noblesse oblige* was one of the expressions she used. Amazing what high principles she has. You don't often find a girl as pretty as that

117

with such high principles. And how pretty she is, isn't she, Bertie? Or, rather, when I say pretty, I mean angelically lovely.'

I agreed that Corky's face wouldn't stop a clock, and he retorted warmly what did I mean it wouldn't stop a clock.

'She's divine. She's the most beautiful girl I've ever seen. It seems so extraordinary that she should be Pirbright's sister. You would think any sister of Pirbright's would be as repulsive as he is.'

'I'd call Catsmeat rather good-looking.'

'I disagree with you. He's a hellhound, and it comes out in his appearance. "There are newts in that fountain, Gussie," he said to me. "Get after them without a second's delay." And wouldn't take No for an answer. Urged me on with sharp hunting cries. "Yoicks!" he said, and "Tallyho!" But what I came about, Bertie,' said Gussie, breaking off abruptly as if this dip into the past pained him, 'was to ask if you could lend me that tie of yours with the pink lozenges on the dove-grey background. I shall be dropping in at the Vicarage to-morrow morning, and I want to look my best.'

Apart from the fleeting thought that he was a bit of an optimist if he expected a tie with pink lozenges on a dove-grey background to undo Nature's handiwork to the extent of making him look anything but a fish-faced gargoyle, my reaction to these words was a feeling of profound relief that I had had that talk with Corky and obtained her promise that she would lose no time in choking Gussie off and putting him on the ice.

For it was plain that there was no time to be lost. Every word this super-heated newt-fancier uttered showed more clearly the extent to which he had got it up his nose. Chatting with Augustus Fink-Nottle about Corky was like getting the inside from Mark Antony on the topic of Cleopatra, and every second he spent out of the Frigidaire was fraught with peril. It was only too plain that The Larches, Wimbledon Common, had ceased to mean a thing in his life and instead of being a holy shrine housing the girl of his dreams, had become just an address in the suburban telephone book.

I gave him the tie, and he thanked me and started out.

'Oh, by the way,' he said, pausing at the door, 'you remember pestering me to write to Madeline. Well, I've done it. I wrote to her this afternoon. Why are you looking like a dying duck?'

I was looking like a dying duck because I had, of course, instantly spotted the snag. What, I was asking myself, was Madeline Bassett going to think when on top of the letter about the sprained wrist she got one in Gussie's handwriting with no reference in it whatever to runaway horses and completely silent on the theme of golden-haired children with lisps?

I revealed to Gussie the recent activities of the Catsmeat-Wooster duo, and he frowned disapprovingly. Most officious, he said, writing people's love letters for them, and not in the best of taste.

'However,' he proceeded, 'it doesn't really matter, because what I said in my letter was that everything was off.'

I tottered and would have fallen, had I not clutched at a passing chest of drawers.

'*Off?*'

'I've broken the engagement. I've been feeling for some days now that Madeline, though a nice girl, won't do. My heart belongs to Corky. Good night again, Bertie. Thanks for the tie.'

He withdrew, humming a sentimental ballad.

15

THE Larches, Wimbledon Common, was one of those eligible residences standing in commodious grounds with Company's own water both h. and c. and the usual domestic offices and all that sort of thing, which you pass on the left as you drive out of London by way of Putney Hill. I don't know who own these joints, though obviously citizens who have got the stuff in sackfuls, and I didn't know who owned The Larches. All I knew was that Gussie's letter to Madeline Bassett would be arriving at that address by the first postal delivery, and it was my intention, should the feat prove to be within the scope of human power, to intercept and destroy it.

In tampering with His Majesty's mails in this manner, I had an idea that I was rendering myself liable to about forty years in the coop, but the risk seemed to me well worth taking. After all, forty years soon pass, and only by preventing that letter reaching its destination could I secure the bit of breathing space so urgently needed in order to enable me to turn round and think things over.

That was why on the following morning the commodious grounds of The Larches, in addition to a lawn, a summer-house, a pond, flower-beds, bushes and an assortment of trees, contained also one Wooster, noticeably cold about the feet and inclined to rise from twelve to eighteen inches skywards every time an early bird gave a sudden *cheep* over its worm. This Wooster to whom I allude was crouching in the interior of a bush not far from the french windows of what, unless the architect had got the place all cockeyed, was the dining-room. He had run up from King's Deverill on the 2.54 milk train.

I say 'run', but perhaps 'sauntered' would be more the *mot juste*. When milk moves from spot to spot, it takes its time, and it was not until very near zero hour that I had sneaked in through the gates and got into position one. By the time I had wedged myself into my bush, the sun was high up in the sky, as Esmond Haddock's Aunt Charlotte would have said, and I found myself musing, as I have so often had occasion to do, on the callous way in which Nature refuses to chip in and do its bit when the human heart is in the soup.

Though howling hurricanes and driving rainstorms would have been a more suitable accompaniment to the run of the action, the morning – or morn, if you prefer to string along with Aunt Charlotte – was bright and fair. My nervous system was seriously disordered, and one of God's less likeable creatures with about a hundred and fourteen legs had crawled down the back of my neck and was doing its daily dozen on the sensitive skin, but did Nature care? Not a hoot. The sky continued blue, and the fatheaded sun which I have mentioned shone smilingly throughout.

Beetles on the spine are admittedly bad, calling for all that a man has of fortitude and endurance, but when embarking on an enterprise which involved parking the carcass in bushes one more or less budgets for beetles. What was afflicting me much more than the activities of the undersigned was the reflection that I didn't know what was going to happen when the postman arrived. It might quite well be, I felt, that everybody at The Larches fed in bed of a morning, in which event a maid would take Gussie's bit of trinitrotoluol up to Madeline's room on a tray, thus rendering my schemes null and void.

It was just as this morale-lowering thought came into my mind that something suddenly bumped against my leg, causing the top of my head to part from its moorings. My initial impression that I had been set upon by a powerful group of enemies lasted, though it seemed a year, for perhaps two seconds. Then, the spots clearing from before my eyes and the world ceasing to do the adagio dance into which it had broken, I was able to perceive that all that had come into my life was a medium-sized ginger cat. Breathing anew, as the expression is, I bent down and tickled it behind the ear, such being my invariable policy when closeted with cats, and was still tickling when there was a bang and a rattle and somebody threw back the windows of the dining-room.

Shortly afterwards, the front door opened and a housemaid came out onto the steps and started shaking a mat in a languid sort of way.

Able now to see into the dining-room and observing that the

table was laid for the morning meal, I found my thoughts taking a more optimistic turn. Madeline Bassett, I told myself, was not the girl to remain sluggishly in bed while others rose. If the gang took their chow downstairs she would be with them. One of those plates now under my inspection, therefore, was her plate, and beside it the fateful letter would soon be deposited. A swift dash, and I should be able to get my hooks on it before she came down. I limbered up the muscles, so as to be ready for instant action, and was on my toes and all set to go, when there was a whistle to the south-west and a voice said 'Oo-oo!' and I saw that the postman had arrived. He was standing at the foot of the steps, giving the housemaid the eye.

'Hallo, beautiful!' he said.

I didn't like it. My heart sank. Now that I could see this postman steadily and see him whole, he stood out without disguise as a jaunty young postman, lissom of limb and a mass of sex-appeal, the sort of postman who, when off duty, is a devil of a fellow at the local hops and, when engaged on his professional rounds, considers the day wasted that doesn't start with about ten minutes intensive flirtation with the nearest domestic handy. I had been hoping for something many years older and much less the Society playboy. With a fellow like this at the helm, the delivery of the first post was going to take time. And every moment that passed made more probable the arrival on the scene of Madeline Bassett and others.

My fears were well founded. The minutes went by and still this gay young postman stood rooted to the spot, dishing out the brilliant badinage as if he were some carefree gentleman of leisure who was just passing by in the course of an early morning stroll. It seemed to me monstrous that a public servant, whose salary I helped to pay, should be wasting the Government's time in this frivolous manner, and it wouldn't have taken much to make me write a strong letter to *The Times* about it.

Eventually, awakening to a sense of his obligations, he handed over a wad of correspondence and with a final sally went on his way, and the housemaid disappeared, to manifest herself a few moments later in the dining-room. There, having read a couple of postcards in rather a bored way, as if she found little in them to grip and interest, she did what she ought to have done at least a quarter of an hour earlier – viz. placed them and the letters beside the various plates.

I perked up. Things, I felt, were moving. What would happen now, I assumed, was that she would pop off and go about her domestic duties, leaving the terrain unencumbered, and it was with something of the emotions of the war-horse that sayeth 'Ha!' among the trumpets that I once more braced the muscles. Ignoring the cat, which was weaving in and out between my legs with a camaraderie in its manner that suggested that it had now got me definitely taped as God's gift to the animal kingdom of Wimbledon, I made ready for the leap.

Picture, then, my chagrin and agony of spirit when, instead of hoofing it out of the door, this undisciplined housemaid came through the window, and having produced a gasper stood leaning against the wall, puffing luxuriously and gazing dreamily at the sky, as if thinking of postmen.

I don't know anything more sickening than being baffled by an unforeseen stymie at the eleventh hour, and it would not be overstating it to say that I writhed with impotent fury. As a rule, my relations with housemaids are cordial and sympathetic. If I meet a housemaid, I beam at her and say 'Good morning', and she beams at me and says 'Good morning', and all is joy and peace. But this one I would gladly have socked on the napper with a brick.

I stood there cursing. She stood there smoking. How long I cursed and she smoked I couldn't say, but I was just wondering if this degrading exhibition was going on for ever when she suddenly leaped, looked hastily over her shoulder and, hurling the gasper from her, legged it round the side of the house. The whole thing rather reminiscent of a nymph surprised while bathing.

And it wasn't long before I was able to spot what had caused her concern. I had thought for a moment that the voice of conscience must have whispered in her ear, but this was not so. Somebody was coming out of the front door, and my heart did a quick double somersault as I saw that it was Madeline Bassett.

And I was just saying 'This is the end', for it seemed inevitable that in another two ticks she would be inside the dining-room absorbing the latest news from Deverill Hall, when my *joie de vivre*, which had hit a new low, was restored by the sight of her turning to the left instead of to the right, and I perceived, what had failed to register in that first awful moment, that she was carrying a basket and gardening scissors. One sprang to the conclusion that she was off for a bit of pre-breakfast nosegay gathering, and one was right. She disappeared, and I was alone once more with the cat.

There is, as Jeeves rather neatly put it once, a tide in the affairs of men which, taken at the flood, leads on to fortune, and I could see clearly enough that this was it. What is known as the crucial moment had unquestionably arrived, and any knowledgeable adviser, had such a one been present, would have urged me to make it snappy and get moving while the going was good.

But recent events had left me weak. The spectacle of Madeline Bassett so close to me that I could have tossed a pebble into her mouth – not that I would, of course – had had the effect of numbing the sinews. I was for the nonce a spent force, incapable even of kicking the cat, which, possibly under the impression that this rigid Bertram was a tree, had now started to sharpen its claws on my leg.

And it was lucky I was – a spent force, I mean, not a tree – for at the very moment when, had I had the horse-power, I would have been sailing through the dining-room window, a girl came out of it carrying a white, woolly dog. And a nice ass I should have looked if I had taken at the flood the tide which leads on to fortune, because it wouldn't have led on to fortune or anything like it. It would have resulted in a nasty collision on the threshold.

She was a solid, hefty girl, of the type which plays five sets of tennis without turning a hair, and from the fact that her face was sombre and her movements on the listless side, I deduced that this must be Madeline Bassett's school friend, the one whose sex life had recently stubbed its toe. Too bad, of course, and one was sorry that she and the dream man hadn't been able to make a go of it, but at the moment I wasn't thinking very much about her troubles, my attention being riveted on the disturbing fact that I was dished. Thanks to the delay caused by the dilatory methods of that sprightly young postman, my plan of campaign was a total loss. I couldn't possibly start to function, with solid girls cluttering up the fairway.

There was but one hope. Her demeanour was that of a girl about to take the dog for a run, and it might be that she and friend would wander far enough afield to enable me to bring the thing off. I was just speculating on the odds for and against this, when she put the dog on the ground and with indescribable emotion I saw that it was heading straight for my bush and in another moment would be noting contents and barking its head off. For no dog, white or not white, woolly or not woolly, accepts with a mere raised eyebrow the presence of strangers in bushes. The thing, I felt, might quite possibly culminate not only in exposure, disgrace and shame, but in a quick nip on the ankle.

It was the cat who eased a tense situation. Possibly because it had not yet breakfasted and wished to do so, or it may be because the charm of Bertram Wooster's society had at last begun to pall, it selected this moment to leave me. It turned on its heel and emerged from the bush with its tail in the air, and the white, woolly dog, sighting it, broke into a canine version of Aunt Charlotte's a-hunting-we-will-go song and with a brief 'Hallo, hallo, hallo, hallo' went a-hunting. The pursuit rolled away over brake and over thorn, with Madeline Bassett's school friend bringing up the rear.

Position at the turn:

1. Cat
2. Dog
3. Madeline Basset's school friend.

The leaders were well up in a bunch. Several lengths separated 2 and 3.

I did not linger and dally. All a passer-by, had there been a passer-by, would have seen, was a sort of blur. Ten seconds later, I was standing beside the breakfast-table, panting slightly, with Gussie's letter in my hand.

To trouser it was with me the work of an instant; to reach the window with a view to the quick getaway that of an instant more. And I was on the point of passing through in the same old bustling way, when I suddenly perceived the solid girl returning with the white, woolly dog in her arms, and I saw what must have happened. These white, woolly dogs lack staying power. All right for the quick sprint, but hopeless across country. This one must have lost the hallo-hallo spirit in the first fifty yards or so and, pausing for breath, allowed itself to be gathered in.

In moments of peril, the Woosters act swiftly. One way out being barred to me, I decided in a flash to take the other. I nipped through the door, nipped across the hall and, still nipping, reached the temporary safety of the room on the other side of it.

16

THE room in which I found myself was bright and cheerful, in which respect it differed substantially from Bertram Wooster. It had the appearance of being the den or snuggery of some female interested in sports and pastimes and was, I assumed, the headquarters of Madeline Bassett's solid school friend. There was an oar over the mantelpiece, a squash racket over the book-shelf, and on the walls a large number of photographs which even at a cursory glance I was able to identify as tennis and hockey groups.

A cursory glance was all I was at leisure to bestow upon them at the moment, for the first thing to which my eye had been attracted on my entry was a serviceable french window, and I made for it like a man on a walking tour diving into a village pub two minutes before closing time. It opened on a sunken garden at the side of the house, and offered an admirable avenue of escape to one whose chief object in life was to detach himself from this stately home of Wimbledon and never set eyes on the bally place again.

When I say that it offered an admirable avenue of escape, it would be more correct to put it that it would have done, had there not been standing immediately outside it, leaning languidly on a spade, a short, stout gardener in corduroy trousers and a red and yellow cap which suggested – erroneously, I imagine – that he was a member of the Marylebone Cricket Club. His shirt was brown, his boots black, his face cerise and his whiskers grey.

I am able to supply this detailed record of the colour scheme because for some considerable time I stood submitting this son of toil to a close inspection. And the closer I inspected him, the less I found myself liking the fellow. Just as I had felt my spirit out of tune with the gasper-smoking housemaid of The Larches, so did I now look askance at the establishment's gardener, feeling very strongly that what he needed was a pound and a half of dynamite exploded under his fat trouser seat.

Presently, unable to stand the sight of him any longer, I turned away and began to pace the room like some caged creature of the wild, the only difference being that whereas a caged creature of the wild would not have bumped into and come within a toucher of upsetting a small table with a silver cup, a golf ball in a glass case and a large framed photograph on it, I did. It was only by an outstanding feat of legerdemain that I succeeded in catching the photograph as it fell, thereby averting a crash which would have brought every inmate of the house racing to the spot. And having caught it, I saw that it was a speaking likeness of Madeline Bassett.

It was one of those full-face speaking likenesses. She was staring straight out of the picture with large, sad, saucerlike eyes, and the lips seemed to quiver with a strange, reproachful appeal. And as I gazed at those sad eyes and took a square look at those quivery lips, something went off inside my bean like a spring. I had had an inspiration.

Events were to prove that my idea, like about ninety-four per cent of Catsmeat's, was just one of those that seem good at the time, but at the moment I was convinced that if I were to snitch this studio portrait and confront Gussie with it, bidding him drink it in and let conscience be his guide, all would be well. Remorse would creep in, his better self would get it up the nose, and all the old love and affection would come surging back. I believe this sort of thing frequently happens. Burglars, catching sight of photographs of their mothers, instantly turn in their tools and resolve to lead a new life, and the same is probably true of footpads, con men and fellows who have not paid their dog licence. I saw no reason to suppose that Gussie would be slower off the mark.

It was at this moment that I heard the sound of a Hoover being wheeled along the hall, and realized that the housemaid was on her way to do the room.

If there is anything that makes you feel more like a stag at bay than being in a room where you oughtn't to be and hearing housemaids coming to do it, I don't know what is. If you described Bertram Wooster at this juncture as all of a doodah, you would not be going far astray. I sprang to the window. The gardener was still there. I sprang back, and nearly knocked the table over again. Finally, thinking quick, I sprang sideways. My eye had been caught by a substantial sofa in the corner of the room, and I could have wished no more admirable cover. I was behind it with perhaps two seconds to spare.

To say that I now breathed freely again would be putting it perhaps too strongly. I was still far from being at my ease. But I did feel that in this little nook of mine I ought to be reasonably secure. One of the things you learn, when you have knocked about the world a bit, is that housemaids don't sweep behind sofas. Having run the Hoover over the exposed portions of the carpet, they consider the day well spent and go off and have a cup of tea and a slice of bread and jam.

On the present occasion even the exposed portions of the carpet did not get their doing, for scarcely had the girl begun to ply the apparatus when she was called off the job by orders from up top.

"Morning, Jane,' said a voice, which from the fact that it was accompanied by a shrill bark such as could have proceeded only from a white, woolly dog I took to be that of the solid school friend. 'Never mind about doing the room now.'

'No, miss,' said the housemaid, seeming well pleased with the idea, and pushed off, no doubt to have another gasper in the scullery. There followed a rustling of paper as the solid girl, seating herself on the sofa, skimmed through the morning journal. Then I heard her say 'Oh, hallo, Madeline', and was aware that the Bassett was with us.

'Good morning, Hilda,' said the Bassett in that soupy, treacly voice which had got her so disliked by all right-thinking men. 'What a lovely, lovely morning.'

The solid girl said she didn't see what was so particularly hot about it, adding that personally she found all mornings foul. She spoke morosely, and I could see that her disappointment in love had soured her, poor soul. I mourned for her distress, and had the circumstances been different, might have reached up and patted her on the head.

'I have been gathering flowers,' proceeded the Bassett. 'Beautiful smiling flowers, all wet with the morning dew. How *happy* flowers seem, Hilda.'

The solid girl said why shouldn't they, what had they got to beef about, and there was a pause. The solid girl said something about the prospects of the Surrey Cricket Club, but received no reply, and a moment later it was evident that Madeline Bassett's thoughts had been elsewhere.

'I have just been in the dining-room,' she said, and one spotted the tremor in the voice. 'There was no letter from Gussie. I'm so worried, Hilda. I think I shall go down to Deverill by an earlier train.'

'Suit yourself.'

'I can't help having an awful feeling that he is seriously injured. He said he had only sprained his wrist, but has he? That is what I ask myself. Suppose the horse knocked him down and trampled on him?'

'He'd have mentioned it.'

'But he wouldn't. That's what I mean. Gussie is so unselfish and considerate. His first thought would be to spare me anxiety. Oh, Hilda, do you think his spine is fractured?'

'What rot! Spine fractured, my foot. If there isn't a letter, all it means is that this other fellow – what's his name – Wooster – has kicked at acting as an amanuensis. I don't blame him. He's dippy about you, isn't he?'

'He loves me very, very dearly. It's a tragedy. I can't describe to you, Hilda, the pathos of that look of dumb suffering in his eyes when we meet.'

'Well, then, the thing's obvious. If you're dippy about a girl, and another fellow has grabbed her, it can't be pleasant to sit at a writing-table, probably with a rotten pen, sweating away while the other fellow dictates "My own comma precious darling period I worship you comma I adore you period How I wish comma my dearest comma that I could press you to my bosom and cover your lovely face with burning kisses exclamation mark". I don't wonder Wooster kicked.'

'You're very heartless, Hilda.'

'I've had enough to make me heartless. I've sometimes thought of ending it all. I've got a gun in that drawer there.'

'Hilda!'

'Oh, I don't suppose I shall. Lot of fuss and trouble. Have you seen the paper this morning? It says there's some talk of altering the leg-before-wicket rule again. Odd how your outlook changes when your heart's broken. I can remember a time when I'd have been all excited if they altered the leg-before-wicket rule. Now I don't give a damn. Let 'em alter it, and I hope they have a fine day for it. What sort of a fellow is this Wooster?'

'Oh, a dear.'

'He must be, if he writes Gussie's love letters for him. Either that or a perfect sap. If I were in your place, I'd give Gussie the air and sign up with him. Being a man, I presume he's a louse, like all other men, but he's rich, and money's the only thing that matters.'

From the way Madeline said, 'Oh, Hilda, *darling*!' – the wealth of reproach in the voice, I mean, and all that sort of thing – I could tell that these cynical words had got in amongst her, shocking her and wounding her finer feelings, and I found myself in complete accord with her attitude. I thoroughly disapproved of this girl and her whole outlook, and wished she wouldn't say things like that. The position of affairs was black enough already, without having old school friends egging Madeline Bassett on to give Gussie the air and sign up with me.

I think that Madeline would have gone on to chide and rebuke, but at this point, instead of speaking, she suddenly uttered a squeal or wordless exclamation, and the solid girl said 'Now what?'

'My photograph!'

'What about it?'

'Where is it?'

'On the table.'

'But it's not. It's gone.'

'Then I suppose Jane has smashed it. She always does smash everything that isn't made of sheet-iron, and I see no reason why she should have made an exception in favour of your photograph. You'd better go and ask her.'

'I will,' said Madeline, and I heard her hurrying out.

A few moments passed, self inhaling fluff and the solid girl presumably scanning her paper for further facts about the leg-before-wicket rule, and then I heard her say 'Sit still', no doubt addressing the white, woolly dog, for shortly afterwards she said 'Oh, all right, blast you, buzz off if you want to', and there was a thud; not a dull, sickening thud but the sort of thud a white, woolly dog makes when landing on a carpet from a sofa of medium height. And it was almost immediately after this that there came a sound of sniffing in my vicinity, and with a considerable lowering of the already low morale I realized that the animal must have picked up the characteristic Wooster smell and was now in the process of tracking it to its source.

And so it proved. Glancing round, I suddenly found its face about six inches from mine, its demeanour that of a dog that can hardly believe its eyes. Backing away with a startled 'Ooops!' it retreated to the centre of the room and began barking.

'What's the matter, you silly ass?' said the solid girl, and then there was a silence. On her part, that is. The white, woolly dog continued to strain its vocal cords.

Madeline Bassett re-entered.

'Jane says – ' she began, then broke off with a piercing scream. '*Hilda!* Oh, Hilda, *what* are you doing with that pistol?'

The solid girl calmed her fears, though leaving mine in *status quo*.

'Don't get excited. I'm not going to shoot myself. Though it would be a pretty good idea, at that. There's a man behind the sofa.'

'Hilda!'

'I've been wondering for some time where that curious, breathing sound was coming from. Percy spotted him. At-a-boy, Percy, nice work. Come on out of it, you.'

Rightly concluding that she meant me, I emerged, and Madeline uttered another of her piercing screams.

'A dressy criminal, though shopsoiled,' said the solid girl, scrutinizing me over the young cannon which she was levelling at my waistcoat. 'One of those Mayfair men you read about, I suppose. Hallo, I see he's got that photograph you were looking for. And probably half a dozen other things as well. I think the first move is to make him turn out his pockets.'

The thought that in one of those pockets lay Gussie's letter caused me to reel and utter a strangled cry, and the solid girl said if I was going to have a fit, that was all right with her, but she would be obliged if I would step through the window and have it outside.

It was at this point that Madeline Bassett most fortunately found speech. During the preceding exchanges, if you can call it exchanges when one person has taken the floor and is doing all the talking, she had been leaning against the wall with a hand to her heart, giving an impersonation, and not at all a bad one either, of a cat with a herring-bone in its throat. She now made her first contribution to the dialogue.

'Bertie!' she cried.

The solid girl seemed puzzled.

'Bertie?'

'This is Bertie Wooster.'

'The complete letter-writer? Well, what's he doing here? And why has he swiped your photograph?'

Madeline's voice sank to a tremulous whisper.

'I think I know.'

'Then you're smarter than I am. Goofy, the whole proceeding strikes me as.'

'Will you leave us, Hilda? I want to speak to Bertie . . . alone.'

'Right ho. I'll be shifting along to the dining-room. I don't suppose, feeling the way I do, there's a dog's chance of my being able to swallow a mouthful, but I can be counting the spoons.'

The solid girl pushed off, accompanied by the white, woolly dog, leaving us all set for a *tête-à-tête* which I for one would willingly have avoided. In fact, though it would, of course, have been a near thing with not much in it either way, I think I would have preferred a *tête-à-tête* with Dame Daphne Winkworth.

17

THE proceedings opened with one of those long, sticky silences which give you the same unpleasant feeling you get when you let them rope you in to play 'Bulstrode, a butler' in amateur theatricals and you go on and find you have forgotten your opening lines. She was standing gazing at me as if I had been a photographer about to squeeze the bulb and take a studio portrait in sepia and silver-grey wash, and after a while it seemed to me that it was about time one of us said something. The great thing on these occasions is to get the conversation going.

'Nice day,' I said. 'I thought I'd look in.'

She enlarged the eyes a bit, but did not utter, so I proceeded.

'It occurred to me that you might be glad to have the latest bulletin about Gussie, so I popped up on the milk train. Gussie, I am glad to say, is getting along fine. The wrist is still stiff, but the swelling is subsiding and there is no pain. He sends his best.'

She remained *sotto voce* and the silent tomb, and I carried on. I thought a word or two touching upon my recent activities might now be in order. I mean, you can't just come bounding up from behind the furniture and let it go at that. You have to explain and clarify your motives. Girls like to know these things.

'You are probably asking yourself,' I said, 'what I was doing behind that sofa. I parked myself there on a sudden whim. You know how one gets these sudden whims. And you may be thinking it a bit odd that I should be going around with this studio portrait in my possession. Well, I'll tell you. I happened to see it on the table there, and I took it to give to Gussie. I thought he would like to have it, to buck him up in your absence. He misses you sorely, of course, and it occurred to me that it would be nice for him to shove it on the dressing-table and study it from time to time. No doubt he already has several of these speaking likenesses, but a fellow can always do with one more.'

Not too bad, it seemed to me, considering that the material had had to be thrown together rather against time, and I was hoping for the bright smile and the cordial 'Why, yes, to be sure, a capital idea'. Instead of which, she waggled her head in a slow, mournful sort of way, and a teardrop stood in her eye.

'Oh, Bertie!' she said.

I have always found it difficult to think of just the right come-back when people say 'Oh, Bertie!' to me. My Aunt Agatha is always doing it, and she has me stymied every time. I found myself stymied now. It is true that this 'Oh, Bertie!' of the Bassett's differed in many respects from Aunt Agatha's 'Oh, Bertie!' its tone being one of soupiness rather than asperity, but the effect was the same. I stood there at a loss.

'Oh, Bertie!' she said again. 'Do you read Rosie M. Banks's novels?' she asked.

I was a bit surprised at her changing the subject like this, but equally relieved. A talk about current literature, I felt, might ease the strain. These booksy chats often do.

'Not very frequently,' I said. 'They sell like hot cakes, Bingo tells me.'

'You have not read *Mervyn Keene, Clubman?*'

'No, I missed that. Good stuff?'

'It is very, very beautiful.'

'I must put it on my library list.'

'You are sure you have not read it?'

'Oh, quite. As a matter of fact, I've always steered rather clear of Mrs Bingo's stuff. Why?'

'It seemed such an extraordinary coincidence . . . Shall I tell you the story of Mervyn Keene?'

'Do.'

She took time out to gulp a bit. Then she carried on in a low voice with a goodish amount of throb to it.

'He was young and rich and handsome, an officer in the Coldstream Guards and the idol of all who knew him. Everybody envied him.'

'I don't wonder, the lucky stiff.'

'But he was not really to be envied. There was a tragedy in his life. He loved Cynthia Grey, the most beautiful girl in London, but just as he was about to speak his love, he found that she was engaged to Sir Hector Mauleverer, the explorer.'

'Dangerous devils, these explorers. You want to watch them

like hawks. In these circs, of course, he would have refrained from speaking his love? Kept it under his hat, I suppose, what?'

'Yes, he spoke no word of love. But he went on worshipping her, outwardly gay and cheerful, inwardly gnawed by a ceaseless pain. And then one night her brother Lionel, a wild young man who had unfortunately got into bad company, came to his rooms and told him that he had committed a very serious crime and was going to be arrested, and he asked Mervyn to save him by taking the blame himself. And, of course, Mervyn said he would.'

'The silly ass! Why?'

'For Cynthia's sake. To save her brother from imprisonment and shame.'

'But it meant going to chokey himself. I suppose he overlooked that?'

'No. Mervyn fully realized what must happen. But he confessed to the crime and went to prison. When he came out, grey and broken, he found that Cynthia had married Sir Hector and he went out to the South Sea Islands and became a beachcomber. And time passed. And then one day Cynthia and her husband arrived at the island on their travels and stayed at Government House, and Mervyn saw her drive by, and she was just as beautiful as ever, and their eyes met, but she didn't recognize him, because of course he had a beard and his face was changed because he had been living the pace that kills, trying to forget.'

I remembered a good one I had read somewhere about the pace that kills nowadays being the slow, casual walk across a busy street, but I felt that this was not the moment to spring it.

'He found out that she was leaving next morning, and he had nothing to remember her by, so he broke into Government House in the night and took from her dressing-table the rose she had been wearing in her hair. And Cynthia found him taking it, and, of course, she was very upset when she recognized him.'

'Oh, she recognized him this time? He'd shaved, had he?'

'No, he still wore his beard, but she knew him when he spoke her name, and there was a very powerful scene in which he told her how he had always loved her and had come to steal her rose, and she told him that her brother had died and confessed on his death-bed that it was he who had been guilty of the crime for which Mervyn had gone to prison. And then Sir Hector came in.'

'Good situation. Strong.'

'And, of course, he thought Mervyn was a burglar, and he shot him, and Mervyn died with the rose in his hand. And, of course, the sound of the shot roused the house, and the Governor came running in and said: "Is anything missing?" And Cynthia in a low, almost inaudible voice said: "Only a rose." That is the story of Mervyn Keene, Clubman.'

Well, it was difficult, of course, to know quite what comment to make. I said 'Oh, ah!' but I felt at the time that it could have been improved on. The fact is, I was feeling a bit stunned. I had always known in a sort of vague, general way that Mrs Bingo wrote the world's worst tripe – Bingo generally changes the subject nervously if anyone mentions the little woman's output – but I had never supposed her capable of bilge like this.

But the Bassett speedily took my mind off literary criticism. She had resumed her saucerlike stare, and the teardrop in the eye was now more noticeable than ever.

'Oh, Bertie,' she said, and her voice, like Cynthia's, was low and almost inaudible, 'I ought to have given you my photograph long ago. I blame myself. But I thought it would be too painful for you, too sad a reminder of all that you had lost. I see now that I was wrong. You found the strain too great to bear. At all costs you had to have it. So you stole into the house, like Mervyn Keene, and took it.'

'What!'

'Yes, Bertie. There need be no pretences between you and me. And don't think I am angry. I am touched, more deeply touched than I can say, and oh, so, so sorry. How sad life is!'

I was with her there.

'You betcher,' I said.

'You saw my friend Hilda Gudgeon. There is another tragedy. Her whole happiness has been ruined by a wretched quarrel with the man she loves, a man called Harold Anstruther. They were playing in the Mixed Doubles in a tennis tournament not long ago and – according to her – I don't understand tennis very well – he insisted on hogging the game, as she calls it. I think she means that when the ball came near her and she was going to strike it, he rushed across and struck it himself, and this annoyed her very much. She complained to him, and he was very rude and said she was a rabbit and had better leave everything to him, and she broke off the engagement directly the game was finished. And now she is broken-hearted.'

I must say she didn't sound very broken-hearted. Just as the Bassett said these words, there came from without the uproar of someone singing, and I identified the voice as that of the solid school friend. She was rendering that old number 'Give yourself a pat on the back', and the general effect was of an exhilarated foghorn. The next moment, she came leaping into the room, and I have never seen anything more radiant. If she hadn't had the white, woolly dog in her arms, I wouldn't have recognized the sombre female of so short a while ago.

'Hi, Madeline,' she cried. 'What do you think I found on the breakfast-table? A grovelling letter from the boy friend, no less. He's surrendered unconditionally. He says he must have been mad to call me a rabbit. He says he can never forgive himself, but can I forgive him. Well, I can answer that one. I'm going to forgive him the day after tomorrow. Not earlier, because we must have discipline.'

'Oh, Hilda! How glad I am!'

'I'm pretty pleased about it myself. Good old Harold! A king among men, but, of course, needs keeping in his place from time to time and has to be taught what's what. But I mustn't run on about Harold. What I came to tell you was that there's a fellow outside in a car who says he wants to see you.'

'To see me?'

'So he says. Name of Pirbright.'

Madeline turned to me.

'Why, it must be your friend Claude Pirbright, Bertie. I wonder what he wants. I'd better go and see.' She threw a quick glance at the solid girl, and seeing that she had stepped through the french window, no doubt to give the gardener the devil about something, came to me and pressed my hand. 'You must be brave, Bertie,' she said in a low, roopy voice. 'Some day another girl will come into your life and you will be happy. When we are both old and grey, we shall laugh together over all this . . . laugh, but I think with a tear behind the smile.'

She popped off, leaving me feeling sick. The solid girl, whom I had dimly heard telling the gardener he needn't be afraid of breaking that spade by leaning on it, came back and immediately proceeded, in which I considered an offensively familiar manner, to give me a hearty slap on the back.

'Well, Wooster, old bloke,' she said.

'Well, Gudgeon, old bird,' I replied courteously.

'Do you know, Wooster, I keep feeling there's something familiar about your name? I must have heard Harold mention it. Do you know Harold Anstruther?'

I had recognized the name directly I heard Madeline Bassett utter it. Beefy Anstruther had been my partner at Rackets my last year at Oxford, when I had represented the establishment at that sport. I revealed this to the solid girl, and she slapped my back again.

'I thought I wasn't wrong. Harold speaks very highly of you, Wooster, old-timer, and I'll tell you something. I have a lot of influence with Madeline, and I'll exert it on your behalf. I'll talk to her like a mother. Dash it all, we can't have her marrying a pill like Gussie Fink-Nottle, when there's a Rackets Blue on her waiting list. Courage, Wooster, old cock. Courage and patience. Come and have a bit of breakfast.'

'Thanks awfully, no,' I said, though I needed it sorely. 'I must be getting along.'

'Well, if you won't, you won't. But I will. I'm going to have the breakfast of a lifetime. I haven't felt so roaring fit since I won the tennis singles at Roedean.'

I had braced myself for another slap on the back, but with a swift change of policy she prodded me in the ribs, depriving me of what little breath her frightful words had left inside me. At the thought of what might result from a girl of her dominating personality talking to Madeline Bassett like a mother, I had wilted where I stood. It was with what are called leaden steps that I passed through the french window and made my way to the road. I was anxious to intercept Catsmeat when he drove out, so that I might learn from him the result of his interview.

And, of course, when he did drive out, he was hareing along at such a pace that it was impossible to draw myself to his attention. He vanished over the skyline as if he had been competing in some event at Brooklands, leaving me standing.

In sombre mood, bowed down with dark forebodings, I went

off to get a bit of breakfast and catch a train back to King's Deverill.

=18=

THE blokes who run the railway don't make it easy for you to get from Wimbledon to King's Deverill, feeling no doubt – and I suppose it's a kindly thought – that that abode of thugs and ghouls is a place you're better away from. You change twice before you get to Basingstoke and then change again and take the branch line. And once you're on the branch line, it's quicker to walk.

The first person I saw when I finally tottered out at journey's end, feeling as if I had been glued to the cushioned seat since early boyhood and a bit surprised that I hadn't put out tendrils like a Virginia creeper, was my cousin Thomas. He was buying motion-picture magazines at the bookstall.

'Oh, hallo,' I said. 'So you got here all right?'

He eyed me coldly and said 'Crumbs!' a word of which he is far too fond. This Thos is one of those tough, hardboiled striplings, a sort of juvenile James Cagney with a touch of Edward G. Robinson. He has carroty hair and a cynical expression, and his manner is supercilious. You would think that anyone conscious of having a mother like my Aunt Agatha and knowing it could be proved against him, would be crushed and apologetic, but this is not the case. He swanks about the place as if he'd bought it, and in conversation with a cousin lacks tact and is apt to verge on the personal.

He became personal now, on the subject of my appearance, which I must confess was not spruce. Night travel in milk trains always tends to remove the gloss, and you can't hobnob with beetles in bushes and remain dapper.

'Crumbs!' he said. 'You look like something the cat brought in.'

You see what I mean? The wrong note. In no frame of mind to bandy words, I clouted the child moodily on the head and passed on. And as I emerged into the station yard, somebody yoo-hooed and I saw Corky sitting in her car.

'Hallo, Bertie,' she said. 'Where did you spring from, moon of my delight?' She looked about her in a wary and conspiratorial manner, as if she had been registering snakiness in a spy film. 'Did you see what was in the station?' she asked, lowering the voice.

'I did.'

'Jeeves delivered him as per memo last night. Uncle Sidney looked a little taken aback for a moment, and seemed as if he were on the point of saying some of the things he gave up saying when he took Orders, but everything has turned out for the best. He loves his game of chess, and it seems that Thomas is the undisputed champion of his school, brimming over with gambits and openings and things, so they get along fine. And I love him. What a sympathetic, sweet-natured boy he is, Bertie.'

I blinked.

'You are speaking of my cousin Thomas?'

'He's so *loyal*. When I told him about the heel Dobbs arresting Sam Goldwyn, he simply boiled with generous indignation. He says he's going to cosh him.'

'To what him?'

'It's something people do to people in detective stories. You use a small but serviceable rubber bludgeon.'

'He hasn't got a small but serviceable rubber bludgeon.'

'Yes, he has. He bought it in Seven Dials when he was staying at your flat. His original idea was to employ it on a boy called Stinker at Bramley-on-Sea, but it is now earmarked for Dobbs.'

'Oh, my God!'

'It will do Dobbs all the good in the world to be coshed. It may prove a turning-point in his life. I have a feeling that things are breaking just right these days and that very shortly an era of universal happiness will set in. Look at Catsmeat, if you want Exhibit A. Have you seen him?'

'Not to speak to,' I said, speaking in a *distrait* manner, for my mind was still occupied with Thos and his plans. The last thing you want, when the nervous system is in a state of hash, are your first cousins socking policemen with rubber bludgeons. 'What about Catsmeat?'

'I met him just now, and he was singing like a linnet all over the place. He had a note from Gertrude last night, and she says that, if and when she can elude her mother's eye, she will elope with him. His cup of joy is full.'

'I'm glad someone's is.'

The sombreness of my tone caused her to look sharply at me, and her eyes widened as she saw the disorder of my outer crust.

'Bertie! My lamb!' she cried, visibly moved. 'What have you been doing to yourself? You look like – '

'Something the cat brought in?'

'I was going to say something excavated from Tutankhamen's tomb, but your guess is as good as mine. What's been happening?'

I passed a weary hand over the brow.

'Corky,' I said, 'I've been through hell.'

'About the only place I thought you didn't have to go through to get to King's Deverill. And how were they all?'

'I have a frightful story to relate.'

'Did somebody cosh you?'

'I've just come from Wimbledon.'

'From Wimbledon? But Catsmeat was attending to the Wimbledon end. He told me all about it.'

'He didn't tell you all about it, because all about it is precisely what he doesn't know. If you've only heard Catsmeat's reminiscences, you simply aren't within a million miles of being in possession of the facts. He barely scratched the surface of Wimbledon, whereas I . . . Would you care to have the ghastly details?'

She said she would love to, and I slipped them to her, and for once she listened attentively from start to finish, an agreeable deviation from her customary deaf-adder tactics. I found her a good audience. She was properly impressed when I spoke of Gussie's letter, nor did she omit to draw the breath in sharply as I touched on the Gudgeon and the sinister affair of the studio portrait. The facts in connection with the white, woolly dog also went over big.

'Golly!' she said, as I wore to a close. 'You do live, don't you, Bertie?'

I agreed that I lived, but expressed a doubt as to whether, the circumstances being what they were it was worthwhile continuing to do so. One was rather inclined, I said, to murmur 'Death, where is thy sting?' and turn the toes up.

'The best one can say,' I concluded, 'is that one has obtained a brief respite, if respite is the word. And that only if Catsmeat was successful in dissuading the Bassett from her awful purpose. For all I know, she may be coming on the next train.'

'No, she's not. He headed her off.'

'You had that straight from the horse's mouth?'

'Direct from his personal lips.'

I drew a deep breath. This certainly put a brighter aspect on the cloud wreck. In fact, it seemed to me that 'Hallelujah!' about summed it up, and I mentioned this.

I was concerned to note that she appeared a bit dubious.

'Yes, I suppose "Hallelujah!" sums it up . . . to a certain extent. I mean you can make your mind easy about her coming here. She isn't coming. But in the light of what you tell me about Mervyn Keene, Clubman, and the studio portrait, it's a pity Catsmeat didn't hit on some other method of heading her off. I do feel that.'

My heart stood still. I clutched at the windscreen for support, and what-whatted.

'The great thing to remember, the thing to bear in mind and keep the attention fixed on, is that he meant well.'

My heart stood stiller. In your walks about London you will sometimes see bent, haggard figures that look as if they had recently been caught in some powerful machinery. They are those of fellows who got mixed up with Catsmeat when he was meaning well.

'What he told Miss Bassett was this. He said that on hearing that she was coming to the Hall you betrayed agitation and concern, and finally he got it out of you what the trouble was. Loving her hopelessly as you do, you shrank from the agony of having to see her day after day in Gussie's society.'

My heart, ceasing to stand still, gave a leap and tried to get out through my front teeth.

'He told Madeline Bassett that?' I quavered, shaking on my stem.

'Yes, and implored her to stay away and not subject you to this anguish. He says he was terrific and wished one or two managers had been there to catch his work, and I think he must have been pretty good, because Miss Bassett cried buckets and said she quite understood and, of course, would cancel her visit, adding something in a low voice about the desire of the moth for the star and how sad life was. What did you say?'

I explained that I had not spoken, merely uttered one of those hollow groans, and she agreed that in the circs hollow groans were perhaps in order.

'But, of course, it wasn't easy for the poor angel to think of a good way of stopping her coming,' she argued. 'And the great thing was to stop her somehow.'

'True.'

'So, if I were you, I would try to look on the bright side. Count your blessings one by one, if you know what I mean.'

This is an appeal which, when addressed to Bertram Wooster, rarely falls on deaf ears. The stunned sensation which her words had induced did not actually leave me, but it diminished somewhat in intensity. I saw her point.

'There is much in what you say,' I agreed, rising on stepping-stones of my dead self to higher things, as I have mentioned is my custom. 'The great thing, as you justly remark, was to stop the Bassett blowing in, and, if that has been accomplished, one does wrong to be fussy about the actual mechanism. And, after all, she was already firmly convinced of my unswerving devotion, so Catsmeat hasn't really plunged me so very much deeper in the broth than I was before.'

'That's my brave little man. That's the way to talk.'

'We now have a respite, and all depends on how quickly you can put Gussie on ice. The moment that is done, the whole situation will clarify. Released from your fatal spell, he will automatically return to the old love, feeling that the cagey thing is to go where he is appreciated. When do you expect to cool him off?'

'Very soon.'

'Why not instanter?'

'Well, I'll tell you, Bertie. There's a little job I want him to do for me first.'

'What job?'

'Ah, here's Thomas at last. He seems to have bought every fan magazine in existence. To read at the concert, if he's sensible. You haven't forgotten the concert is this evening? Well, mind you don't. And when you see Jeeves, ask him how that claque of Esmond's has come out. Hop in, Thomas.'

Thos hopped in, giving me another of his supercilious looks, and when in, leaned across and slipped a penny into my hand, saying 'Here, my poor man' and urging me not to spend it on drink. At any other moment this coarse ribaldry would have woken the fiend that sleeps in Bertram Wooster and led to the young pot of poison receiving another clout on the head, but I had no time now for attending to Thoses. I fixed Corky with a burning eye.

'What job?' I repeated.

'Oh, it wouldn't interest you,' she said. 'Just a trivial little job about the place.'

And she drove off, leaving me a prey to a nameless fear.

I was hoofing along the road that led to the Hall, speculating dully as to what precisely she had meant by the expression 'trivial little job', when, as I rounded a corner, something large and Norfolk-coated hove in sight, and I identified it as Esmond Haddock.

=19=

O WING to the fact that on the instructions of Dame Daphne ('Safety First') Winkworth port was no longer served after dinner and the male and female members of the gang now left the table in a body at the conclusion of the evening repast, I had not enjoyed a *tête-à-tête* with Esmond Haddock since the night of my arrival. I had seen him around the place, of course, but always in the company of a brace of assorted aunts or that of his cousin Gertrude, in each case looking Byronic. (Checking up with Jeeves, I find that that is the word all right. Apparently it means looking like the late Lord Byron, who was a gloomy sort of bird, taking things the hard way.)

We came together, he approaching from the nor'-nor'-east and self approaching from the sou'-sou'-west, and he greeted me with a moody twitch of the cheek muscles, as if he had thought of smiling and then thought again and said 'Oh, to hell with it'.

'Hallo,' he said.

'Hallo,' I said.

'Nice day,' he said.

'Yes,' I said. 'Out for a walk?'

'Yes,' he said. 'You out for a walk?'

Prudence compelled me to descend to subterfuge.

'Yes,' I said. 'I'm out for a walk. I just ran into Miss Pirbright.'

At the mention of that name, he winced as if troubled by an old wound.

'Oh?' he said. 'Miss Pirbright, eh?'

He swallowed a couple of times. I could see a question trembling on his lips, but it was plainly one that nauseated him, for after uttering the word 'Was' he kept right along swallowing. I was just about to touch on the situation in the Balkans in order to keep the conversation going, when he got it out.

'Was Wooster with her?'

'No, she was alone.'

'You're sure?'

'Certain.'

'He may have been lurking in the background. Behind a tree or something.'

'The meeting occurred in the station yard.'

'He wasn't skulking in a doorway?'

'Oh, no.'

'Strange. You don't often see her without Wooster these days,' he said, and ground his teeth a trifle.

I had a shot at trying to mitigate his anguish, which I could see was considerable. He, too, had obviously noted Gussie's spotty work, and it was plain that what is technically known as the green-eyed monster had been slipping it across him properly.

'They're old friends, of course,' I said.

'Are they?'

'Oh, rather. We – I should say they – have known each other since childhood. They went to the same dancing class.'

The moment I had mentioned that, I was wishing I hadn't, for it seemed to affect him as though some hidden hand had given him the hotfoot. You couldn't say his brow darkened because it had been dark to start with, but he writhed visibly. Like Lord Byron reading a review of his last slim volume of verse and finding it a stinker. I wasn't surprised. A man in love and viewing with concern the competition of a rival does not like to think of the adored object and that rival pirouetting about together at dancing classes and probably splitting a sociable milk and biscuit in the eleven o'clock interval.

'Oh?' he said, and gave a sort of whistling sigh like the last whoosh of a dying soda-water syphon. 'The same dancing class? The same dancing class, eh?'

He brooded a while. When he spoke again, his voice was hoarse and rumbling.

'Tell me about this fellow Wooster, Gussie. He is a friend of yours?'

'Oh, yes.'

'Known him long?'

'We were at school together.'

'I suppose he was a pretty loathsome boy? The pariah of the establishment?'

'Oh, no.'

'Changed after he grew up, eh? Well, he certainly made up

leeway all right, because of all the slinking snakes it has ever been my misfortune to encounter, he is the slimiest.'

'Would you call him a slinking snake?'

'I did call him a slinking snake, and I'll do it again as often as you wish. The fishfaced trailing arbutus!'

'He's not a bad chap.'

'That may be your opinion. It is not mine, nor, I should imagine, that of most decent-minded people. Hell is full of men like Wooster. What the devil does she see in him?'

'I don't know.'

'Nor anyone else. I've studied the fellow carefully and without bias, and he seems to me entirely lacking in charm. Have you ever turned over a flat stone?'

'From time to time.'

'And what came crawling out? A lot of obscene creatures that might have been his brothers. I tell you, Gussie, if you were to put a bit of gorgonzola cheese on the slide of a microscope and tell me to take a look, the first thing I'd say on getting it focused would be: "Why, hallo, Wooster!" '

He brooded Byronically for a moment.

'I know the specious argument you are going to put forward, Gussie,' he proceeded. 'You are going to say that it is not Wooster's fault that he looks like a slightly enlarged cheesemite. Very true. One strives to be fair. But it is not only the man's revolting appearance that distresses the better element. He is a menace to the community.'

'Oh, come.'

'What do you mean, "Oh, come"? You heard what my Aunt Daphne was telling us at dinner the night you arrived. About this ghastly Wooster perpetually stealing policemen's helmets.'

'Not perpetually. Just as a treat on Boat Race night.'

He frowned.

'I don't like the way you stick up for the fellow, Gussie. You probably consider that you are being broadminded, but you want to be careful how you let that so-called broadmindedness grow on you. It is apt to become mere moral myopia. The facts are well documented. Whenever Wooster has a spare moment, he goes about London persecuting unfortunate policemen, assaulting them, hampering them in their duties, making their lives a hell on earth. That's the kind of man Wooster is.'

He paused, and became for a moment lost in thought. Then there flitted across his map another of those quick twitches which he seemed to be using nowadays, on the just-as-good principle, as a substitute for smiles.

'Well, I'll tell you one thing, Gussie. I only hope he intends to start something on those lines here, because we're ready for him.'

'Eh?'

'Ready and waiting. You know Dobbs?'

'The flatty?'

'Our village constable, yes. A splendid fellow, tireless in the performance of his duties.'

'I've not met him. I hear his engagement is broken off.'

'So much the better, for it will remove the last trace of pity and weakness from his heart. I have told Dobbs all about Wooster and warned him to be on the alert. And he is on the alert. He is straining at the leash. Let Wooster so much as lift a finger in the direction of Dobbs's helmet, and he's for it. You might not think so at a casual glance, Gussie, but I'm a Justice of the Peace. I sit on the Bench at our local Sessions and put it across the criminal classes when they start getting above themselves. It is my earnest hope that the criminal streak in Wooster will come to the surface and cause him to break out, because in that event Dobbs will be on him like a leopard and he will come up before me and I shall give him thirty days without the option, regardless of his age or sex.'

I didn't like the sound of this.

'You wouldn't do that, Esmond?'

'I would. I'm looking forward to it. Let Wooster stray one inch from the straight and narrow path – just one inch – and you can kiss him good-bye for thirty days. Well, I'll be moving along, Gussie. I find it helps a little to keep walking.'

He disappeared over the horizon at five m.p.h., and I stood there aghast. The sense of impending peril was stronger on the wing than ever. 'Oh, that Jeeves were here!' I said to myself.

I found he was. For some little time past I had been conscious of some substance in the offing that was saying 'Good morning, sir', and, turning to see where the noise was coming from, I beheld him at my side, looking bronzed and fit, as if his visit to Bramley-on-Sea had done him good.

20

Good morning, sir,' he said. 'May I make a remark?'
'Certainly, Jeeves. Carry on. Make several.'

'It is with reference to your appearance, sir. If I might take the liberty of suggesting – '

'Go on. Say it. I look like something the cat found in Tutankhamen's tomb, do I not?'

'I would not go so far as that, sir, but I have unquestionably seen you more *soigné*.'

It crossed my mind for an instant that with a little thought one might throw together something rather clever about 'Way down upon the *soigné* river', but I was too listless to follow it up.

'If you will allow me, sir, I will take the suit which you are wearing and give it my attention.'

'Thank you, Jeeves.'

'I will sponge and press it.'

'Thank you, Jeeves.'

'Very good, sir. A beautiful morning, is it not, sir?'

'Thank you, Jeeves.'

He raised an eyebrow.

'You appear *distrait*, sir.'

'I am *distrait*, Jeeves. About as *distrait* as I can stick. And there's enough to make me *distrait*.'

'But surely, sir, matters are proceeding most satisfactorily. I delivered Master Thomas at the Vicarage. And I learn from my Uncle Charlie that her ladyship, your aunt, has postponed her visit to the Hall.'

'Quite. But these things are mere side issues. I don't say they aren't silver linings in their limited way, but take a look at the clouds that lower elsewhere. First and foremost, that man is in again.'

'Sir?'

I pulled myself together with a strong effort, for I saw that I was being obscure.

'Sorry to speak in riddles, Jeeves,' I said. 'What I meant was that Gussie had once more become a menace of the first water.'

'Indeed, sir? In what way?'

'I will tell you. What started all this rannygazoo?'

'The circumstances of Mr Fink-Nottle being sent to prison, sir.'

'Exactly. Well, it's an odds on bet that he's going to be sent to prison again.'

'Indeed, sir?'

'I wish you wouldn't say "Indeed, sir?" Yes, the shadow of the Pen is once more closing in on Augustus Fink-Nottle. The Law is flexing its muscles and waiting to pounce. One false step – and he's bound to make at least a dozen in the first minute – and into the coop he goes for thirty days. And we know what'll happen then, don't we?'

'We do indeed, sir.'

'I don't mind you saying "Indeed, sir" if you tack it on to something else like that. Yes, we know what will happen, and the flesh creeps, what?'

'Distinctly, sir.'

I forced myself to a sort of calm. Only a frozen calm, but frozen calms are better than nothing.

'Of course, it may be, Jeeves, that I am mistaken in supposing that this old lag is about to resume his life of crime, but I don't think so. Here are the facts. Just now I encountered Miss Pirbright in the station yard. We naturally fell into conversation, and after a while the subject of Gussie came up. And we had been speaking of him for some moments when she let fall an observation that filled me with a nameless fear. She said there was a little job she was getting him to do for her. And when I said "What job?" she replied "Oh, just a trivial little job about the place". And her manner was evasive. Or shall I say furtive?'

'Whichever you prefer, sir.'

'It was the manner of a girl guiltily conscious of being in the process of starting something. "What ho!" I said to myself. "Hallo, hallo, hallo, hallo!" '

'If I might interrupt for a moment, sir, I am happy to inform you that my efforts to secure a claque for Mr Esmond Haddock at the concert have been crowned with gratifying success. The back of the hall will be thronged with his supporters and well-wishers.'

I frowned.

'This is excellent news, Jeeves, but I'm dashed if I can see what it's got to do with the *res* under discussion.'

'No, sir. I am sorry. It was your observing "Hallo, hallo, hallo, hallo", that put the matter into my mind. Pardon me, sir. You were saying – '

'Well, what *was* I saying? I've forgotten.'

'You were commenting on Miss Pirbright's furtive and evasive manner, sir.'

'Ah, yes. It suggested that she was in the process of starting something. And the thought that smote me like a blow was this. If Corky is starting something, it's a hundred to eight it's something in the nature of reprisals against Constable Dobbs. Am I right or wrong, Jeeves?'

'The probability certainly lies in that direction, sir.'

'I know Corky. Her psychology is an open book to me. Even in the distant days when she wore rompers and had a tooth missing in front, hers was always a fiery and impulsive nature, quick to resent anything in the shape of oompus-boompus. And it is inevitably as oompus-boompus that she will have classed the zealous officer's recent arrest of her dog. And if she had it in for him merely on account of their theological differences, how much more will she have it in for him now. The unfortunate hound is languishing in a dungeon with gyves upon his wrists, and a girl of her spirit is not likely to accept such a state of things supinely.'

'No, sir.'

'You're right, No, sir. The facts are hideous, but we must face them. Corky is planning direct action against Constable Dobbs, taking we cannot say what form, and it seems only too sickeningly certain that Gussie, whom it is so imperative to keep from getting embroiled again with the Force, is going to lend himself as an instrument to her sinister designs. And here's something that'll make you say "Indeed, sir?" I've just been talking to Esmond Haddock, and he turns out to be a J.P. He has the powers of the High, the Middle and the Low Justice in King's Deverill, and is consequently in a position to give anyone thirty days without the option as soon as look at them. And what's more, he has taken a violent dislike to Gussie and told me in so many words that it is his dearest wish to see the darbies clapped on him. Try that one on your pianola, Jeeves.'

He seemed about to speak, but I raised a restraining hand.

'I know what you're going to say, and I quite agree. Left to himself, with Conscience as his guide, Gussie is the last person likely to commit a tort or malfeasance and start JPs ladling out exemplary sentences. Quite true. From boyhood up, his whole policy, instilled into him, no doubt, at his mother's knee, has been to give the primrose path a solid miss and sedulously avoid those rash acts which put wilder spirits in line for thirty days in the jug. But one knows that he is easily swayed. Catsmeat, for instance, swayed him in Trafalgar Square by threatening to bean him with a bottle. I shall be vastly surprised if Corky doesn't sway him, too. And I know from personal experience,' I said, thinking of that orange at the dancing school, 'that when Corky sways people, the sky is the limit.'

'You think that Mr Fink-Nottle will lend a willing ear to the young lady's suggestions?'

'Her word is law to him. He will be wax in her hands. I tell you, Jeeves, the spirits are low. I don't know if you have ever been tied hand and foot to a chair in front of a barrel of gunpowder with an inch of lighted candle on top of it?'

'No, sir, I have not had that experience.'

'Well, that's how I am feeling. I'm just clenching the teeth and waiting for the bang.'

'Would you wish me to speak a word to Mr Fink-Nottle, sir, warning him of the inadvisability of doing anything rash?'

'There's nothing I'd like better. He might listen to you.'

'I will make a point of doing so at the earliest opportunity, sir.'

'Thank you, Jeeves. It's a black business, isn't it?'

'Extremely, sir.'

'I don't know when I've come across a blacker. Very, very murky everything is.'

'With perhaps the exception of the affairs of Mr Pirbright, sir?'

'Ah, yes, Catsmeat. I was informed of his lucky strike. His hat is on the side of his head, they tell me.'

'It was distinctly in that position when I last saw him, sir.'

'Well, that's something. Yes, that cheers the heart a bit,' I said, for even when preoccupied with the stickiness of their own concerns, the Woosters can always take time out to rejoice over a buddy's bliss. 'One may certainly chalk up Catsmeat's happy ending as a ray of light. And you say that the village toughs are going to rally round Mr Haddock this evening?'

'In impressive numbers, sir.'

'Well, dash it, that's two rays of light. And if you can talk Gussie out of making an ass of himself, that'll be three. We're getting on. All right, Jeeves, push off and see what you can do with him. I should imagine you will find him at the Vicarage.'

'Very good, sir.'

'Oh, and, Jeeves, most important. When at the Vicarage, get in touch with young Thos and remove from his possession a blunt instrument known as a cosh, which he has managed to acquire. It's a species of rubber bludgeon, and you know as well as I do how reluctantly one would trust him with such a thing. You could go through the telephone book from A to Z without hitting on the name of anyone one wouldn't prefer to see with his hooks on a rubber bludgeon. You will get an idea of what I mean when I tell you that he speaks freely of beaning Constable Dobbs with the weapon. So choke it out of him without fail. I shan't be easy in my mind till I know you've got it.'

'Very good, sir. I will give the matter my attention,' he said and we parted with mutual civilities, he to do his day's good deed at the Vicarage, I to resume my hoofing in the opposite direction.

And I had hoofed perhaps a matter of two hundred yards, when I was jerked out of the reverie into which I had fallen by a sight which froze the blood and caused the two eyes, like stars, to start from their spheres. I had seen Gussie coming out of a gate of a picturesque cottage standing back from the road behind a neat garden.

King's Deverill was one of those villages where picturesque cottages breed like rabbits, but what distinguished this picturesque cottage from the others was that over its door were the Royal Arms and the words

POLICE STATION

And evidence that the above legend was not just a gag was supplied by the fact that accompanying Gussie, not actually with a hand on his collar and another gripping the seat of his trousers but so nearly so that the casual observer might have been excused for supposing that this was a pinch, was a stalwart figure in a blue uniform and a helmet, who could be no other than Constable Ernest Dobbs.

21

IT was the first time I had been privileged to see this celebrated rozzer, of whom I had heard so much, and I think that even had the circumstances been less tense I would have paused to get an eyeful, for his, like Silversmith's, was a forceful personality, arresting the attention and causing the passer-by to draw the breath in quite a bit.

The sleepless guardian of the peace of King's Deverill was one of those chunky, nobbly officers. It was as though Nature, setting out to assemble him, had said to herself 'I will not skimp'. Nor had she done so, except possibly in the matter of height. I believe that in order to become a member of the Force you have to stand five feet nine inches in your socks, and Ernest Dobbs can only just have got his nose under the wire. But this slight perpendicular shortage had the effect of rendering his bulk all the more impressive. He was plainly a man who, had he felt disposed, could have understudied the village blacksmith and no questions asked, for it could be seen at a glance that the muscles of his brawny arms were strong as iron bands.

To increase the similarity, his brow at the moment was wet with honest sweat. He had the look of a man who has recently passed through some testing emotional experience. His eyes were aglow, his moustache a-bristle and his nose a-wiggle.

'Grrh!' he said and spat. Only that and nothing more. A man of few words, apparently, but a good spitter.

Gussie, having reached the great open spaces, smiled weakly. He, too, appeared to be in the grip of some strong emotion. And as I was, also, that made three of us.

'Well, good day, officer,' he said.

'Good day, sir,' said the constable shortly.

He went back into the cottage and banged the door, and I sprang at Gussie like a jumping bean.

'What's all this?' I quavered.

The door of the cottage opened, and Constable Dobbs reappeared. He had a shovel in his hand, and in this shovel one noted what seemed to be frogs. Yes, on a closer inspection, definitely frogs. He gave the shovel a jerk, shooting the dumb chums through the air as if he had been scattering confetti. They landed on the grass and went about their business. The officer paused, directed a hard look at Gussie, spat once more with all the old force and precision and withdrew, and Gussie, removing his hat, wiped his forehead.

'Let's get out of this,' he urged, and it was not until we were some quarter of a mile distant that he regained a certain measure of calm. He removed his glasses, polished them, replaced them on his nose and seemed the better for it. His breathing became more regular.

'That was Constable Dobbs,' he said.

'So I deduced.'

'From the uniform, no doubt?'

'That and the helmet.'

'Quite,' said Gussie. 'I see. Quite. I see. Quite. I see.'

It seemed possible that he would go rambling on like this for a goodish while, but after saying 'Quite' about another six times and 'I see' about another seven he snapped out of it.

'Bertie,' he said, 'you have frequently been in the hands of the police, haven't you?'

'Not frequently. Once.'

'It is a ghastly experience, is it not? Your whole life seems to rise before you. By Jove, I could do with a drink of orange juice!'

I paused for a moment, to allow a dizzy feeling to pass.

'What was happening?' I asked, when I felt stronger.

'Eh?'

'What had you been doing?'

'Who, me?'

'Yes, you.'

'Oh,' said Gussie in an offhand way, as if it were only what might have been expected of an English gentleman, 'I had been strewing frogs.'

I goggled.

'Doing *what*?'

'Strewing frogs. In Constable Dobbs's boudoir. The Vicar suggested it.'

'The Vicar?'

'I mean it was he who gave Corky the idea. She had been brooding a lot, poor girl, on Dobbs's high-handed behaviour in connection with her dog, and last night the Vicar happened to speak of Pharaoh and all those Plagues he got when he wouldn't let the Children of Israel go. You probably recall the incident? His words started a train of thought. It occurred to Corky that if Dobbs were visited by a Plague of Frogs, it might quite possibly change his heart and make him let Sam Goldwyn go. So she asked me to look in at his cottage and attend to the matter. She said it would please her and be good for Dobbs and would only take a few minutes of my time. She felt that the Plague of Lice might be even more effective, but she is a practical, clear-thinking girl and realized that lice are hard to come by, whereas you can find frogs in any hedgerow.'

Every mouse in my interior sprang into renewed life. With a strong effort I managed to refrain from howling like a lost soul. It seemed incredible to me that this super-goof should have gone through life all this while without fetching up in some loony bin. You would have thought that some such establishment as Colney Hatch, with its talent scouts out all over the place, would have snapped him up years ago.

'Tell me exactly what happened. He caught you?'

'Fortunately, no. He came in about half a minute too late. I had bided my time, and having ascertained that the cottage was empty I went in and distributed my frogs.'

'And he was somewhere round the corner?'

'Exactly. In a sort of shed place by the back door, where I think he must have been potting geraniums or something, for his hands were all covered with mould. I suppose he had come in to wash them. It was a most embarrassing moment. One didn't quite know how to begin the conversation. Eventually I said "Oh, hallo, there you are!" and he stared at the frogs for some time, and then he said, "What's all this?" They were hopping about a bit. You know how frogs hop.'

'Hither and thither, you mean?'

'That's right. Hither and thither. Well, I kept my presence of mind. I said "What's all what, officer?" And he said "All these frogs". And I said "Ah, yes, there do seem to be quite a few frogs in here. You are fond of them?" He then asked if these frogs were my doing. And I said "In what sense do you use the word 'doing', officer?" and he said "Did you bring these frogs in here?" Well, then, I'm afraid, I wilfully misled him, for I said No. It went against the grain to tell a deliberate falsehood, of course, but I do think there are times when one is justified in – '

'Get on!'

'You bustle me so, Bertie. Where was I? Ah, yes. I said No, I couldn't account for their presence in any way. I said it was just one of those things we should never be able to understand. Probably, I said, we were not meant to understand. And, of course, he could prove nothing. I mean, anyone could wander innocently into a room where there happened to be some frogs hopping about – the Archbishop of Canterbury or anyone. I think he must have appreciated this, for all he did was mutter something about it being a very serious offence to bring frogs into a police station and I said I supposed it was and what a pity one could never hope to catch the fellow who had done it. And then he asked me what I was doing there, and I said I had come to ask him to release Sam Goldwyn, and he said he wouldn't because he had now established that the bite Sam had given him was his second bite and that the animal was in a very serious position. So I said "Oh, well, then, I think I'll be going", and I went. He came with me, as you saw, growling under his breath. I can't say I liked the man. His manner is bad. Brusque. Abrupt. Not at all the sort of chap likely to win friends and influence people. Well, I suppose I had better be getting along and reporting to Corky. That stuff about the second bite will worry her, I'm afraid.'

Repeating his remark about being in the vein for a drink of orange juice, he set a course for the Vicarage and pushed off, and I resumed my progress to the Deverilleries, speculating dully as to what would be the next horror to come into my life. It only needed a meeting with Dame Daphne Winkworth, I felt sombrely, to put the tin hat on this dark day.

My aim was to sneak in unobserved, and it seemed at first as though luck were with me. From time to time, as I slunk through the grounds, keeping in the shelter of the bushes and trying not to let a twig snap beneath my feet, I could hear the distant baying of aunts, but I wasn't spotted. With something approaching a 'Tra-la' on my lips I passed through the front door into the hall, and – *bing* – right in the middle of the fairway, arranging flowers at a table, Dame Daphne Winkworth.

Well, I suppose Napoleon or Attila the Hun or one of those fellows would just have waved a hand and said 'Aha, there!' and hurried on, but the feat was beyond me. Her eye, swivelling round, stopped me like a bullet. The Wedding Guest, if you remember, had the same trouble with the Ancient Mariner.

'Ah, there you are, Augustus.'

It was fruitless to deny it. I stood on one leg and dashed a bead of persp from the brow.

'I had no time to ask you last night. Have you written to Madeline?'

'Oh, yes, rather.'

'I hope you were properly apologetic.'

'Oh, rather, yes.'

'And why are you looking as if you had slept in your clothes?' she asked, giving the upholstery a look of distaste.

The thing about the Woosters is that they know when to speak out and when not to speak out. Something told me that here was where manly frankness might pay dividends.

'Well, as a matter of fact,' I said, 'I did. I ran up to Wimbledon last night on the milk train. To see Madeline, don't you know. You know how it is. You can't say all you want to in letters, and I thought . . . well, the personal touch, if you see what I mean.'

It couldn't have gone better. I have never actually seen a shepherd welcoming a strayed lamb back into the fold, but I should imagine that his manner on such an occasion would closely parallel that of this female twenty-minute egg as she heard my words. The eyes softened. The face split in a pleased smile. That wrinkling of the nose which had been so noticeable a moment before, as if I had been an escape of gas or a not-quite-up-to-sample egg, disappeared totally. It would not be putting it too strongly to say that she beamed.

'Augustus!'

'I think it was a good move.'

'It was, indeed. It is just the sort of thing that would appeal to Madeline's romantic nature. Why, you are quite a Romeo, Augustus. In the *milk* train? You must have been travelling all night.'

'Pretty well.'

'You poor boy! I can see you're worn out. I will ring for Silversmith to bring you some orange juice.'

She pressed the bell. There was a stage wait. She pressed it again, and there was another stage wait. She was on the point of giving it a third prod, when the hour produced the man. Uncle Charlie entered left, and I was amazed to see that there was an indulgent smile on his face. It is true that he switched it off immediately and resumed his customary aspect of a respectful chunk of dough, but the facial contortion had unquestionably been there.

'I must apologize for my delay in answering the bell, m'lady,' he said. 'When your ladyship rang, I was in the act of making a speech, and it was not until some moments had elapsed that I became aware of the summons.'

Dame Daphne blinked. Me, too.

'Making a speech?'

'In honour of the happy event, m'lady. My daughter Queenie has become affianced, m'lady.'

Dame Daphne oh-really-ed, and I very nearly said 'Indeed, sir?' for the information had come as a complete surprise. For one thing I hadn't suspected for an instant that ties of blood linked this bulging butler and that lissom parlourmaid, and for another, it seemed to me that she had got over her spot of Dobbs trouble pretty snappily. So this is what Woman's constancy amounts to, is it, I remember saying to myself, and I'm not at all sure I didn't add the word 'Faugh!'

'And who is the happy man, Silversmith?'

'A nice steady young fellow, m'lady. A young fellow called Meadowes.'

I had a feeling I had heard the name before somewhere, but I couldn't place it. Meadowes? Meadowes? No, it eluded me.

'Indeed? From the village?'

'No, m'lady. Meadowes is Mr Fink-Nottle's personal attendant,' said Silversmith, now definitely unshipping a smile and directing it at me. He seemed to be trying to indicate that after this he looked on me as one of the boys and practically a relation by marriage and that, on his side at least, no more would be said of my weakness for singing hunting songs over the port and introducing into country houses dogs that bit like serpents.

I suppose the gasp that had escaped my lips sounded to Dame Daphne like the gurgle of a man dying of thirst, for she instantly put in her order for orange juice.

'Silversmith had better take it to your room. You will be wanting to change your clothes.'

'He might tell Meadowes to bring it,' I said faintly.

'Why, of course. You will want to wish him happiness.'

'That's right,' I said.

It was not immediately that Catsmeat presented himself. No doubt if you have made all your plans for marrying the daughter of the house and then suddenly find yourself engaged to the parlourmaid you need a little time to adjust the faculties. When he finally did appear, it seemed to me from his dazed expression that he had still a longish way to go in that direction. His air was that of a man who has recently been coshed by a small but serviceable rubber bludgeon.

'Bertie,' he said, 'a rather unfortunate thing has happened.'

'I know.'

'Oh, you know, do you? Then what do you advise?'

There could be but one answer to this.

'You'd better place the whole matter before Jeeves.'

'I will. That great brain may find a formula. I'll lay the facts before Jeeves and bid him brood on them.'

'But what are the facts? How did it happen?'

'I'll tell you. Do you want this orange juice?'

'No.'

'Then I'll have it. It may help a little.'

He drank deeply, and mopped the forehead.

'It all comes of letting that Dickens spirit creep over you, Bertie. The advice I give to every young man starting life is Never get Dickensy. You remember I told you that for some days I have been bursting with a sort of yeasty benevolence? This morning it came to a head. I had had Gertrude's note saying that she would elope with me, and I was just a solid chunk of sweetness and light. In ecstasies myself, I wanted to see happiness all around me. I loved my species and yearned to do it a bit of good. And with these sentiments fizzing about inside me, with the milk of human kindness sloshing up against my back teeth, I wandered into the servants' hall and found Queenie there in tears.'

'Your heart bled?'

'Profusely. I said "There, there". I took her hand and patted it. And then, as I didn't seem to be making any headway, almost unconsciously I drew her on to my knee and put my arm around her waist and started kissing her. Like a brother.'

'H'm.'

'Don't say "H'm", Bertie. It was only what Sir Galahad or someone like that would have done in my place. Dash it, there's nothing wrong, is there, in acting like a sympathetic elder brother when a girl is in distress? Pretty square behaviour, I should have thought. But don't run away with the idea that I don't wish I hadn't yielded to the kindly impulse. I regret it sincerely, because at that moment Silversmith came in. And what do you think? He's her father.'

'I know.'

'You seem to know everything.'

'I do.'

'Well, there's one thing you don't know, and that is that he was accompanied by Gertrude.'

'Gosh!'

'Yes. Her manner on beholding me was a bit reserved. Silversmith's, on the other hand, wasn't. He looked like a minor prophet without a beard suddenly confronted with the sins of the people, and started in immediately to thunder denunciations. There are fathers who know how to set about an erring daughter, and fathers who do not. Silversmith is one of the former. And then, in a sort of dream, I heard Queenie telling him that we were engaged. She has since informed me that it seemed to her the only way out. It did, of course, momentarily ease the strain.'

'How did Gertrude appear to take it?'

'Not very blithely. I've just had a brief note from her, cancelling our arrangements.'

He groaned the sort of hollow groan I had been groaning so much of late.

'You see before you, Bertie, a spent egg, a man in whom hope is dead. You don't happen to have any cyanide on you?' He groaned another hollow one. 'And on top of all this,' he said, 'I've got to put on a green beard and play Mike in a knockabout cross-talk act!'

I was sorry for the unhappy young blister, of course, but it piqued me somewhat that he seemed to consider that he was the only one who had any troubles.

'Well, I've got to recite Christopher Robin poems.'

'Pah!' he said. 'It might have been Winnie the Pooh.'

Well, there was that, of course.

22

THE village hall stood in the middle of the High Street, just abaft the duck-pond. Erected in the year 1881 by Sir Quintin Deverill, Bart, a man who didn't know much about architecture but knew what he liked, it was one of those mid-Victorian jobs in glazed red brick which always seem to bob up in these olde-worlde hamlets and do so much to encourage the drift to the towns. Its interior, like those of all the joints of its kind I've ever come across, was dingy and fuggy and smelled in about equal proportions of apples, chalk, damp plaster, Boy Scouts and the sturdy English peasantry.

The concert was slated to begin at eight-fifteen, and a few minutes before the kick-off, my own little effort not being billed till after the intermission, I wandered in and took my place among the standees at the back, noting dully that I should be playing to absolute capacity. The populace had rolled up in droves, though I could have warned them that they were asking for it. I had seen the programme, and I knew the worst.

The moment I scanned the bill of fare, I was able to understand why Corky, that afternoon at my flat, had spoken so disgruntedly of the talent at her disposal, like a girl who has been thwarted and frustrated and kept from fulfilling herself and what not. I knew what had happened. Starting out to arrange this binge with high hopes and burning ideals and all that sort of thing, poor child, she had stubbed her toe on the fatal snag which always lurks in the path of the impresario of this type of entertainment. I allude to the fact that at every village concert there are certain powerful vested interests which have to be considered. There are, that is to say, divers local nibs who, having always done their bit, are going to be pretty cold and sniffy if not invited to do it again this time. What Corky had come up against was the Kegley-Bassington clan.

To a man of my wide experience, such items as 'Solo: Miss Muriel Kegley-Bassington' and 'Duologue (A Pair of Lunatics): Colonel and Mrs R. P. Kegley-Bassington' told their own story;

and the same thing applied to 'Imitations: Watkyn Kegley-Bassington'; 'Card Tricks: Percival Kegley-Bassington' and 'Rhythmic Dance: Miss Poppy Kegley-Bassington'. Master George Kegley-Bassington, who was down for a recitation, I absolved from blame. I strongly suspected that he, like me, had been thrust into his painful position by *force majeure* and would have been equally willing to make a cash settlement.

In the intervals of feeling a brotherly sympathy for Master George and wishing I could run across him and stand him a commiserating gingerbeer, I devoted my time to studying the faces of my neighbours, hoping to detect in them some traces of ruth and pity and what is known as kind indulgence. But not a glimmer. Like all rustic standees, these were stern, implacable men, utterly incapable of taking the broad, charitable view and realizing that a fellow who comes on a platform and starts reciting about Christopher Robin going hoppity-hoppity-hop (or, alternatively, saying his prayers) does not do so from sheer wantonness but because he is a helpless victim of circumstances beyond his control.

I was gazing with considerable apprehension at a particularly dangerous specimen on my left, a pleasure-seeker with hair oil on his head and those mobile lips to which the raspberry springs automatically, when a mild splatter of applause from the two-bob seats showed that we were off. The vicar was opening the proceedings with a short address.

Apart from the fact that I was aware that he played chess and shared with Catsmeat's current *fiancée* a dislike for hearing policemen make cracks about Jonah and the Whale, the Rev. Sidney Pirbright had hitherto been a sealed book to me, and this was, of course, the first time I had seen him in action. A tall, drooping man, looking as if he had been stuffed in a hurry by an incompetent taxidermist, it became apparent immediately that he was not one of those boisterous vicars who, when opening a village concert, bound on the stage with a whoop and a holler, give the parishioners a huge Hallo, slam across a couple of travelling-salesman-and-farmer's-daughter stories and bound off, beaming. He seemed low-spirited, as I suppose he had every right to be. With Corky permanently on the premises, doing the little Mother, and Gussie rolling up for practically every meal, and on top of that a gorilla like young Thos coming and parking himself in the spare bedroom, you could scarcely expect him to bubble over with *joie de vivre*. These things take their toll.

At any rate, he didn't. His theme was the Church Organ, in aid of which these grim doings had been set afoot, and it was in a vein of pessimism that he spoke of its prospects. The Church Organ, he told us frankly, was in a hell of a bad way. For years it had been going around with holes in its socks, doing the Brother-can-you-spare-a-dime stuff, and now it was about due to hand in its dinner pail. There had been a time when he had hoped that the pull-together spirit might have given it a shot in the arm, but the way it looked to him at the moment, things had gone too far and he was prepared to bet his shirt on the bally contrivance going down the drain and staying there.

He concluded by announcing sombrely that the first item on the programme would be a Violin Solo by Miss Eustacia Pulbrook, managing to convey the suggestion that, while he knew as well as we did that Eustacia was going to be about as corny as they come, he advised us to make the most of her, because after that we should have the Kegley-Bassington family at our throats.

Except for knowing that when you've heard one, you've heard them all, I'm not really an authority on violin solos, so cannot state definitely whether La Pulbrook's was or was not a credit to the accomplices who had taught her the use of the instrument. It was loud in spots and less loud in other spots, and it had that quality which I have noticed in all violin solos, of seeming to last much longer than it actually did. When it eventually blew over, one saw what the sainted Sidney had meant about the Kegley-Bassingtons. A minion came on the stage carrying a table. On this table he placed a framed photograph, and I knew that we were for it. Show Bertram Wooster a table and a framed photograph, and you don't have to tell him what the upshot is going to be. Muriel Kegley-Bassington stood revealed as a 'My Hero' from *The Chocolate Soldier* addict.

I thought the boys behind the back row behaved with extra-ordinary dignity and restraint, and their suavity gave me the first faint hope I had had that when my turn came to face the firing-squad I might be spared the excesses which I had been anticipating. I would rank 'My Hero' next after 'The Yeoman's Wedding Song' as a standee-rouser, and when a large blonde appeared and took up the photograph and gave it a soulful look and rubbed her hands in the rosin and inflated her lungs, I was expecting big things. But these splendid fellows apparently did not war on women. Not only did they refrain from making uncouth noises with the tongue between the lips, one or two actually clapped – an imprudent move, of course, because, taken in conjunction with the applause of the two-bobbers, who applaud everything, it led to 'Oh, who will o'er the downs with me' as an encore.

Inflamed by this promising start, Muriel would, I think, willingly have continued, probably with 'The Indian Love Call', but something in our manner must have shown her that she couldn't do that here, for she shrank back and withdrew. There was a brief stage wait, and then a small, bullet-headed boy in an Eton jacket came staggering on like Christopher Robin going hoppity-hoppity-hop, in a manner that suggested that blood relations in the background had overcome his reluctance to appear by putting a hand between his shoulder-blades and shoving. Master George Kegley-Bassington, and no other. My heart went out to the little fellow. I knew just how he was feeling.

One could picture so clearly all that must have led up to this rash act. The first fatal suggestion by his mother that it would please the vicar if George gave that recitation which he did so nicely. The agonized 'Hoy!' The attempted rebuttal. The family pressure. The sullen scowl. The calling in of Father to exercise his authority. The reluctant acquiescence. The dash for freedom at the eleventh hour, foiled, as we have seen, by that quick thrust between the shoulder-blades.

And here he was, out in the middle.

He gave us an unpleasant look, and said:

' "Ben Battle." '

I pursed the lips and shook the head. I knew this 'Ben Battle', for it had been in my own repertoire in my early days. One of those gruesome antiques with a pun in every other line, the last thing to which any right-minded boy would wish to lend himself, and quite unsuited to this artiste's style. If I had had the ear of Colonel and Mrs R. P. Kegley-Bassington, I would have said to them: 'Colonel, Mrs Kegley-Bassington, be advised by an old friend. Keep George away from comedy, and stick to good sound "Dangerous Dan McGrews". His forte is grimness.'

Having said 'Ben Battle', he paused and repeated the
unpleasant look. I could see what was passing through his mind.
He wished to know if anybody out front wanted to make anything of this. The pause was a belligerent pause. But it was
evident that it had been misinterpreted by his nearest and dearest, for two voices, both loud and carrying, spoke simul-
taneously from the wings. One had a parade-ground rasp, the
other was that of the songstress who had so recently My-Hero-
ed.

'Ben Battle was a soldier bold . . .'

'All *right*!' said George, transferring the unpleasant look in
that direction. '*I* know. Ben-Battle-was-a-soldier-bold-and-
used-to-war's-alarms, A-cannon-ball-took-off-his-legs-so-he-
laid-down-his-arms,' he added, crowding the thing into a single
word. He then proceeded.

Well, really, come, come, I felt, as he did so, this is most
encouraging. Can it be, I asked myself, that these rugged
exteriors around me hide hearts of gold? It certainly seemed so,
for despite the fact that it would have been difficult, nay impossible, to imagine anything lousier than Master George Kegley-
Bassington's performance, it was producing nothing in the
nature of a demonstration from the standees. They had not
warred on women, and they did not war on children. Might it
not quite easily happen, I mused, that they would not war on
Woosters? Tails up, Bertram, I said to myself, and it was with
almost a light heart that I watched George forget the last three
stanzas and shamble off, giving us that unpleasant look again
over his shoulder, and in the exuberance with which I greeted
the small man with the face like an anxious marmoset – Adrian
Higgins, I gathered from my programme; by profession, I subsequently learned, King's Deverill's courteous and popular
grave-digger – there was something that came very close to
being carefree.

Adrian Higgins solicited our kind attention for Impressions
of Woodland Songsters Which Are Familiar To You All, and
while these did not go with any particular bang, the farmyard
imitations which followed were cordially received, and the
drawing of a cork and pouring out a bottle of beer which took
him off made a solid hit, leaving the customers in excellent
mood. With the conclusion of George's recitation, they were

feeling that the worst was behind them and a few clenched teeth would see them through the remainder of the Kegley-Bassington offensive. There was a general sense of relaxation, and Gussie and Catsmeat could not have had a better spot. When they came on, festooned in green beards, they got a big hand.

It was the last time they did. The act died standing up. Right from the start I saw that it was going to be a turkey, and so it proved. It was listless. It lacked fire and oomph. The very opening words struck a chill.

'Hallo, Pat,' said Catsmeat in a dull, toneless voice.

'Hallo, Mike,' said Gussie, with equal moodiness. 'How's your father?'

'He's not enjoying himself just now.'

'What's he doing?'

'Seven years,' said Catsmeat glumly, and went on in the same depressed way to speak of his brother Jim, who, having obtained employment as a swimming teacher, was now often in low water.

Well, I couldn't see what Gussie could have on his mind, unless he was brooding on the Church Organ, but Catsmeat's despondency was, of course, susceptible of a ready explanation. From where he stood he had an excellent view of Gertrude Winkworth in row one of the two-bob seats, and the sight of her, looking pale and proud in something which I should say at a venture was *mousseline*, must have been like a sword-thrust through the bosom. Just as you allow a vicar a wide latitude in the way of gloom when his private life has become cluttered up with Corkies and Gussies and Thoses, so should you, if a fairminded man, permit a tortured lover, confronted with the girl he has lost, to sink into the depths a bit.

Well, that's all right. I'm not saying you shouldn't, and, as a matter of fact, I did. If you had come along and asked me, 'Has Claude Cattermole Pirbright your heartfelt sympathy, Wooster?' I would have replied, 'You betcher he has my heartfelt sympathy. I mourn in spirit.' All I do say is that this Byronic outlook doesn't help you bang across your points in a Pat and Mike knockabout cross-talk act.

The whole performance gave one a sort of grey, hopeless feeling, like listening to the rain at three o'clock on a Sunday afternoon in November. Even the standees, tough, rugged men who would not have recognized the finer feelings if you had served them up on a plate with watercress round them, obviously felt the pathos of it all. They listened in dejected silence, shuffling their feet, and I didn't blame them. There should be nothing so frightfully heartrending in one fellow asking another fellow who that lady was he saw him coming down the street with and the other fellow replying that there was no lady, that was his wife. An amusing little misunderstanding, you would say. But when Gussie and Catsmeat spoke the lines, they seemed to bring home to you all the underlying sadness of life.

At first, I couldn't think what the thing reminded me of. Then I got it. At the time when I was engaged to Florence Craye and she was trying to jack up my soul, one of the methods she employed to this end was to take me on Sunday nights to see Russian plays; the sort of things where the old home is being sold up and people stand around saying how sad it all is. If I had to make a criticism of Catsmeat and Gussie, I should say that they got too much of the Russian spirit into their work. It was a relief to one and all when the poignant slice of life drew to a close.

'My sister's in the ballet,' said Catsmeat despondently.

There was a pause here, because Gussie had fallen into a sort of trance and was standing staring silently before him as if the Church Organ had really got him down at last, and Catsmeat, realizing that only moral support, if that, was to be expected from this quarter, was obliged to carry on the conversation by himself, a thing which I always think spoils the effect on these occasions. The essence of a cross-talk act is that there should be wholesome give and take, and you never get the same snappy zip when one fellow is asking the questions and answering them himself.

'You say your sister's in the ballet?' said Catsmeat with a catch in his voice. 'Yes, begorrah, my sister's in the ballet. What does your sister do in the ballet?' he went on, taking a look at Gertrude Winkworth and quivering in agony. 'She comes rushin' in and she goes rushin' out. What does she have to rush like that for?' asked Catsmeat with a stifled sob. 'Faith and begob, because it's a Rushin' ballet.'

And, too broken in spirit to hit Gussie with his umbrella, he took him by the elbow and directed him to the exit. They moved slowly off with bowed heads, like a couple of pallbearers who have forgotten their coffin and had to go back for it, and to the rousing strains of 'Hallo, hallo, hallo, hallo, a-hunting we will go, pom pom', Esmond Haddock strode masterfully onto the stage.

Esmond looked terrific. Anxious to omit no word or act which would assist him in socking the clientele on the button, he had put on full hunting costume, pink coat and everything, and the effect was sensational. He seemed to bring into that sombre hall a note of joy and hope. After all, you felt, there was still happiness in the world. Life, you told yourself, was not all men in green beards saying 'Faith' and 'Begorrah'.

To the practised eye like mine it was apparent that in the interval since the conclusion of the scratch meal which had taken the place of dinner the young Squire had been having a couple, but, as I often say, why not? There is no occasion on which a man of retiring disposition with an inferiority complex and all the trimmings needs the old fluid more than when he is about to perform at a village concert, and with so much at stake it would have been madness on his part not to get moderately ginned.

It is to the series of quick ones which he had absorbed that I attribute the confident manner of his entry, but the attitude of the audience must speedily have convinced him that he could really have got by perfectly well on limejuice. Any doubt lingering in his mind as to his being the popular pet must have been dispelled instantly by the thunders of applause from all parts of the house. I noted twelve distinct standees who were whistling through their fingers, and those who were not whistling were stamping on the floor. The fellow with the hair oil on my left was doing both.

And now, of course, came the danger spot. A feeble piping at this point, like gas escaping from a pipe, or let us say a failure to remember more than an odd word or two of the subject matter, and a favourable first impression might well be undone. True, the tougher portion of the audience had been sedulously stood beers over a period of days and in return had entered into a gentleman's agreement to be indulgent, but nevertheless it was unquestionably up to Esmond Haddock to deliver the goods.

He did so abundantly and in heaping measure. That first night over the port, when we had been having our run-through, my thoughts at the outset had been centred on the lyric and I had been too busy polishing up Aunt Charlotte's material to give much attention to the quality of his voice. And later on, of course, I had been singing myself, which always demands complete concentration. When I was on the chair, waving my decanter, I had been aware in a vague sort of way of some kind of disturbance in progress on the table, but if Dame Daphne Winkworth on her entry had asked me my opinion of Esmond Haddock's timbre and brio, I should have had to reply that I really hadn't noticed them much.

He now stood forth as the possessor of a charming baritone – full of life and feeling and, above all, loud. And volume of sound is what you want at a village concert. Make the lights flicker and bring plaster down from the ceiling, and you are home. Esmond Haddock did not cater simply for those who had paid the price of admission, he took in strollers along the High Street and even those who had remained at their residences, curled up with a good book. Catsmeat, you may recall, in speaking of the yells which Dame Daphne and the Misses Deverill had uttered on learning of his betrothal to Gertrude Winkworth, had hazarded the opinion that they could have been heard at Basingstoke. I should say that Basingstoke got Esmond Haddock's hunting song nicely.

If so, it got a genuine treat and one of some duration, for he took three encores, a couple of bows, a fourth encore, some more bows and then the chorus once over again by way of one for the road. And even then his well-wishers seemed reluctant to let him go.

This reluctance made itself manifest during the next item on the programme – Glee (Oh, come unto these yellow sands) by the Church Choir, conducted by the school-mistress – in murmurs at the back and an occasional 'Hallo', but it was not until Miss Poppy Kegley-Bassington was performing her rhythmic dance that it found full expression.

Unlike her sister Muriel, who had resembled a Criterion barmaid of the old school, Poppy Kegley-Bassington was long and dark and supple, with a sinuous figure suggestive of a snake with hips; one of those girls who do rhythmic dances at the drop of a hat and can be dissuaded from doing them only with a meat-axe. The music that accompanied her act was Oriental in nature, and I should be disposed to think that the thing had started out in life as a straight Vision of Salome but had been toned down and had the whistle blown on it in spots in deference to the sensibilities of the Women's Institute. It consisted of a series of slitherings and writhings, punctuated with occasional pauses when, having got herself tied in a clove-hitch, she seemed to be waiting for someone who remembered the combination to come along and disentangle her.

It was during one of these pauses that the plug-ugly with the hair oil make an observation. Since Esmond's departure he had been standing with a rather morose expression on his face, like an elephant that has had its bun taken from it, and you could see how deeply he was regretting that the young Squire was no longer with us. From time to time he would mutter in a peevish undertone, and I seemed to catch Esmond's name. He now spoke, and I found that my hearing had not been at fault.

'We want Haddock,' he said. 'We want Haddock, we want Haddock, we want Haddock, we want HADDOCK!'

He uttered the words in a loud, clear, penetrating voice, not unlike that of a costermonger informing the public that he has blood oranges for sale, and the sentiment expressed evidently chimed in with the views of those standing near him. It was not long before perhaps twenty or more discriminating concert-goers were also chanting:

'We want Haddock, we want Haddock, we want Haddock, we want Haddock, we want HADDOCK!'

And it just shows you how catching this sort of thing is. It wasn't more than about five seconds later that I heard another voice intoning.

'We want Haddock, we want Haddock, we want Haddock, we want Haddock, we want HADDOCK!' and discovered with a mild surprise that it was mine. And as the remainder of the standees, some thirty in number, also adopted the slogan, this made us unanimous.

To sum up, then, the fellow with the hair oil, fifty other fellows, also with hair oil, and I had begun to speak simul-taneously and what we said was:

'We want Haddock, we want Haddock, we want Haddock, we want Haddock, we want HADDOCK!'

There was some shushing from the two-bobbers, but we were firm, and though Miss Kegley-Bassington pluckily continued to slither for a few moments longer, the contest of wills could have but one ending. She withdrew, getting a nice hand, for we were generous in victory, and Esmond came on, all boots and pink coat. And what with him going a-hunting at one end of the hall and our group of thinkers going a-hunting at the other, the thing might have occupied the rest of the evening quite agreeably, had not some quick-thinking person dropped the curtain for the intermission.

You might have supposed that my mood, as I strolled from the building to enjoy a smoke, would have been one of elation. And so, for some moments, it was. The whole aim of my foreign policy had been to ensure the making of a socko by Esmond, and he had made a socko. He had slain them and stopped the show. For perhaps the space of a quarter of a cigarette I rejoiced unstintedly.

Then my uplifted mood suddenly left me. The cigarette fell from my nerveless fingers, and I stood rooted to the spot, the lower jaw resting negligently on the shirt front. I had just realized that, what with one thing and another – my disturbed night, my taxing day, the various burdens weighing on my mind and so forth – every word of those Christopher Robin poems had been expunged from my memory.

And I was billed next but two after intermission.

23

How long I stood there, rooted to the s., I cannot say. A goodish while, no doubt, for this wholly unforeseen development had unmanned me completely. I was roused from my reverie by the sound of rustic voices singing 'Hallo, hallo, hallo, hallo, a-hunting we will go, my lads, a-hunting we will go' and discovered that the strains were proceeding from the premises of the Goose and Cowslip on the other side of the road. And it suddenly struck me – I can't think why it hadn't before – that here might possibly be the mental tonic of which I was in need. It might be that all that was wrong with me was that I was faint for lack of nourishment. Hitching up the lower jaw, I hurried across and plunged into the saloon bar.

The revellers who were singing the gem of the night's Hit Parade were doing so in the public bar. The only occupant of the more posh saloon bar was a godlike man in a bowler hat with grave, finely chiselled features and a head that stuck out at the back, indicating great brain power. To cut a long story short, Jeeves. He was having a meditative beer at the table by the wall.

'Good evening, sir,' he said, rising with his customary polish. 'I am happy to inform you that I was successful in obtaining the cosh from Master Thomas. I have it in my pocket.'

I raised a hand.

'This is no time for talking about coshes.'

'No, sir. I merely mentioned it in passing. Mr Haddock's was an extremely gratifying triumph, did you not think, sir?'

'Nor is it a time for talking about Esmond Haddock, Jeeves,' I said, 'I'm sunk.'

'Indeed, sir?'

'Jeeves!'

'I beg your pardon, sir. I should have said "Really, sir?" '

' "Really, sir?" is just as bad. What the crisis calls for is a "Gosh!" or a "Gorblimey!" There have been occasions, numerous occasions, when you have beheld Bertram Wooster in the bouillon, but never so deeply immersed in it as now. You know those damned poems I was to recite? I've forgotten every word of them. I need scarcely stress the gravity of the situation. Half an hour from now I shall be up on that platform with the Union Jack behind me and before me an expectant audience, waiting to see what I've got. And I haven't got anything. I shan't have a word to say. And while an audience at a village concert justifiably resents having Christopher Robin poems recited at it, its resentment becomes heightened if the reciter merely stands there opening and shutting his mouth in silence like a goldfish.'

'Very true, sir. You cannot jog your memory?'

'It was in the hope of jogging it that I came in here. Is there brandy in this joint?'

'Yes, sir. I will procure you a double.'

'Make it two doubles.'

'Very good, sir.'

He moved obligingly to the little hatch thing in the wall and conveyed his desire to the unseen provider on the other side, and presently a hand came through with a brimming glass and he brought it to the table.

'Let's see what this does,' I said. 'Skin off your nose, Jeeves.'

'Mud in your eye, sir, if I may use the expression.'

I drained the glass and laid it down.

'The ironical thing,' I said, while waiting for the stuff to work, 'is that though, except for remembering in a broad, general way that he went hoppity-hoppity-hop, I am a spent force as regards Christopher Robin, I could do them "Ben Battle" without a hitch. Did you hear Master George Kegley-Bassington on the subject of "Ben Battle"?'

'Yes, sir. A barely adequate performance, I thought.'

'That is not the point, Jeeves. What I'm trying to tell you is that listening to him has had the effect of turning back time in its flight, if you know what I mean, so that from the reciting angle I am once more the old Bertram Wooster of bygone days and can remember every word of "Ben Battle" as clearly as in the epoch when it was constantly on my lips. I could do the whole thing without fluffing a syllable. But does that profit me?'

'No, sir.'

'No, sir, is correct. Thanks to George, saturation point has been reached with this particular audience as far as "Ben Battle" is concerned. If I started to give it them, too, I shouldn't get beyond the first stanza. There would be an ugly rush for the platform, and I should be roughly handled. So what do you suggest?'

'You have obtained no access of mental vigour from the refreshment which you have been consuming, sir?'

'Not a scrap. The stuff might have been water.'

'In that case, I think you would be well advised to refrain from attempting to entertain the audience, sir. It would be best to hand the whole conduct of the affair over to Mr Haddock.'

'Eh?'

'I am confident that Mr Haddock would gladly deputize for you. In the uplifted frame of mind in which he now is, he would welcome an opportunity to appear again before his public.'

'But he couldn't learn the stuff in a quarter of an hour.'

'No, sir, but he could read it from the book. I have a copy of the book on my person, for I had been intending to station myself at the side of the stage in order to prompt you, as I believe the technical expression is, should you have need of my services.'

'Dashed good of you, Jeeves. Very white. Very feudal.'

'Not at all, sir. Shall I step across and explain the position of affairs to Mr Haddock and hand him the book?'

I mused. The more I examined his suggestion, the better I liked it. When you are slated to go over Niagara Falls in a barrel, the idea of getting a kindly friend to take your place is always an attractive one; the only thing that restrains you, as a rule, from making the switch being the thought that it is a bit tough on the kindly f. But in the present case this objection did not apply. On this night of nights Esmond Haddock could get away with anything. There was, I seemed to remember dimly, a poem in the book about Christopher Robin having ten little toes. Even that, dished out by the idol of King's Deverill, would not provoke mob violence.

'Yes, buzz straight over and fix up the deal, Jeeves,' I said, hesitating no longer. 'As always, you have found the way.'

He adjusted the bowler hat which he had courteously doffed at my entry, and went off on his errand of mercy. And I, too agitated to remain sitting, wandered out into the street and began to pace up and down outside the hostelry. And I had paused for a moment to look at the stars, wondering, as I always did when I saw stars, why Jeeves had once described them to me as quiring to the young-eyed Cherubim, when a tapping on my arm and a bleating voice saying 'I say, Bertie' told me that some creature of the night was trying to arrest my attention. I turned and beheld something in a green beard and a check suit of loud pattern which, as it was not tall enough to be Catsmeat, the only other person likely to be going about in that striking get-up, I took correctly to be Gussie.

'I say, Bertie,' said Gussie, speaking with obvious emotion, 'do you think you could get me some brandy?'

'You mean orange juice?'

'No, I do not mean orange juice. I mean brandy. About a bucketful.'

Puzzled, but full of the St-Bernard-dog spirit, I returned to the saloon bar and came back with the snifter. He accepted it gratefully and downed about half of it at a gulp, gasping in a struck-by-lightning manner, as I have seen men gasp after taking one of Jeeves's special pick-me-ups.

'Thanks,' he said, when he had recovered. 'I needed that. And I didn't like to go in myself with this beard on.'

'Why don't you take it off?'

'I can't get it off. I stuck it on with spirit gum, and it hurts like sin when I pull at it. I shall have to get Jeeves to see what he can do about it later. Is this stuff brandy?'

'That's what they told me.'

'What appalling muck. Like vitriol. How on earth can you and your fellow topers drink it for pleasure?'

'What are you drinking it for? Because you promised your mother you would?'

'I am drinking it, Bertie, to nerve myself for a frightful ordeal.'

I gave his shoulder a kindly pat. It seemed to me that the man's mind was wandering.

'You're forgetting, Gussie. Your ordeal is over. You've done your act. And pretty lousy it was,' I said, unable to check the note of censure. 'What was the matter with you?'

He blinked like a chidden codfish.

'Wasn't I good?'

'No, you were not good. You were cheesy. Your work lacked fire and snap.'

'Well, so would your work lack fire and snap, if you had to play in a knockabout cross-talk act and knew that directly the thing was over, you were going to break into a police station and steal a dog.'

The stars, ceasing for a moment to quire to the young-eyed Cherubim, did a quick buck-and-wing.

'Say that again!'

'What's the point of saying it again? You heard. I've promised Corky I'll go to Dobbs's cottage and extract that dog of hers. She will be waiting in her car near at hand and will gather the animal in and whisk it off to the house of some friends of hers who live about twenty miles along the London road, well out of Dobbs's sphere of influence. So now you know why I wanted brandy.'

I wanted brandy, too. Either that or something equally restorative. Oh, I was saying to myself, for a beaker full of the warm south, full of the true, the blushful Hippocrene. I have spoken earlier of the tendency of the spirit of the Woosters to rise when crushed to earth, but there is a limit, and this limit had now been reached. At these frightful words, the spirit of the Woosters felt as if it had been sat on by an elephant. And not one of your streamlined, schoolgirl-figured elephants, either. A big, fat one.

'Gussie! You mustn't!'

'What do you mean, I mustn't? Of course I must. Corky wishes it.'

'But you don't realize the peril. Dobbs is laying for you. Esmond Haddock is laying for you. They're just waiting to spring.'

'How do you know that?'

'Esmond Haddock told me so himself. He dislikes you intensely and it is his dearest hope some day to catch you bending and put you behind the bars. And he's a JP, so is in a strong position to bring about the happy ending. You'll look pretty silly when you find yourself doing thirty days in the jug.'

'For Corky's sake I'd do a year. As a matter of fact,' said Gussie in a burst of confidence, 'though you might not think it from the way I've been calling for brandy, there's no chance of my being caught. Dobbs is watching the concert.'

This, of course, improved the outlook. I don't say I breathed freely, but I breathed more freely than I had been breathing.

'You're sure of that?'

'I saw him myself.'

'You couldn't have been mistaken?'

'My dear Bertie, when Dobbs has come into a room in which you have been strewing frogs and stood face to face with you for an eternity, chewing his moustache and grinding his teeth at you, you know him when you see him again.'

'But all the same – '

'It's no good saying "All the same". Corky wants me to extract her dog, and I'm going to do it. "Gussie", she said to me, "you're such a *help*", and I intend to be worthy of those words.'

And, having spoken thus, he gave his beard a hitch and vanished into the silent night, leaving me to pay for the brandy.

I had just finished doing so when Jeeves returned.

'Everything has been satisfactorily arranged, sir,' he said. 'I have seen Mr Haddock, and, as I anticipated, he is more than willing to deputize for you.'

A great weight seemed to roll off my mind.

'Then God bless Mr Haddock!' I said. 'There is splendid stuff in these young English landowners, Jeeves, is there not?'

'Unquestionably, sir.'

'The backbone of the country, I sometimes call them. But I gather from the fact that you have been gone the dickens of a time that you had to do some heavy persuading.'

'No, sir. Mr Haddock consented immediately and with enthusiasm. My delay in returning was due to the fact that I was detained in conversation by Police Constable Dobbs. There were a number of questions of a theological nature on which he was anxious to canvass my views. He appears particularly interested in Jonah and the Whale.'

'Is he enjoying the concert?'

'No, sir. He spoke in disparaging terms of the quality of the entertainment provided.'

'He didn't like George Kegley-Bassington much?'

'No, sir. On the subject of Master Kegley-Bassington he expressed himself strongly, and was almost equally caustic when commenting upon Miss Kegley-Bassington's rhythmic dance. It is in order to avoid witnessing the efforts of the remaining members of the family that he has returned to his cottage, where he plans to pass what is left of the evening with a pipe and the works of Colonel Robert G. Ingersoll.'

24

So that was that. You get the picture. Above, in the serene sky, the stars quiring to the Cherubim. Off-stage, in the public bar, the local toughies quiring to the potboy. And down centre Jeeves, having exploded his bombshell, regarding me with the eye of concern, as if he feared that all was not well with the young master, in which conjecture he was one hundred per cent right. The young master was feeling as if his soul had just received the Cornish Riviera express on the seat of its pants.

I gulped perhaps half a dozen times before I was able to utter.

'Jeeves, you didn't really say that, did you?'

'Sir?'

'About Constable Dobbs going back to his cottage.'

'Yes, sir. He informed me that it was his intention to do so. He said he desired solitude.'

'Solitude!' I said. 'Ha!'

And in a dull, toneless voice, like George Kegley-Bassington reciting 'Ben Battle', I gave him the lowdown.

'That is the situation in what is sometimes called a nutshell, Jeeves,' I concluded. 'And, not that it matters, for nothing matters now, I wonder if you have spotted how extraordinarily closely the present set-up resembles that of Alfred, Lord Tennyson's well-known poem, "The Charge of the Light Brigade", which is another of the things I used to recite in happier days. I mean to say, someone has blundered and Gussie, like the Six Hundred, is riding into the Valley of Death. His not to reason why, his but to do or – '

'Pardon me, sir, for interrupting you – '

'Not at all, Jeeves. I had nearly finished.'

' – but would it not be advisable to take some form of action?'

I gave him the lack-lustre eye.

'Action, Jeeves? How can that help us now? And what form of it would you suggest? I should have said the thing had got beyond the scope of human power.'

'It might be possible to overtake Mr Fink-Nottle, sir, and apprise him of his peril.'

I shrugged the shoulders.

'We can try, if you like. I see little percentage in it, but I suppose one should leave no stone unturned. Can you find your way to *chez* Dobbs?'

'Yes, sir.'

'Then shift ho,' I said listlessly.

As we made our way out of the High Street into the dark regions beyond, we chatted in desultory vein.

'I noticed, Jeeves, that when I started telling you the bad news just now, one of your eyebrows flickered.'

'Yes, sir. I was much exercised.'

'Don't you ever get exercised enough to say "Coo!"?'

'No, sir.'

'Or "Crumbs!"?'

'No, sir.'

'Strange. I should have thought you might have done so at a moment like that. I would say this was the end, wouldn't you?'

'While there is life, there is hope, sir.'

'Neatly put, but I disagree with you. I see no reason for even two-pennorth of hope. We shan't overtake Gussie. He must have got there long ago. About now, Dobbs is sitting on his chest and slipping the handcuffs on him.'

'The officer may not have proceeded directly to his home, sir.'

'You think there is a possibility that he paused at a pub for a gargle? It may be so, of course, but I am not sanguine. It would mean that Fate was handing out lucky breaks, and my experience of Fate –'

I would have spoken further and probably been pretty deepish, for the subject of Fate and its consistent tendency to give good men the elbow was one to which I had devoted considerable thought, but at this moment I was accosted by another creature of the night, a soprano one this time, and I perceived a car drawn up at the side of the road.

'Yoo-hoo, Bertie,' said a silvery voice. 'Hi-ya, Jeeves.'

'Good evening, miss,' said Jeeves in his suave way. 'Miss Pirbright, sir,' he added, giving me the office in an undertone.

I had already recognized the silvery v.

'Hallo, Corky,' I said moodily. 'You are waiting for Gussie?'

'Yes, he went by just now. What did you say?'

'Oh, nothing,' I replied, for I had merely remarked by way of a passing comment that cannons to left of him, cannons to right of him volleyed and thundered. 'I suppose you know that you have lured him on to a doom so hideous that the brain reels, contemplating it?'

'What do you mean?'

'He will find Dobbs at journey's end reading Robert G. Ingersoll. How long the officer will continue reading Robert G. Ingersoll after discovering that Gussie has broken in and is de-dogging the premises, one cannot – '

'Don't be an ass. Dobbs is at the concert.'

'He *was* at the concert. But he left early and is now – '

Once more I was interrupted when about to speak further. From down the road there had begun to make itself heard in the silent night a distant barking. It grew in volume, indicating that the barker was heading our way, and Corky sprang from the car and established herself as a committee of welcome in the middle of the fairway.

'What a chump you are, Bertie,' she said with some heat, 'pulling a girl's leg and trying to scare her stiff. Everything has gone according to plan. Here comes Sam. I'd know his voice anywhere. At-a-boy, Sam! This way. Come to Mother.'

What ensued was rather like the big scene in *The Hound of the Baskervilles*. The baying and the patter of feet grew louder, and suddenly out of the darkness Sam Goldwyn clocked in, coming along at a high rate of speed and showing plainly in his manner how keenly he appreciated the termination of the sedentary life he had been leading these last days. He looked good for about another fifty miles at the same pace, but the sight of us gave him pause. He stopped, looked and listened. Then, as our familiar odour reached his nostrils, he threw his whole soul into a cry of ecstasy. He bounded at Jeeves as if contemplating licking his face, but was checked by the latter's quiet dignity. Jeeves views the animal kingdom with a benevolent eye and is the first to pat its head and offer it a slice of whatever is going, but he does not permit it to lick his face.

'Inside, Sam,' said Corky, when the rapture of reunion had had the first keen edge taken off it and we had all simmered down a bit. She boosted him into the car, and resumed her place at the wheel. 'Time to be leaving,' she said. 'The quick fade-out is what the director would suggest here, I think. I'll be seeing you at the Hall later, Bertie. Uncle Sidney has been asked to look in for coffee and sandwiches after the show, and I was included in the invitation, I don't think. Still, I shall assume I was.'

She clapped spurs to her two-seater and vanished into the darkness. Sam Goldwyn's vocal solo died away, and all was still once more.

No, not all, to be absolutely accurate, for at this moment there came to the ear-drum an odd sort of hammering noise in the distance which at first I couldn't classify. It sounded as if someone was doing a tap-dance, but it seemed improbable that people would be doing tap-dances out of doors at this hour. Then I got it. Somebody – no, two people – was – or I should say were – haring towards us along the road, and I was turning to cock an enquiring eyebrow at Jeeves, when he drew me into the shadows.

'I fear the worst, sir,' he said in a hushed voice, and, sure enough, along it came.

In addition to the stars quiring to the young-eyed Cherubim, there was now in the serene sky a fair-sized moon, and as always happens under these conditions the visibility was improved. By its light one could see what was in progress.

Gussie and Constable Dobbs were in progress, in the order named. Not having been present at the outset of the proceedings, I can only guess at what had occurred in the early stages, but anyone entering a police station to steal a dog and finding Constable Dobbs on the premises would have lost little time in picking up the feet, and I think we can assume that Gussie had got off to a good start. At any rate, at the moment when the runners came into view he had established a nice lead and appeared to be increasing it.

It is curious how you can be intimate with a fellow from early boyhood and yet remain unacquainted with one side of him. Mixing constantly with Gussie through the years, I had come to know him as a newt-fancier, a lover and a fathead, but I had never suspected him of possessing outstanding qualities as a sprinter on the flat, and I was amazed at the high order of ability he was exhibiting in this very specialized form of activity. He was coming along like a jack-rabbit of the western prairie, his head back and his green beard floating in the breeze. I liked his ankle work.

Dobbs, on the other hand, was more laboured in his movements and to an eye like mine, trained in the watching of point-to-point races, had all the look of an also-ran. One noted symptoms of roaring, and I am convinced that had Gussie had the intelligence to stick to his job and make a straight race of it, he would soon have out-distanced the field and come home on a tight rein. Police constables are not built for speed. Where you catch them at their best is standing on street corners saying 'Pass along there'.

But, as I was stressing a moment ago, Augustus Fink-Nottle, in addition to being a flat racer of marked ability, was also a fathead, and now, when he had victory in his grasp, the fat-headed streak in him came uppermost. There was a tree standing at the roadside and, suddenly swerving off the course, he made for it and hoisted himself into its branches. And what he supposed that was going to get him, only his diseased mind knew. Ernest Dobbs may not have been one of Hampshire's brightest thinkers, but he was smart enough to stand under a tree.

And this he proceeded to do. Determination to fight it out on these lines if it took all summer was written on every inch of his powerful frame. His back being towards me, I couldn't see his face, but I have no doubt it was registering an equal amount of resolution, and nothing could have been firmer than his voice as he urged upon the rooster above the advisability of coming down without further waste of time. It was a fair cop, said Ernest Dobbs, and I agreed with him. To shut out the painful scene which must inevitably ensue, I closed my eyes.

It was an odd, chunky sound, like some solid substance striking another solid substance, that made me open them. And when they were opened, I could hardly believe them. Ernest Dobbs, who a moment before had been standing with his feet apart and his thumbs in his belt like a statue of Justice Putting It Across the Evil-Doer, had now assumed what I have heard described as a recumbent position. To make what I am driving at clear to the meanest intelligence, he was lying in the road with his face to the stars, while Jeeves, like a warrior sheathing his sword, replaced in his pocket some object which instinct told me was small but serviceable and constructed of india-rubber.

I tottered across, and drew the breath in sharply as I viewed the remains. The best you could have said of Constable Ernest Dobbs was that he looked peaceful.

'Good Lord, Jeeves!' I said.

'I took the liberty of coshing the officer, sir,' he explained respectfully. 'I considered it advisable in the circumstances as the simplest method of averting unpleasantness. You will find it safe to descend now, sir,' he proceeded, addressing Gussie. 'If I might offer the suggestion, speed is of the essence. One cannot guarantee that the constable will remain indefinitely immobile.'

This opened up a new line of thought.

'You don't mean he'll recover?'

'Why, yes, sir, almost immediately.'

'I'd have said that all he wanted was a lily in the right hand, and he'd be set.'

'Oh, no, sir. The cosh produces merely a passing malaise. Permit me, sir,' he said, assisting Gussie to alight. 'I anticipate that Dobbs, on coming to his senses, will experience a somewhat severe headache, but – '

'Into each life some rain must fall?'

'Precisely, sir. I think it would be prudent of Mr Fink-Nottle to remove his beard. It presents too striking a means of identification.'

'But he can't. It's stuck on with spirit gum.'

'If Mr Fink-Nottle will permit me to escort him to his room, sir, I shall be able to adjust that without difficulty.'

'You will? Then get on with it, Gussie.'

'Eh?' said Gussie, being just the sort of chap who would stand about saying 'Eh?' at a moment like this. He had a dazed air, as if he, too, had stopped one.

'Push off.'

'Eh?'

I gave a weary gesture.

'Remove him, Jeeves,' I said.

'Very good, sir.'

'I would come along with you, but I shall be occupied else-where. I need about six more of those brandies, and I need them quick. You're sure about this living corpse?'

'Sir?'

'I mean, "living" really is the *mot juste*?'

'Oh, yes, sir. If you will notice, the officer is already commencing to regain consciousness.'

I did notice it. Ernest Dobbs was plainly about to report for duty. He moved, he stirred, he seemed to feel the rush of life along his keel. And, this being so, I deemed it best to withdraw. I had no desire to be found standing at the sick-bed when a fellow of his muscular development and uncertain temper came to and started looking about for responsible parties. I returned to the Goose and Cowslip at a good speed, and proceeded to put big business in the way of the hand that came through the hatch. Then, feeling somewhat restored, I went back to the Hall and dug in in my room.

I had, as you will readily understand, much food for thought. The revelation of this deeper, coshing side to Jeeves's character had come as something of a shock to me. One found oneself wondering how far the thing would spread. He and I had had our differences in the past, failing to see eye to eye on such matters as purple socks and white dinner jackets, and it was inevitable, both of us being men of high spirit, that similar differences would arise in the future. It was a disquieting thought that in the heat of an argument about, say, soft-bosomed shirts for evening wear he might forget the decencies of debate and elect to apply the closure by hauling off and socking me on the frontal bone with something solid. One could but trust that the feudal spirit would serve to keep the impulse in check.

I was still trying to adjust the faculties to the idea that I had been nursing in my bosom all these years something that would be gratefully accepted as a muscle guy by any gang on the look out for new blood, when Gussie appeared, minus the shrubbery. He had changed the check suit for a dinner jacket, and with a start I realized that I ought to be dressing, too. I had forgotten that Corky had said that a big coffee-and-sandwiches binge was scheduled to take place in the drawing-room at the conclusion of the concert, which must by now be nearing the 'God Save The King' stage.

There seemed to be something on Gussie's mind. His manner was nervous. As I hurriedly socked, shirted and evening shoe-ed myself, he wandered about the room, fiddling with the *objets d'art* on the mantelpiece, and as I slid into the form-fitting trousers there came to my ears the familiar sound of a hollow groan – whether hollower than those recently uttered by self and Catsmeat I couldn't say, but definitely hollow. He had been staring for some moments at a picture on the wall of a girl in a poke bonnet cooing to a pigeon with a fellow in a cocked hat and tight trousers watching her from the background, such as you will always find in great profusion in places like Deverill Hall, and he now turned and spoke.

'Bertie, do you know what it is to have the scales fall from your eyes?'

'Why, yes. Scales have frequently fallen from my eyes.'

'They have fallen from mine,' said Gussie. 'And I'll tell you the exact moment when it happened. It was when I was up in that tree gazing down at Constable Dobbs and hearing him describe the situation as a fair cop. That was when the scales fell from my eyes.'

I ventured to interrupt.

'Half a second,' I said. 'Just to keep the record straight, what are you talking about?'

'I'm telling you. The scales fell from my eyes. Something happened to me. In a flash, with no warning, love died.'

'Whose love?'

'Mine, you ass. For Corky. I felt that a girl who could subject a man to such an ordeal was not the wife for me. Mind you, I still admire her enormously, and I think she would make an excellent helpmeet for somebody of the Ernest Hemingway type who likes living dangerously, but after what has occurred to-night, I am quite clear in my mind that what I require as a life partner is someone slightly less impulsive. If you could have seen Constable Dobbs's eyes glittering in the moonlight!' he said, and broke off with a strong shudder.

A silence ensued, for my ecstasy at this sensational news item was so profound that for an instant I was unable to utter. Then I said 'Whoopee!' and in doing so may possibly have raised my voice a little, for he leaped somewhat and said he wished I wouldn't suddenly yell 'Whoopee!' like that, because I had made him bite his tongue.

'I'm sorry,' I said, 'but I stick to it. I said "Whoopee!" and I meant "Whoopee!" "Whoopee!" with the possible exception of

"Hallelujah!" is the only word that meets the case, and if I yelled it, it was merely because I was deeply stirred. I don't mind telling you now, Gussie, that I have viewed your passion for young Corky with concern, pursing the lips and asking myself dubiously if you were on the right lines. Corky is fine and, as you say, admirably fitted to be the bride of the sort of man who won't object to her landing him on the whim of the moment in a cell in one of our popular prisons, but the girl for you is obviously Madeline Bassett. Now you can go back to her and live happily ever after. It will be a genuine pleasure to me to weigh in with the silver egg-boiler or whatever you may suggest as a wedding gift, and during the ceremony you can rely on me to be in a ringside pew, singing "Now the labourer's task is o'er" like nobody's business.'

I paused at this point, for I noticed that he was writhing rather freely. I asked him why he writhed, and he said, Well, wouldn't anybody writhe who had got himself into the jam he had, and he wished I wouldn't stand there talking rot about going back to Madeline.

'How can I go back to Madeline, dearly as I would like to, after writing that letter telling her it was all off?'

I saw that the time had come to slip him the good news.

'Gussie,' I said, 'all is well. No need for concern. Others have worked while you slept.'

And without further preamble I ran through the Wimbledon continuity.

At the outset he listened dumbly, his eyes bulging, his lips moving like those of a salmon in the spawning season.

Then, as the gist penetrated, his face lit up, his horn-rimmed spectacles flashed fire and he clasped my hand, saying rather handsomely that while as a general rule he yielded to none in considering me the world's premier half-wit, he was bound to own that on this occasion I had displayed courage, resource, enterprise and an almost human intelligence.

'You've saved my life, Bertie!'

'Quite all right, old man.'

'But for you – '

'Don't mention it. Just the Wooster service.'

'I'll go and telephone her.'

'A sound move.'

He mused for a moment.

'No, I won't, by Jove. I'll pop right off and see her. I'll get my car and drive to Wimbledon.'

'She'll be in bed.'

'Well, I'll sleep in London and go out there first thing in the morning.'

'You'll find her up and about shortly after eight. Don't forget your sprained wrist.'

'By Jove, no. I'm glad you reminded me. What sort of a child was it you told her I had saved?'

'Small, blue-eyed, golden-haired and lisping.'

'Small, blue-eyed, golden-haired and lisping. Right.'

He clasped my hand once more and bounded off, pausing at the door to tell me to tell Jeeves to send on his luggage, and I, having completed the toilet, sank into a chair to enjoy a quick cigarette before leaving for the drawing-room.

I suppose in this moment of *bien être*, with the heart singing within me and the good old blood coursing through my veins, as I believe the expression is, I ought to have been saying to myself, 'Go easy on the rejoicing, cocky. Don't forget that the tangled love-lives of Catsmeat, Esmond Haddock, Gertrude Winkworth, Constable Dobbs and Queenie the parlourmaid remain still unstraightened out', but you know how it is. There come times in a man's life when he rather tends to think only of self, and I must confess that the anguish of the above tortured souls was almost completely thrust into the background of my consciousness by the reflection that Fate after a rocky start had at last done the square thing by Bertram Wooster.

My mental attitude, in short, was about that of an African explorer who by prompt shinning up a tree has just contrived to elude a quick-tempered crocodile and gathers from a series of shrieks below that his faithful native bearer had not been so fortunate. I mean to say he mourns, no doubt, as he listens to the doings, but though his heart may bleed, he cannot help his primary emotion being one of sober relief that, however sticky life may have become for native bearers, he, personally, is sitting on top of the world.

I was crushing out the cigarette and preparing to leave, feeling just ripe for a cheery sandwich and an invigorating cup of coffee, when there was a flash of pink in the doorway, and Esmond Haddock came in.

25

Iɴ dishing up this narrative for family consumption, it has been my constant aim throughout to get the right word in the right place and to avoid fobbing the customers off with something weak and inexpressive when they have a right to expect the telling phrase. It means a bit of extra work, but one has one's code.

We will therefore expunge that 'came' at the conclusion of the previous spasm and substitute for it 'curvetted'. There was a flash of pink, and Esmond Haddock curvetted in. I don't know if you have ever seen a fellow curvet, but war-horses used to do it rather freely in the old days, and Esmond Haddock was doing it now. His booted feet spurned the carpet in a sort of rhythmic dance something on the lines of that of the recent Poppy Kegley-Bassington, and it scarcely needed the ringing hunting cries which he uttered to tell me that here stood a bird who was about as full of beans and buck as a bird could be.

I Hallo-Esmonded and invited him to take a seat, and he stared at me in an incredulous sort of way.

'You don't seriously think that on this night of nights I can *sit down*?' he said. 'I don't suppose I shall sit down again for months and months and months. It's only by the exercise of the greatest will-power that I'm keeping myself from floating up to the ceiling. Yoicks!' he proceeded, changing the subject. 'Hard for'ard! Tally ho! Loo-loo-loo-loo-loo-loo!'

It had become pretty plain by now that Jeeves and I, while budgeting for a certain uplift of the spirit as the result of the success on the concert platform, had underestimated the heady results of a popular triumph. Watching this Haddock as he curvetted and listening to his animal cries, I felt that it was lucky for him that my old buddy Sir Roderick Glossop did not happen to be among those present. That zealous loony doctor would long ere this have been on the telephone summoning horny-handed assistants to rally round with the straight waistcoat and dust off the padded cell.

'Well, be that as it may,' I said, after he had loo-loo-looed for perhaps another minute and a quarter, 'I should like, before going any further, to express my gratitude to you for your gallant conduct in taking on those poems of mine. Was everything all right?'

'Terrific.'

'No mob violence?'

'Not a scrap. They ate 'em.'

'That's good. One felt that you were so solidly established with the many-headed that you would be in no real danger. Still, you were taking a chance, and thank Heaven that all has ended well. I don't wonder you're bucked,' I said, interrupting him in a fresh outbreak of loo-loo-looing. 'Anyone would be after making the sort of hit you did. You certainly wowed them.'

He paused in his curvetting to give me another incredulous look.

'My good Gussie,' he said, 'you don't think I'm floating about like this just because my song got over?'

'Aren't you?'

'Certainly not.'

'Then why do you float?'

'Because of Corky, of course. Good Lord!' he said, smiting his brow and seeming a moment later to wish he hadn't, for he had caught it a rather juicy wallop. 'Good Lord! I haven't told you, have I? And that'll give you a rough idea of the sort of doodah I'm in, because it was simply in order to tell you that I came here. You aren't abreast, Gussie. You haven't heard the big news. The most amazing front-page stuff has been happening, and you know nothing about it. Let me tell you the whole story.'

'Do,' I said, adding that I was agog.

He simmered down a bit, not sufficiently to enable him to take a seat but enough to make him cheese the curvetting for a while.

'I wonder, Gussie, if you remember a conversation we had the first night you were here? To refresh your memory, it was the last time we were allowed to get at the port; the occasion when you touched up that lyric of my Aunt Charlotte's in such a masterly way, strengthening the weak spots and making it box-office. If you recall?'

I said I recalled.

'In the course of that conversation I told you that Corky had given me the brusheroo. If you recollect?'

I said I recollected.

'Well, tonight – You know, Gussie,' he said, breaking off, 'it's the most extraordinary sensation, swaying a vast audience . . .'

'Would you call it a vast audience?'

The question seemed to ruffle him.

'Well, the two bob, shilling and eightpenny seats were all sold out and there must have been fully fifty threepenny standees at the back,' he said, a bit stiffly. 'Still, call it a fairly vast audience, if you prefer. It makes no difference to the argument. It's the most extraordinary sensation, swaying a fairly vast audience. It does something to you. It fills you with a sense of power. It makes you feel that you're a pretty hot number and that you aren't going to stand any nonsense from anyone. And under the head of nonsense you find yourself classing girls giving you the brusheroo. I mention this so that you will be able to understand what follows.'

I smiled one of my subtle smiles.

'I know what follows. You got hold of Corky and took a strong line.'

'Why, yes,' he said, seeming a little flattened. 'As a matter of fact that was what I was leading up to. How did you guess?'

I smiled another subtle one.

'I foresaw what would happen if you slew that fairly vast audience. I knew you were one of those birds on whom popular acclamation has sensational effects. Yours has been a repressed life, and you have, no doubt, a marked inferiority complex. The cheers of the multitude frequently act like a powerful drug upon bimbos with inferiority complexes.'

I had rather expected this to impress him, and it did. His lower jaw fell a notch, and he gazed at me in a reverent sort of way.

'You're a deep thinker, Gussie.'

'I always have been. From a child.'

'One wouldn't suspect it, just to look at you.'

'It doesn't show on the surface. Yes,' I said, getting back to the *res*, 'matters have taken precisely the course which I antici-pated. With the cheers of the multitude ringing in your ears, you came off that platform a changed man, full of yeast and breathing flame through the nostrils. You found Corky. You backed her into a corner. You pulled a dominant male on her and fixed everything up. Right?'

'Yes, that was just what happened. Amazing how you got it all taped out.'

'Oh, well, one studies the psychology of the individual, you know.'

'Only I didn't back her into a corner. She was in her car, just driving off somewhere, and I shoved my head in at the window.'

'And – ?'

'Oh, we kidded back and forth,' he said a little awkwardly, as if reluctant to reveal what had passed at that sacred scene. 'I told her she was the lodestar of my life and all that sort of thing, adding that I intended to have no more rot about her not marrying me, and after a bit of pressing she came clean and admitted that I was the tree on which the fruit of her life hung.'

Those who know Bertram Wooster best are aware that he is not an indiscriminate back-slapper. He picks and chooses. But there was no question in my mind that here before me stood a back which it would be churlish not to slap. So I slapped it.

'Nice work,' I said. 'Then everything's all right?'

'Yes,' he assented. 'Everything's fine . . . except for one small detail.'

'What is that in round numbers?'

'Well, it's a thing I don't know if you will quite understand. To make it clear I shall have to go back to that time when we were engaged before. She severed relations then because she considered that I was a bit too much under the domination of my aunts, and she didn't like it.'

Well, of course, I knew this, having had it from her personal lips, but I wore the mask and weighed in with a surprised 'Really?'

'Yes. And unfortunately she hasn't changed her mind. Nothing doing in the orange-blossom and wedding-cake line, she says, until I have defied my aunts.'

'Well, go ahead. Defy them.'

My words seemed to displease him. With a certain show of annoyance he picked up a statuette of a shepherdess on the mantelpiece and hurled it into the fireplace, reducing it to hash and removing it from the active list.

'It's all very well to say that. It's a thing that presents all sorts of technical difficulties. You can't just walk up to an aunt and say "I defy you". You need a cue of some sort. I'm dashed if I know how to set about it.'

I mused.

'I'll tell you what,' I said. 'It seems to me that here is a matter on which you would do well to seek advice from Jeeves.'

'Jeeves?'

'My man.'

'I thought your man's name was Meadowes.'

'A slip of the tongue,' I said hastily. 'I meant to say Wooster's man. He is a bird of extraordinary sagacity and never fails to deliver the goods.'

He frowned a bit.

'Doesn't one rather want to keep visiting valets out of this?'

'No, one does not want to keep visiting valets out of this,' I said firmly. 'Not when they're Jeeves. If you didn't live all the year round in this rural morgue, you'd know that Jeeves isn't so much a valet as a Mayfair consultant. The highest in the land bring their problems to him. I shouldn't wonder if they didn't give him jewelled snuff-boxes.'

'And you think he would have something to suggest?'

'He always has something to suggest.'

'In that case,' said Esmond Haddock, brightening, 'I'll go and find him.'

With a brief 'Loo-loo-loo' he pushed off, clicking his spurs, and I settled down to another cigarette and a pleasant reverie.

Really, I told myself, things were beginning to straighten out. Deverill Hall still housed, no doubt, its quota of tortured souls, but the figures showed a distinct downward trend. I was all right. Gussie was all right. It was only on the Catsmeat front that the outlook was still unsettled and the blue bird a bit slow in picking up its cues.

I pondered on Catsmeat's affairs for a while, then turned to the more agreeable theme of my own, and I was still doing so, feeling more braced every moment, when the door opened.

There was no flash of pink this time, because it wasn't Esmond home from the hunt. It was Jeeves.

'I have extricated Mr Fink-Nottle from his beard, sir,' he said, looking modestly pleased with himself, like a man who has fought the good fight, and I said Yes, Gussie had been paying me a neighbourly call and I had noticed the absence of the fungoid growth.

'He told me to tell you to pack his things and send them on. He's gone back to London.'

'Yes, sir. I saw Mr Fink-Nottle and received his instructions in person.'

'Did he tell you why he was going to London?'

'No, sir.'

I hesitated. I yearned to share the good news with him, but I was asking myself if it wouldn't involve bandying a woman's name. And, as I have explained earlier, Jeeves and I do not bandy women's names.

I put out a feeler.

'You've been seeing a good deal of Gussie recently, Jeeves?'

'Yes, sir.'

'Constantly together, swapping ideas, what?'

'Yes, sir.'

'I wonder if by any chance . . . in some moment of expansiveness, if that's the word . . . he ever happened to let fall anything that gave you the impression that his heart, instead of sticking like glue to Wimbledon, had skidded a bit in another direction?'

'Yes, sir. Mr Fink-Nottle was good enough to confide in me regarding the emotions which Miss Pirbright had aroused in his bosom. He spoke freely on the subject.'

'Good. Then I can speak freely, too. All that's off.'

'Indeed, sir?'

'Yes. He came down from that tree feeling that Corky was not the dream mate he had supposed her to be. The scales fell from his eyes. He still admires her many fine qualities and considers that she would make a good wife for Sinclair Lewis, but – '

'Precisely, sir. I must confess that I had rather anticipated some such contingency. Mr Fink-Nottle is of the quiet, domestic type that enjoys a calm, regular life, and Miss Pirbright is perhaps somewhat – '

'More than somewhat. Considerably more. He sees that now. He realizes that association with young Corky, though having much to be said for it, must inevitably lead in the end to a five-year stretch in Wormwood Scrubs or somewhere, and his object in going to London to-night is to get a good flying start for an early morning trip to Wimbledon Common to-morrow. He is very anxious to see Miss Bassett as soon as possible. No doubt they will breakfast together, and having downed a couple of rashers and a pot of coffee, saunter side by side through the sunlit grounds.'

'Most gratifying, sir.'

'Most. And I'll tell you something else that's gratifying. Esmond Haddock and Corky are engaged.'

'Indeed, sir?'

'Provisionally, perhaps I ought to say.'

And I sketched out for him the set-up at the moment of going to press.

'I advised him to consult you,' I said, 'and he went off to find you. You see the posish, Jeeves? As he rightly says, however much you may want to defy a bunch of aunts, you can't get started unless they give you something to defy them about. What we want is some situation where they're saying "Go", like the chap in the Bible, and instead of going he cometh. If you see what I mean?'

'I interpret your meaning exactly, sir, and I will devote my best thought to the problem. Meanwhile, I fear I must be leaving you, sir. I promised to help my Uncle Charlie serve the refreshments in the drawing-room.'

'Scarcely your job, Jeeves?'

'No, sir. But one is glad to stretch a point to oblige a relative.'

'Blood is thicker than water, you mean?'

'Precisely, sir.'

He withdrew, and about a minute later Esmond blew in again, looking baffled, like a Master of Hounds who has failed to locate the fox.

'I can't find the blighter,' he said.

'He has just this moment left. He's gone to the drawing-room to help push around the sandwiches.'

'And that's where we ought to be, my lad,' said Esmond. 'We're a bit late.'

He was right. Silversmith, whom we encountered in the hall, informed us that he had just shown out the last batch of alien guests, the Kegley-Bassington gang, and that apart from members of the family only the vicar, Miss Pirbright and what he called 'the young gentleman', a very loose way of describing my cousin Thomas, remained on the burning deck. Esmond exhibited pleasure at the news, saying that now we should have a bit of elbow room.

'Smooth work, missing those stiffs, Gussie. What England needs is fewer and better Kegley-Bassingtons. You agree with me, Silversmith?'

'I fear I have not formulated an opinion on the subject, sir.'

'Silversmith,' said Esmond, 'you're a pompous old ass,' and, incredible as it may seem, he poised a finger and with a cheery 'Yoicks!' drove it into the other's well-covered ribs.

And it was as the stricken butler reeled back and tottered off with an incredulous stare of horror in his gooseberry eyes, no doubt to restore himself with a quick one in the pantry, that Dame Daphne came out of the drawing-room.

'Esmond!' she said in the voice which in days gone by had reduced so many Janes and Myrtles and Gladyses to tearful pulp in the old study. 'Where have you been?'

It was a situation which in the pre-Hallo-hallo epoch would have had Esmond Haddock tying himself in apologetic knots and perspiring at every pore: and no better evidence of the changed conditions prevailing in the soul of King's Deverill's Bing Crosby could have been afforded than by the fact that his brow remained unmoistened and he met her eye with a pleasant smile.

'Oh, hallo, Aunt Daphne,' he said. 'Where are you off to?'

'I am going to bed. I have a headache. Why are you so late, Esmond?'

'Well, if you ask me,' said Esmond cheerily, 'I'd say it was because I didn't arrive sooner.'

'Colonel and Mrs Kegley-Bassington were most surprised. They could not understand why you were not here.'

Esmond uttered a ringing laugh.

'Then they must be the most priceless fatheads,' he said. 'You'd think a child would have realized that the solution was that I was somewhere else. Come along, Gussie. Loo-loo-loo-loo-loo,' he added in a dispassionate sort of way, and led me into the drawing-room.

Even though the drawing-room had been cleansed of Kegley-Bassingtons, it still gave the impression of being fairly well filled up. Four aunts, Corky, young Thos, Gertrude Winkworth and the Rev. Sidney Pirbright might not be absolute capacity, but it was not at all what you would call a poor house. Add Esmond and self and Jeeves and Queenie moving to and fro with the refreshments, and you had quite a quorum.

I had taken a couple of sandwiches (sardine) off Jeeves and was lolling back in my chair, feeling how jolly this all was, when Silversmith appeared in the doorway, still pale after his recent ordeal.

He stood to attention and inflated his chest.

'Constable Dobbs,' he announced.

26

THE reactions of a gaggle of coffee and sandwich chewers in the drawing-room of an aristocratic home who, just as they are getting down to it, observe the local flatty muscling in through the door, vary according to what Jeeves calls the psychology of the individual. Thus, while Esmond Haddock welcomed the newcomer with a genial 'Loo-loo-loo', the aunts raised their eyebrows with a good deal of To-what-are-we-indebted-for-the-honour-of-this-visitness and the vicar drew himself up austerely, suggesting in his manner that one crack out of the zealous officer about Jonah and the Whale and he would know what to do about it. Gertrude Winkworth, who had been listless, continued listless, Silversmith preserved the detached air which butlers wear on all occasions, and the parlourmaid Queenie turned pale and uttered a stifled 'Oo-er!' giving the impression of a woman on the point of wailing for her demon lover. I, personally, put in a bit of quick gulping. The mood of *bien être* left me, and I was conscious of a coolness about the feet. When the run of events has precipitated, as Jeeves would say, a situation of such delicacy as existed at Deverill Hall, it jars you to find the place filling up with rozzers.

It was to Esmond Haddock that the constable directed his opening remark.

'I've come on an unpleasant errand, sir,' he said, and the chill in the Wooster feet became accentuated. 'But before I go into that there,' he proceeded, now addressing himself to the Rev. Sidney Pirbright, 'there's this here. I wonder if I might have a word with you, sir, on a spiritual subject?'

I saw the sainted Sidney stiffen, and knew that he was saying to himself 'Here it comes'.

'It's with ref to my having seen the light, sir.'

Somebody gave a choking gasp, like a Pekingese that has taken on a chump chop too large for its frail strength, and looking around I saw that it was Queenie. She was staring at Constable Dobbs wide-eyed and parted-lipped.

204

This choking gasp might have attracted more attention had it not dead-heated with another, equally choking, which proceeded from the thorax of the Rev. Sidney. He, too, was staring wide-eyed. He looked like a vicar who has just seen the outsider on whom he has placed his surplice nose its way through the throng of runners and flash in the lead past the judge's box.

'Dobbs! What did you say? You have seen the light?'

I could have told the officer he was a chump to nod so soon after taking that juicy one on the napper from the serviceable rubber instrument, but he did so, and the next thing he said was 'Ouch!' But the English policeman is made of splendid stuff, and after behaving for a moment like a man who has just swallowed one of Jeeves's morning specials he resumed his normal air, which was that of a stuffed gorilla.

'R,' he said. 'And I'll tell you how it come about, sir. On the evening of the twenty-third inst . . . well, to-night, as a matter of fact . . . I was proceeding about my duties, chasing a marauder up a tree, when I was unexpectedly struck by a thunderbolt.'

That, as might have been expected, went big. The vicar said 'A thunderbolt', two of the aunts said 'A *thunderbolt*?' and Esmond Haddock said 'Yoicks'.

'Yes, sir,' proceeded the officer, 'a thunderbolt. Caught me on the back of the head, it did, and hasn't half raised a lump.'

The vicar said 'Most extraordinary', the other two aunts said 'Tch, tch' and Esmond said 'Tally ho'.

'Well, sir, I'm no fool,' continued Ernest Dobbs. 'I can take a hint. "Dobbs," I said to myself, "no use kidding yourself about what *this* is, Dobbs. It's a warning from above, Dobbs," I said to myself. "If it's got as far as thunderbolts, Dobbs," I said to myself, "it's time you made a drawstic revision of your spiritual outlook, Dobbs," I said to myself. So, if you follow my meaning, sir, I've seen the light, and what I wanted to ask you, sir, was Do I have to join the Infants' Bible Class or can I start singing in the choir right away?'

I mentioned earlier in this narrative that I had never actually seen a shepherd welcoming a strayed lamb back into the fold, but watching Dame Daphne Winkworth on the occasion to which I allude I had picked up a pointer or two about the technique, so was able to recognize that this was what was going to happen now. You could see from his glowing eyes and benevolent smile, not to mention the hand raised as if about to bestow a blessing, that this totally unexpected reversal of form on the part of the local backslider had taken the Rev. Sidney's mind right off the church organ. I think that in about another couple of ticks he would have come across with something pretty impressive in the way of simple, manly words, but, as it so happened, he hadn't time to get set. Even as his lips parted, there was a noise like a rising pheasant from the outskirts and some solid object left the ranks and hurled itself on Constable Dobbs's chest.

Closer inspection showed this to be Queenie. She was clinging to the representative of the Law like a poultice, and from the fact that she was saying 'Oh, Ernie!' and bedewing his uniform with happy tears I deduced, being pretty shrewd, that what she was trying to convey was that all was forgiven and forgotten and that she was expecting the prompt return of the ring, the letters and the china ornament with 'A Present from Blackpool' on it. And as it did not escape my notice that he, on his side, was covering her upturned face with burning kisses and saying 'Oh, Queenie!' I gathered that Tortured Souls Preferred had taken another upward trend and that one could chalk up on the slate two more sundered hearts reunited in the springtime.

These tender scenes affect different people in different ways. I myself, realizing Catsmeat's honourable obligations to this girl might now be considered cancelled, was definitely bucked by the spectacle. But the emotion aroused in Silversmith was plainly a shuddering horror that such goings-on should be going on in the drawing-room of Deverill Hall. Pulling a quick Stern Father, he waddled up to the happy pair and with a powerful jerk of the wrist detached his child and led her from the room.

Constable Dobbs, though still dazed, recovered himself sufficiently to apologize for his display of naked emotion, and the Rev. Sidney said he quite, quite understood.

'Come and see me to-morrow, Dobbs,' he said benevolently, 'and we will have a long talk.'

'Very good, sir.'

'And now,' said the Rev. Sidney, 'I think I will be wending my way homeward. Will you accompany me, Cora?'

Corky said she thought she would stick on for a bit, and

Thos, keenly alive to the fact that there were still stacks of sandwiches on tap, also declined to shift, so he beamed his way out of the room by himself, and it was only after the door had closed that I realized that Constable Dobbs was still standing there and remembered that his opening words had been that he had come upon an unpleasant errand. Once more the temperature of the feet fell, and I eyed him askance.

He was not long in getting down to the agenda. These flatties are trained to snap into it.

'Sir,' he said, addressing Esmond.

Esmond interrupted to ask him if he would like a sardine sandwich, and he said 'No, sir, I thank you', and when Esmond said that he did not insist on sardine but would be equally gratified if the other would wade into the ham, tongue, cucumber or potted meat, explained that he would prefer to take no nourishment of any kind, because of this unpleasant errand he had come on. Apparently, when policemen come on unpleasant errands, they lay off the vitamins.

'I'm looking for Mr Wooster, sir,' he said.

In the ecstasy of this recent reunion with the woman he loved I imagine that Esmond had temporarily forgotten how much he disliked Gussie, but at these words it was plain that all the old distaste for one who had made passes at the adored object had come flooding back, for his eyes gleamed, his face darkened and he did a spot of brow-knitting. The sweet singer of King's Deverill had vanished, leaving in his place the stern, remorseless Justice of the Peace.

'Wooster, eh?' he said, and I saw him lick his lips. 'You wish to see him officially?'

'Yes, sir.'

'What has he been doing?'

'Effecting burglarious entries, sir.'

'Has he, by Jove!'

'Yes, sir. On the twenty . . . This evening, sir a burglarious entry was effected by the accused into my police station and certain property of the Crown abstracted – to wit, one dog, what was in custody for having effected two bites. I copped him in the very act, sir,' said Constable Dobbs, simplifying his narrative style. 'He was the marauder I was chasing up trees at the moment when I was inadvertently struck by that thunderbolt.'

Esmond continued to knit his brow. It was evident that he took a serious view of the matter. And when Justices of the Peace take serious views of matters, you want to get out from under.

'You actually found him abstracting this to wit one dog?' he said keenly, looking like Judge Jeffreys about to do his stuff.

'Yes, sir. I come into my police station and he was in the act of unloosing it and encouraging it to buzz off. It proceeded to buzz off, and I proceeded to say "Ho!" whereupon, becoming cognizant of my presence, he also proceeded to buzz off, with me after him lickerty-split. I proceeded to pursue him up a tree and was about to effect an arrest, when along come this here thunderbolt, stunning me and depriving me of my senses. When I come to, the accused had departed.'

'And what makes you think it was Wooster?'

'He was wearing a green beard, sir, and a check suit. This rendered him conspicuous.'

'I see. He had not changed after his performance.'

'No, sir.'

Esmond licked his lips again.

'Then the first thing to do,' he said, 'is to find Wooster. Has anybody seen him?'

'Yes, sir. Mr Wooster has gone to London in his car.'

It was Jeeves who spoke, and Esmond gave him a rather surprised look.

'Who are you?' he asked.

'My name is Jeeves, sir. I am Mr Wooster's personal attendant.'

Esmond eyed him with interest.

'Oh, you're Jeeves? I'd like a word with you, Jeeves, some time.'

'Very good, sir.'

'Not now. Later on. So Wooster has gone to London, has he?'

'Yes, sir.'

'Fleeing from justice, eh?'

'No, sir. Might I make a remark, sir?'

'Carry on, Jeeves.'

'Thank you, sir. I merely wished to say that the officer is mistaken in supposing that the miscreant responsible for the outrage was Mr Wooster. I was continuously in Mr Wooster's society from the time he left the concert hall. I accompanied him to his room, and we remained together until he took his departure for London. I was assisting him to remove his beard, sir.'

'You mean you give him an alibi?'

'A complete alibi, sir.'

'Oh?' said Esmond, looking baffled, like the villain in a melo-drama. One could sense that the realization that he was not to be able to dish out a sharp sentence on Gussie had cut him to the quick.

'Ho!' said Constable Dobbs, not, probably, with an idea of contributing anything vital to the debate but just because police-men never lose a chance of saying 'Ho!' Then suddenly a strange light came into his face and he said 'Ho!' again, this time packing a lot of meaning into the word.

'Ho!' he said. 'Then if it wasn't the accused Wooster, it must have been the other chap. That fellow Meadowes, who was doing Mike. He was wearing a green beard, too.'

'Ah!' said Esmond.

'Ha!' said the aunts.

'Oh!' said Gertrude Winkworth, starting visibly.

'Hoy!' said Corky, also starting visibly.

I must say I felt like saying 'Hoy!' too. It astonished me that Jeeves had not spotted what must inevitably ensue if he gave Gussie that alibi. Just throwing Catsmeat to the wolves, I mean to say. It was not like him to overlook a snag like that.

I caught Corky's eye. It was the eye of a girl seeing a loved brother going down for the third time in the soup. And then my gaze, swivelling round, picked up Gertrude Winkworth.

Gertrude Winkworth was plainly wrestling with some strong emotion. Her face was drawn, her bosom heaved. Her fragile handkerchief, torn by a sudden movement of the fingers, came apart in her hands.

Esmond was being very Justice-of-the-Peace-y.

'Bring Meadowes here,' he said curtly.

'Very good, sir,' said Jeeves, and pushed off.

When he had gone, the aunts started to question Constable

Dobbs, demanding more details, and when it had been brought home to them that the dog in question was none other than the one which had barged into the drawing-room on the night of my arrival and chased Aunt Charlotte to and fro, they were solidly in favour of Esmond sentencing this Meadowes to the worst the tariff would allow, Aunt Charlotte being particularly vehement.

They were still urging Esmond to display no weakness, when Jeeves returned, ushering in Catsmeat. Esmond gave him the bleak eye.

'Meadowes?'

'Yes, sir. You wished to speak to me?'

'I not only wished to speak to you,' said Esmond nastily, 'I wished to give you thirty days without the option.'

I heard Constable Dobbs snort briefly, and recognized his snort as a snort of ecstasy. The impression I received was that a weaker man, not trained in the iron discipline of the Force, would have said 'Whoopee!' For, just as Esmond Haddock had got it in for Gussie for endeavouring to move in on Corky, so had Constable Dobbs got it in for Catsmeat for endeavouring to move in on the parlourmaid, Queenie. Both were strong men, who believed in treating rivals rough.

Catsmeat seemed puzzled.

'I beg your pardon, sir?'

'You heard,' said Esmond. He intensified the bleakness of his eye. 'Let me ask you a few simple questions. You sustained the role of Pat in the Pat-and-Mike entertainment this evening?'

'Yes, sir.'

'You wore a green beard?'

'Yes, sir.'

'And a check suit?'

'Yes, sir.'

'Then you're for it,' said Esmond crisply, and the four aunts said So they should think, indeed, Aunt Charlotte going on to ask Esmond rather pathetically if thirty days was really all that the book of rules permitted. She had been reading a story about life in the United States, she said, and there, it seemed, even comparatively trivial offences rated ninety.

She was going on to say that the whole trend of modern life in England was towards a planned Americanization and that she, for one, approved of this, feeling that we had much to learn from our cousins across the sea, when there was a brusque repetition of that rising pheasant effect which had preceded the Hobbs-Queenie one-act sketch and the eye noted that Gertrude Winkworth had risen from her seat and precipitated herself into Catsmeat's arms. No doubt she had picked up a hint or two from watching Queenie's work for in its broad lines her performance was modelled on that of the recent parlourmaid. The main distinction was that whereas Silversmith's ewe lamb had said 'Oh, Ernie!' she was saying 'Oh, Claude!'

Esmond Haddock stared.

'Hallo!' he said, adding another three hallos from force of habit.

You might have thought that a fellow in Catsmeat's position, faced with the prospect of going up the river for a calendar month, would have been too perturbed to have time for hugging girls, and it would scarcely have surprised me if he had extricated himself from Gertrude Winkworth's embrace with a 'Yes, yes, quite, but some other time, what?' Not so, however. To clasp her to his bosom was with him the work of a moment, and you could see that he was regarding this as the important part of the evening's proceedings, giving him little scope for attending to Justices of the Peace.

'Oh, Gertrude!' he said. 'Be with you in a minute,' he added to Esmond. 'Oh, Gertrude!' he proceeded, once more addressing his remarks to the lovely burden. And, precisely as Constable Dobbs had done in a similar situation, he covered her upturned face with burning kisses.

'Eeek!' said the aunts, speaking as one aunt.

I didn't blame them for being fogged and unable to follow the run of the scenario. It is unusual for a niece to behave towards a visiting valet as their niece Gertrude was behaving as of even date, and if they squeaked like mice, I maintain they had every right to do so. Theirs had been a sheltered life, and this was all new stuff to them.

Esmond, too, seemed a bit not abreast.

'What's all this?' he said, a remark which would have proceeded more fittingly from the lips of Constable Dobbs. In fact, I saw the officer shoot a sharp look at him, as if stung by this infringement of copyright.

Corky came forward and slipped her arm through his. It was plain that she felt the time had come for a frank, manly explanation.

'It's my brother Catsmeat, Esmond.'

'What is?'

'This is.'

'What, that?'

'Yes. He came here as a valet for love of Gertrude, and a darned good third-reel situation, if you ask me.'

Esmond wrinkled his brow. He looked rather as he had done when discussing that story of mine with me on the night of my arrival.

'Let's go into this,' he said. 'Let's thresh it out. This character is not Meadowes?'

'No.'

'He's not a valet?'

'No.'

'But he *is* your brother Catsmeat?'

'Yes.'

Esmond's face cleared.

'Now I've got it,' he said. 'Now it's all straight. How are you, Catsmeat?'

'I'm fine,' said Catsmeat.

'That's good,' said Esmond heartily. 'That's splendid.'

He paused, and started. I suppose the baying that arose at this point from the pack of aunts, together with the fact that he had just tripped over his spurs, had given him the momentary illusion that he was in the hunting field, for a 'Yoicks' trembled on his lips and he raised an arm as if about to give his horse one on the spot where it would do most good.

The aunts were a bit on the incoherent side, but gradually what you might call a message emerged from their utterances. They were trying to impress on Esmond that the fact that the accused was Corky's brother Catsmeat merely deepened the blackness of his crime and that he was to carry on and administer the sentence as planned.

Their observations would have gone stronger with Esmond if he had been listening to them. But he wasn't. His attention was riveted on Catsmeat and Gertrude, who had seized the

opportunity afforded by the lull in the proceedings to exchange
a series of burning kisses.

'Are you and Gertrude going to get married?' he asked.

'Yes,' said Catsmeat.

'Yes,' said Gertrude.

'No,' said the aunts.

'Please,' said Esmond, raising a hand. 'What's the procedure?'
he asked, once more addressing himself to Catsmeat.

Catsmeat said he thought the best scheme would be for them
to nip up to London right away and put the thing through on
the morrow. He had the licence all ready and waiting, he
explained, and he saw no difficulties ahead that a good registry
office couldn't solve. Esmond said he agreed with him, and
suggested that they should borrow his car, and Catsmeat said
that was awfully good of him, and Esmond said Not at all.
'Please,' he added to the aunts, who were now shrieking like
Banshees.

It was at this point that Constable Dobbs thrust himself
forward.

'Hoy,' said Constable Dobbs.

Esmond proved fully equal to the situation.

'I see what you're driving at, Dobbs. You very naturally wish
to make a pinch. But consider, Dobbs, how slender is the evidence which you can bring forward to support your charge.
You say you chased a man in a green beard and a check suit
up a tree. But the visibility was very poor, and you admit
yourself that you were being struck by thunderbolts all the time,
which must have distracted your attention, so it is more than
probable that you were mistaken. I put it to you, Dobbs, that
when you thought you saw a man in a green beard and a
check suit, it may quite easily have been a clean-shaven man in
something quiet and blue?'

He paused for a reply, and one could divine that the officer
was thinking it over.

The thing that poisons life for a country policeman, the thing
that makes him pick at the coverlet and brings him out in rashes,
is the ever-present fear that one of these days he may talk out
of turn and get in wrong with a Justice of the Peace. He knows
what happens when you get in wrong with Justices of the Peace.
They lay for you. They bide their time. And sooner or later they

catch you bending, and the next thing you know you've drawn a strong rebuke from the Bench. And if there is one experience the young copper wishes to avoid, it is being in the witness-box and having the Bench look coldly at him and say something beginning with 'Then are we to understand, officer . . . ?' and culminating in the legal equivalent of the raspberry or Bronx cheer. And it was evident to him that defiance of Esmond on the present occasion must inevitably lead to that.

'I put it to you, Dobbs,' said Esmond.

Constable Dobbs sighed. There is, I suppose, no spiritual agony so keen as that of the rozzer who has made a cop and seen it turn blue on him. But he bowed to the inev.

'Perhaps you're right, sir.'

'Of course I'm right,' said Esmond heartily. 'I knew you would see it when it was pointed out to you. We don't want any miscarriages of justice, what?'

'No, sir.'

'I should say not. If there's one thing that gives me the pip, it's a miscarriage of justice. Catsmeat, you are dismissed without a stain on your character.'

Catsmeat said that was fine, and Esmond said he thought he would be pleased.

'I suppose you and Gertrude aren't going to hang around, spending a lot of time packing?'

'No, we thought we'd leg it instanter.'

'Exactly what I would suggest.'

'If Gertrude wants clothes,' said Corky, 'she can get them at my apartment.'

'Splendid,' said Esmond. 'Then the quickest way to the garage is along there.'

He indicated the french windows, which, the night being balmy, had been left open. He slapped Catsmeat on the back, and shook Gertrude by the hand, and they trickled out.

Constable Dobbs, watching them recede, heaved another sigh, and Esmond slapped his back, too.

'I know just how you're feeling, Dobbsy,' he said. 'But when you think it over, I'm sure that you'll be glad you haven't been instrumental in throwing a spanner into the happiness of two young hearts in springtime. If I were you, I'd pop off to the kitchen and have a word with Queenie. There must be much that you want to discuss.'

Constable Dobbs's was not a face that lent itself readily to any great display of emotion. It looked as if it had been carved out of some hard kind of wood by a sculptor who had studied at a Correspondence School and had got to about Lesson Three. But at this suggestion it definitely brightened.

'You're right, sir,' he said, and with a brief 'Good night, all' vanished in the direction indicated, his air that of a policeman who is feeling that life, while greyish in spots, is not without its compensations.

'So that's that,' said Esmond.

'That's that,' said Corky. 'I think your aunts are trying to attract your attention, angel.'

All through the preceding scene, though pressure of other matter prevented me mentioning it, the aunts had been extremely vocal. Indeed, it would not be putting it too strongly to say that they had been kicking up the hell of a row. And this row must have penetrated to the upper regions of the house, for at this moment the door suddenly opened, revealing Dame Daphne Winkworth. She wore a pink dressing-gown, and had the appearance of a woman who has been taking aspirins and bathing her temples with eau-de-Cologne.

'Really!' she said. She spoke with a goodish bit of asperity, and one couldn't fairly blame her. When you go up to your bedroom with a headache, you don't want to be dragged down again half an hour later by disturbances from below. 'Will someone be so kind as to tell me what is the reason for this uproar?'

Four simultaneous aunts were so kind. The fact that they all spoke together might have rendered their remarks hard to follow, had not the subject matter been identical. Gertrude, they said, had just eloped with Miss Pirbright's brother, and Esmond had not only expressed his approval of the move but had actually offered the young couple his car.

'There!' they said, as the sound of an engine gathering speed and the cheery toot-toot of a klaxon made themselves heard in the silent night, pointing up their statement.

Dame Daphne blinked as if she had been struck on the mazard with a wet dishcloth. She turned on the young squire menacingly, and one could understand her peevishness. There are few things more sickening for a mother than to learn that her only child has eloped with a man whom she has always regarded as a blot on the species. Not surprising if it spoils her day.

'Esmond! Is this true?'

The voice in which she spoke would have had me clambering up the wall and seeking refuge on the chandelier, had she been addressing me, but Esmond Haddock did not wilt. The man seemed fearless. He was like the central figure in one of those circus posters which show an intrepid bozo in a military uniform facing with death-defying determination twelve murderous, man-eating monarchs of the jungle.

'Quite true,' he replied. 'And I really cannot have any discussion and argument about it. I acted as I deemed best, and the subject is closed. Silence, Aunt Daphne. Less of it, Aunt Emmeline. Quiet, Aunt Charlotte. Desist, Aunt Harriet. Aunty Myrtle, put a sock in it. Really, the way you're going on, one would scarcely suppose that I was the master of the house and the head of the family and that my word was law. I don't know if you happen to know it, but in Turkey all this insubordinate stuff, these attempts to dictate to the master of the house and the head of the family, would have led long before this to you being strangled with bowstrings and bunged into the Bosporus. Aunt Daphne, you have been warned. One more yip out of you, Aunt Myrtle, and I stop your pocket-money. Now, then,' said Esmond Haddock, having obtained silence, 'let me give you the strength of this. The reason I abetted young Gertrude in her matrimonial plans was that the man she loves is a good egg. I have this on the authority of his sister Corky, who speaks extremely well of him. And, by the way, before I forget, his sister Corky and I are going to be married ourselves. Correct?'

'In every detail,' said Corky.

She was gazing at him with shining eyes. One got the feeling that if she had had a table with a photograph on it, she would have been singing 'My Hero'.

'Come, come,' said Esmond kindly, as the yells of the personnel died away, 'no need to be upset about it. It won't affect you dear old souls. You will go on living here, if you call it living, just as you have always done. All that'll happen is that you will be short one Haddock. I propose to accompany my wife to

216

Hollywood. And when she's through with her contract there, we shall set up a shack in some rural spot and grow pigs and cows and things. I think that covers everything, doesn't it?'

Corky said she thought it did.

'Right,' said Esmond. 'Then how about a short stroll in the moonlight?'

He led her lovingly through the french windows, kissing her en route and I edged to the door and made my way upstairs to my room. I could have stayed on and chatted with the aunts, if I had wanted to, but I didn't feel in the mood.

27

M^Y first act on reaching the sleeping quarters was to take pencil and paper and sit down and make out a balance sheet. As follows:

Sundered Hearts	Reunited Hearts
(1) Esmond	(1) Esmond
(2) Corky	(2) Corky
(3) Gussie	(3) Gussie
(4) Madeline	(4) Madeline
(5) Officer Dobbs	(5) Officer Dobbs
(6) Queenie	(6) Queenie
(7) Catsmeat	(7) Catsmeat
(8) Gertrude	(8) Gertrude

It came out exactly square. Not a single loose end left over. With a not unmanly sigh, for if there is one thing that is the dish of the decent-minded man, it is seeing misunderstanding between loving hearts cleared up, especially in the springtime, I laid down the writing materials and was preparing to turn in for the night, when Jeeves came shimmering in.

'Oh, hallo, Jeeves,' I said, greeting him cordially. 'I was rather wondering if you would show up. A big night, what?'

'Extremely, sir.'

I showed him the balance sheet.

'No flaws in that, I think?'

'None, sir.'

'Gratifying, what?'

'Most gratifying, sir.'

'And, as always, due to your unremitting efforts.'

'It is very kind of you to say so, sir.'

'Not at all, Jeeves. We chalk up one more of your triumphs on the slate. I will admit that for an instant during the proceedings, when you gave Gussie that alibi, I experienced a momentary doubt as to whether you were on the right lines, feeling that you were but landing Catsmeat in the bouillon. But calmer reflection told me what you were up to. You felt that if Catsmeat stood in peril of receiving an exemplary sentence, Gertrude Winkworth would forget all that had passed and would cluster round him, her gentle heart melted by his distress. Am I right?'

'Quite right, sir. The poet Scott – '

'Pigeon-hole the poet Scott for a moment, or I shall be losing the thread of my remarks.'

'Very good, sir.'

'But I know what you mean. Oh, Woman in our hours of ease, what?'

'Precisely, sir. Uncertain, coy and hard to please. When – '

' – pain and anguish wring the brow, a ministering angel thou and so on and so forth. You can't stump me on the poet Scott. That is one more of the things I used to recite in the old days. First "Charge of Light Brigade" or "Ben Battle": then, in response to gales of applause, the poet Scott as an encore. But to return to what I was saying . . . There, as I suspected would be the case, Jeeves, I can't remember what I was saying. I warned you what would happen if you steered the conversation to the poet Scott.'

'You were speaking of the reconciliation between Miss Winkworth and Mr Pirbright, sir.'

'Of course. Well, I was about to say that having studied the psychology of the individual you foresaw what would occur. And you knew that Catsmeat wouldn't be in any real peril. Esmond Haddock was not going to jug the brother of the woman he loved.'

'Exactly, sir.'

'You can't get engaged to a girl with one hand and send her brother up for thirty days with the other.'

'No, sir.'

'And your subtle mind also spotted that this would lead to Esmond Haddock defying his aunts. I thought the intrepid Haddock was splendidly firm, didn't you?'

'Unquestionably, sir.'

'It's nice to think that he and Corky are now headed for the centre aisle.' I paused, and looked at him sharply. 'You sighed, Jeeves.'

'Yes, sir.'

'Why did you sigh?'

'I was thinking of Master Thomas, sir. The announcement of Miss Pirbright's betrothal came as a severe blow to him.'

I refused to allow my spirits to be lowered by any such side issues.

'Waste no time commiserating with young Thos, Jeeves. His is a resilient nature, and the agony will pass. He may have lost Corky, but there's always Betty Grable and Dorothy Lamour and Jennifer Jones.'

'I understand those ladies are married, sir.'

'That won't affect Thos. He'll be getting their autographs, just the same. I see a bright future ahead of him. Or, rather,' I said, correcting myself, 'fairly bright. There is that interview with his mother to be got over first.'

'It has already occurred, sir.'

I goggled at the man.

'What do you mean?'

'My primary motive in intruding upon you at this late hour, sir, was to inform you that her ladyship is downstairs.'

I quivered from brilliantine to shoe sole.

'Aunt Agatha?'

'Yes, sir.'

'Downstairs?'

'Yes, sir. In the drawing-room. Her ladyship arrived some few moments ago. It appears that Master Thomas, unwilling to occasion her anxiety, wrote her a letter informing her that he was safe and well, and unfortunately the postmark "King's Deverill" on the envelope – '

'Oh, my gosh! She came racing down?'

'Yes, sir.'

'And – ?'

'A somewhat painful scene took place between mother and son, in the course of which Master Thomas happened to – '

'Mention me?'

'Yes, sir.'

'He blew the gaff?'

'Yes, sir. And I was wondering whether in these circumstances you might not consider it advisable to take an immediate departure down the waterpipe. I understand there is an excellent milk

220

train at two fifty-four. Her ladyship is expressing a desire to see you, sir.'

It would be deceiving my public to say that for an instant I did not quail. I quailed, as a matter of fact, like billy-o. And then, suddenly, it was as if strength had descended upon me.

'Jeeves,' I said, 'this is grave news, but it comes at a moment when I am well fitted to receive it. I have just witnessed Esmond Haddock pound the stuffing out of five aunts, and I feel that after an exhibition like that it would ill beseem a Wooster to curl up before a single aunt. I feel strong and resolute, Jeeves. I shall now go downstairs and pull an Esmond Haddock on Aunt Agatha. And if things look like becoming too sticky, I can always borrow that cosh of yours, what?'

I squared the shoulders and strode to the door, like Childe Roland about to fight the paynim.